S.J. MARTIN

Betrayal

Beguiled. Betrayed. Banished.

To Margaret,

I hope you enjoy the rest of the series.

Sarah Jane Martin

This book is dedicated to my amazing partner, Greg.
This series could not have been published without his tireless
attention to detail and professionalism when it came to
proof-reading and formatting all of the manuscripts.
Add to this his enthusiasm and encouragement and I know these
books could not have been published without him.

Contents

Map of Brittany

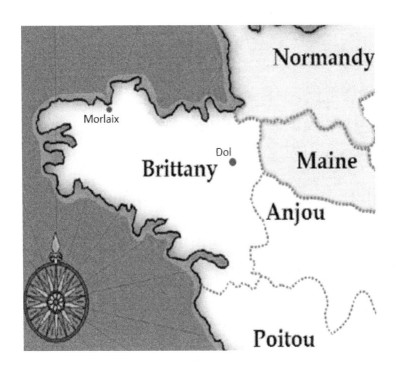

Map of Normandy

The Breton Horse Warrior Series

Character List

Fictional characters in *Italics*

Morlaix

Luc De Malvais
Merewyn De Malvais - his wife
Lusian, Chantal and Garret – their children
Morvan de Malvais – Luc's younger brother
Marie De Malvais – their mother
Sir Gerard – their mentor, sword master and family friend
Benedot – Captain of the Horse Warriors

Caen

King William of England & Duke of Normandy
Queen Matilda
Robert Curthose – eldest son heir to Normandy
William Rufus – heir to England
Henry – youngest son
Constance – daughter at court
Robert De Montgomery, Earl of Shrewsbury- senior advisor
Eustace De Boulogne –senior advisor
Hugh De Grandmesnil – senior advisor
Richard Fitz Gilbert - the Earl of Clare – senior advisor

Toki of Wigod – loyal Saxon retainer of William
Alan Fergant (Iron glove) – heir to the Dukedom of Brittany

Ghent in Flanders

Count Robert of Flanders – brother of Queen Matilda
Robert De Belleme, Seigneur Viscount de Hiemos – follower of Robert
Roger-Fitz-Richard De Clare – follower of Robert
Gilbert De Sorrell – follower of Robert
William of Breteuil – follower of Robert
Yves & Aubrey Grandesmil – followers of Robert
Hugh de Chateauneuf en Thymerais – follower of Robert
Piers de Chatillon – Papal envoy, spy and assassin
Odo de Chatillon – Cardinal and Prior of Cluny. (later Pope Urban II 1088)

Paris

King Philip
Gervais de la Ferte – Seneschal of France
Alina de la Ferte – his wife
Etienne de la Ferte – his eldest son
Minette de la Ferte (Ette) – his youngest daughter.
Dauferio – Abbot of Montecassino, Cardinal of St Cecillia (later Pope Victor III 1085)
Monseigneur Gironde –Catholic prelate to the Dukes of Brittany

Others

Pope Gregory VII– the Vatican, the Holy See (1073-1085)
Fulk – Count of Anjou

Chapter One

The group of horsemen galloped down into the village of Saint-Pabu. Luc De Malvais pulled up his great warhorse Espirit and glanced around the small quiet village sitting on the banks of the river Aber-Benoir. He looked around the scattered wooden houses and identified the most prominent house; as he rode towards it, a man emerged from the open door leading to a dark interior.

Luc smiled; the man who appeared was the epitome of a western Breton chieftain with his dark braided hair and long moustaches. This was a remote, scarcely populated and isolated area where little had changed for hundreds of years. The chieftain regarded the horsemen solemnly for several moments and then raised a hand in greeting as Luc's brother Morvan pulled his horse alongside Espirit.

Morvan De Malvais, who had planned this expedition, waved one of the young Horse Warriors forward. 'Benedot, I believe you understand the Celtic patois in this area?' he asked.

The dark young man nodded. 'Yes, my mother, she comes from this area,' he said as he went forward and greeted the village leader, explaining the reason behind their arrival. The man looked at them in astonishment, and running his hand over his moustaches and chin, he gave a great guffaw of laughter and calling out his sons to hear the tale. Although they eyed the Horse Warriors on their huge Destriers with wary respect, the two young men were similarly amused and talked animatedly together. The older man stepped forward and gesticulated at Benedot before pointing down the estuary and describing what seemed to be a sweep south along the coast.

Morvan's black stallion was impatiently stamping its feet, and he whirled it round in a circle to quieten it as he shouted, 'what is he saying? Has he seen her? Does he know where she is?' Luc smiled at Morvan. After several days of fruitless searches, he knew just how frustrated his younger brother was; Luc hoped this information would be valuable in helping them find her. Young Benedot thanked the village elder and turned back to the two Malvais brothers.

'She was seen only yesterday by the village fishermen. She was in the forest along the cliffs that run down to the beach of the Tres Moutons, but they say we should go now as they think she will soon be moving inland again for the winter,' he replied with a satisfied smile.

Morvan tightened the reins on his restless stallion; he had waited several years to find her again. So many false sightings and now they were so close. 'Do you know where this beach is, Benedot?' he asked.

The young man nodded his head. 'If we follow the banks of the estuary for a few miles, it will bring us to the coast, and we can turn south into the pine forests he describes.' The older man laughed again and added something else. Benedot smiled in understanding to the chieftain, 'He says you will never take her; if she sees you coming, she will disappear and melt into the forests like one of the ghosts on Samhain or All Hallows.'

Luc smiled back; he knew how difficult this would be, but they had travelled a long way, and they had to try to find her. He raised a fist in salute to the man and his sons and slowly led his Horse Warriors out of the village and down along the sandy shores of the wide Aber-Benoir river estuary.

He had only agreed to join his brother's quest to the west, as things had been tranquil in Brittany for a time. Many Breton Lords had retreated to their lands after the siege and battle last year at La Fleche. They still undertook the usual Horse Warrior patrols of the eastern borders to stop the marauding raids by the Angevins into Maine and Brittany, but his right-hand man, Sir Gerard, could handle those while they were away. In addition, he reflected that it was also good to spend some time with his younger brother. Morvan had spent the last few years away from his home in Morlaix at the Norman court of King William in Caen, the capital of Normandy. Here he was forming and training a new cohort of Breton Horse Warriors for the King.

An hour later, they reached the coast and rode up through the pine scrub forests and rocky outcrops to stand on a small bluff overlooking the long silver sand beaches of the western shoreline. It was a wild and rocky coast, but scattered throughout were these beautiful beaches surrounded by pink granite cliffs and coves—vast stretches of white sand and crystal clear turquoise waters when the weather was calm. As he gazed at the beautiful vista, the western salt sea breeze sweeping the dark hair back from his face, Luc realised that it had been far too long since he had ridden this way, too many years embroiled instead in the politics and wars of the Lords and King he served.

Suddenly there was a shout from one of the outriders as he pulled up behind them, 'We think we have found her Sire. To the southeast, we think we sighted her going down onto the beach. High cliffs surround it, and there seems to be just one entrance.'

Luc shaded his eyes, looking south, but it was the far end of the beach they were indicating past a rocky outcrop that went into the sea, and he could see little. However, he could feel the tension in his brother, who sat beside him; Morvan was shortening his reins and peering along the beach at the cliffs and shadows in the distance.

Morvan stood up in his stirrups to address the men. 'You all know what to do, spread out in formation, she must not escape; I refuse to let her slip through my hands this time.'

The group turned back into the pine forests and made their way quietly south, trotting almost parallel to the long beach. Not a word was spoken; not a whinny was heard as they fanned out in a wide circle following the outriders and heading for the shallow rocky gully that led down onto the beach.

They emerged from the trees and picked their way carefully down through the craggy rocks and boulders; a small bluff still hid them from her sight, so she had no idea that they were there. Luc and Morvan rode carefully forward and stopped, raising a hand to keep the rest of the troop back. There she was, on the shoreline, stood in the surf, staring out across the Atlantic Ocean. As Luc gazed at her, she took his breath away; he had forgotten quite how beautiful she was.

Morvan waited for the rest of the men to catch up and then whispered, 'she has not seen us yet, so we have a chance to cut across and catch her when she tries to run; the cliffs surrounding the beach should contain her.' He gestured to the three men at the back. 'You three stay here and ensure she does not escape back up through the gully.' He turned back to Luc.

'We have found her Luc. Finally, I will be taking her back home,' he said, a grin on his face as he shortened his reins and prepared to gallop down to the water's edge.

Chapter Two

Her name was Midnight. She was the most beautiful, wild, and wilful mare they had ever owned. Morvan was riding her son, whom he had named Midnight Shadow for the faint dapple on his sides courtesy of his father, Espirit. She had her back to them, she was leading a wild herd of about twenty horses, and Luc could see a few older colts and yearlings that could be hers. They had come down to the shoreline as the wild horses did to nibble and lick the salty rock seaweed.

Suddenly Espirit whickered, the western wind was blowing off the sea, and he caught the scent of the mare; she whirled around, nostrils flaring, and then, she was off, racing down the beach with the startled herd trying to follow her. Morvan, shouting orders, set off in hot pursuit with Luc and the rest of the men. She had the advantage as the other horses were carrying riders, but gradually, Morvan cut the distance between them. He scanned ahead, but he could see no apparent break in the cliffs where she could escape. However knowing her temperament, he would put nothing past her, so he would leave nothing to chance. The Horse Warriors fanned out, all holding ropes or leather lariats to try to lasso her. She slowed as she reached the rocky outcrop at the end of the beach, and for a few seconds, Morvan feared that she was contemplating going into the sea and swimming around. He knew he had to try to get her away from the rocks so that he could use the weighted ropes to entangle her legs and bring her down. She turned and stood facing them, all four feet firmly planted, snorting loudly and rolling her eyes in a fury.

Without warning, the black mare exploded into action and ran straight at them, hoping to break through the ranks of Horse Warriors facing her. She veered west into the surf at the last minute, and Morvan raced across the sand to cut her off. He whirled the weighted rope above his head before throwing it expertly at her back legs. This wrapped itself tightly around her hocks and brought her to a stop, and she dropped to her haunches in the water, her forelegs frantically pawing at the sand to pull herself back up.

Morvan leapt off his horse, followed by Luc as they threw themselves on the furious mare to wrestle her head and neck down while avoiding the snapping teeth. Two others ran up, and they managed to get several ropes and a leather head halter on her. All four of them knee-deep in the surf were holding on to the ropes, they knew that as soon as her back legs were free, she would be kicking, biting and striking out. They pulled her slowly out of the surf onto the beach and let her vent her anger for some time; kicking, bucking and plunging, she pulled the men back into the surf and along the beach until she eventually began to tire. Morvan relaxed his grip and shook out his aching arms as he turned to grin at Luc; they finally had her. After years of sightings, they had her back. Luc grinned and slapped his brother on his back in approbation. He then directed some of the men to catch and rope some of her promising offspring in the herd, who were milling around nervously at a distance, unsure what to do without their hellish matriarch.

They made camp in one of the coves for the night after ensuring that the mare was firmly staked out with extra hobbling ropes around her rear legs. They set men to watch her in shifts; she had always had a reputation for chewing her way through ropes and lead reins. They intended to set off early the following day for their home in Morlaix; they had been away searching for the mare for nearly nine days. Luc had seen little of his younger brother over the past two years while he was with King William's contingent in Caen and Rouen, but now it felt as if they had never been apart.

Luc was worried about Morvan, for although he was now a capable and fearless warrior in his own right, he knew that his brother was deeply in love with Constance, the youngest daughter of King William and Queen Matilda. This was a love affair that was doomed to fail, for although Constance reciprocated his love, she was a royal princess. Her parents would never let her marry a minor Breton Knight, even though he was the brother of the legendary leader and swordsman that was Luc De Malvais. Luc had warned his brother about the danger of their relationship repeatedly to no avail; Morvan was now too involved and would not listen to reason from Luc, Gerard, their friend and mentor or his mother Marie; it would not end well.

They sat around the campfire that night, happy and tired, their cloaks wrapped around them, as the breezes from the Atlantic turned cold at this time of year. They had shared a few wineskins with the other men, but now the brothers sat in companionable silence. Luc knew that Morvan was elated he had captured his beautiful, fiery broodmare; she had kicked her stable to pieces at Morlaix during a storm one night and then escaped, that was nearly three years ago. She was now in her prime and would still produce several more foals that would become some of the famous Morlaix Destriers. These were a cross between the big Breton horses and the Arab strain that their father had introduced many years before, resulting in intelligent lethal warhorses trained to attack and fight in battle.

Watching Morvan pile more driftwood on the fire, Luc remembered the last time they had sat around a campfire together like this. They had been exhausted and bloody from the battle at La Fleche. He gazed through the flames and wood smoke at his brother, 'I believe King William is finally coming to terms with Count Fulk of Anjou and Philip of France,' he enquired. Morvan took another long slug of wine, 'You should have finished Count Fulk off while you had a chance at La Fleche Luc; he will always be a thorn in our side. I do not believe that the pact he is signing with the King will make a great deal of difference. Within months, Fulk will be raiding, burning and killing over the border again.' Luc nodded grimly in agreement thinking back to the events of the last troubled few years.

It had taken King William some time to come to terms with his surprising and first ignominious defeat at the Siege of Dol in 1076. He had been fighting against Count Fulk of Anjou and Earl Ralph De Gael, an English rebel and now the leader of the rebel Breton Lords. There was no doubt that after months of siege, William had the upper hand; the citadel at Dol was about to fall. Then suddenly King Philip of France had arrived without warning with his army to relieve the siege. This meant that William, now significantly outnumbered, was forced to retreat, abandoning an absolute fortune in weapons, horses and siege machines behind as he fled for his life with the help of Morvan and the Horse Warriors. This was the first serious check that William had experienced in over twenty years.

Luc had been seriously injured in the attack by an Angevin enemy, and for some time, he thought that he might lose the use of his right sword arm. Fortunately, the King had provided his own personal Arab doctor for Luc. The skilled physician had carried out surgery on Luc's arm, and now, although it had been a gruelling first year, Luc had pushed himself hard and was almost back to full fitness.

However, Luc knew that William had suffered a severe setback at Dol, financially and more importantly, to his prestige. In early 1077 Fulk, allied with several Breton Lords, had tried to capitalise on William's losses by attacking La Fleche, a fortress on the border of Maine and Anjou, which was loyal to William. Lord Jean de la Fleche managed to hold out until William arrived with the Horse Warriors in his vanguard. Luc and his brother Morvan led the charge against Fulk's forces, forcing them back, and in the heat of the battle, Luc suddenly found himself face to face with Count Fulk, who was still surrounded by several of his Angevin Knights. Luc had numerous scores to settle with the surly Angevin leader, and disregarding Fulk's entourage, he viciously attacked and delivered what should have been a killing blow. However, at the last moment, one of the Angevin Knight's shoulder charged Luc's horse who responded by lashing out with his front hooves. Still, having been severely wounded by Luc's deflected swinging blow, Fulk was quickly bustled away by the remaining Knights.

In fury and frustration, Luc had turned on his attacker and, riding him down; he had delivered a sword thrust through his throat, giving him only a small amount of satisfaction as Count Fulk had escaped. Shortly afterwards, their leader, now sorely wounded, the Angevin forces began to retreat, leaving William victorious, and the siege lifted. An uneasy truce between Normandy and Anjou had followed the battle at La Fleche, and now a pact was to be signed between William and Count Fulk.

'What news of King Philip of France?' asked Luc throwing another large piece of driftwood on the fire; he knew that Morvan's position at the heart of William's court in Caen would give him access to all the recent news.

'William's defeat and losses at Dol gave Philip the opportunity he needed to extend his influence into eastern Vexin unopposed. As you know, the province of Vexin in the north has always acted as a buffer zone between France and Normandy; it has always been allied to Normandy and has also strategically controlled the traffic between Normandy and Paris,' he said.

Luc was shocked; he was aware that the defeat at Dol had weakened William but not to the extent that he would allow the French King such licence in the Vexin.

'How did this come about?' He asked in amazement. Morvan sighed and shook his head. 'Simon de Crepi, the new ruler of Vexin, decided to enter a monastery and renounce the world on his wedding night. That left the province without a ruler, and in chaos, Philip immediately occupied the eastern part of the Vexin right up to the Normandy border on the River Epte. This move by Philip of France followed fast on William's defeat at Dol, so he was not in a position to repel the incursion. We have been dealing with French raids over the border into Normandy ever since,' answered Morvan. He ran his hands through his dark shoulder-length hair in frustration.

Luc stared at his brother in concern at what he had heard as he wrapped himself in his blanket. William had always been a victorious and defiant leader, a tour de force in the last ten years of Luc's life; he found it difficult to believe that William would accept and give in to such a blatant move by the avaricious French King. More importantly, what did that mean for his future and the future and safety of his family? The Lords of Malvais had always served Alain Rufus, who was his liege lord, but they both served and were loyal to King William, who maintained a powerful presence across this western area of Europe. He just hoped that William was purely licking his wounds and regrouping and that he would emerge triumphant once more and drive these intruders from his borders.

Chapter Three

Constance sat quietly in the window seat of the solar. Her mother, Queen Matilda and several of her ladies were engaged in embroidering a large tapestry to adorn her parent's chamber wall. As they deftly sewed, they gossiped as usual about the court intrigues and scandals. However, Constance was sat in quiet reflection; she was reading the canticle of St Eulalie, an old story that recounted the martyrdom of a young girl. It was a court favourite as the young girl resits torture and survives being burnt at the stake before finally being beheaded. Still, she then ascends to heaven in the form of a dove—a typical parody of sin, punishment, and popular redemption. Constance found empathy in this as she considered her own life in court a form of martyrdom. The restraints of her position, a royal princess, ordered by tradition and duty, she had little control over her life no matter how much her parents loved her.

She had walked down to the market yesterday on a pleasant errand for her mother, shadowed by the usual maidservant and man at arms. As she waited for a lace merchant to display his wares, she watched the bustling crowds, listened to the shouts of the hawkers and the lowing of the milk cows for sale. The weekly market in Caen was very busy, and people came from miles around to sell their goods, to barter or buy the necessities that they could not make. She watched the scandalous banter that went on between the young squires and apprentices to the shocked serving girls, the smacking of lips and lewd gestures as the girls turned their backs. However, she knew that the same girls would be slipping out of the postern gate to meet these boys on the riverbank later. She took a deep breath to relieve the constriction around her chest; she would love to have the same freedom.

She was now twenty-two and still lived at home, this was unusual for a King's daughter, but she was her mother's favourite. Her older brothers and sisters had all been directed in their choices and betrothals. The merchant appeared with the length of beautiful Breton lace she required, and Constance directed the serving girl to pay. It was a fine late autumn morning, and she decided to walk down to Saint Etienne, the Abbaye-aux-Hommes. She knew that they would be making the final preparations for the dedication of the church and Abbey tomorrow. Many Norman and Breton Lords had been invited, bringing their wives and entourage, so the town was bursting at the seams with tents and pavilions set up in the meadows. Her mother had a raft of servants under the direction of the Steward, setting up truckle beds and making arrangements for those lords privileged enough to be staying inside William's impressive fortress at Caen.

Suddenly, there was a loud clatter of hooves and shouted orders for people to move aside as the large troop of Horse Warriors came through the archway and trotted up towards the Bailey. Her breath caught in her throat as she watched them, the enormous, magnificent Destriers, their coats gleaming, the warriors on their backs with the distinctive crossed swords and laced leather doublets. They were riding bareback, as they had been out for morning training and down to the river to wash the horses in preparation for tomorrow's procession. From habit, she quickly scanned the leaders, but she knew he was not there. Morvan De Malvais was still at his home in Brittany. He had been gone for nearly two months and every day without him felt like a lifetime. The truth was that she was in love with the Breton Knight; however, she also knew that her love was doomed, so it was bittersweet; it could never be. King William respected and admired the young Knight; he often ate at their table in the Great Hall, he spent time with her brothers, but the King would never tolerate him as a suitor for his daughter.

Luc and Morvan had arrived back at their home in Morlaix, elated at their success in capturing the black mare. She had been bred at Morlaix out of the same dam as Espirit, but her sire had been Thunder, a troublesome stallion with a bad-tempered mean streak that they had eventually sold on to a Knight in Flanders. The same fiery temperament had transferred to the black mare and hence to her son, Morvan's great battle Destrier Midnight Shadow. It was a crisp September morning as Luc and Sir Gerard leant on the paddock fence and watched Morvan and one of his men trying to control and calm the mare. He had attached two lunge reins to her head collar, and she fought them every inch of the way as they turned her in a circle one way and then back again, running alongside her while she snapped and lashed out at them with front and back hooves.

Gerard watched with an amused smile; he had raised and trained both the Malvais brothers in warfare and swordsman-ship, and he knew they had tenacity and determination. 'Please tell me he will not try to ride her,' he said, shaking his head and laughing.

Luc laughed, 'I do not think so; he wants to get her used to being lunged and handled again.'

Gerard snorted in derision. 'Again? She would not let anyone near her the first time. He leaves soon to go back to Caen, I believe, so that means we will be left with her on our hands.'

Luc smiled, 'Yes, and although I know he has enjoyed his time back here with his family, his duty to William is of paramount importance now.' Gerard nodded; duty came first. 'There is a message here for you from Count Eudo, have you read it?' he asked, raising an eyebrow. Luc sighed, 'Not yet; it will probably be more Angevin raiders coming into his lands on the borders.'

Eudo was the father of Luc's Patron, Alain Rufus; he was an experienced old warrior who was the Count of Penthievre. He was a force to be reckoned with, a tall virile man still, with over a dozen children legitimate and illegitimate scattered here and there.

'I think you will find the message may be more than that; I spent some time with the young Knight that brought it,' he added. Luc laughed, Gerard like his mother Marie De Malvais, had his own ways and means of gathering information before anyone else. 'Just tell me, Gerard,' he said in a resigned voice.

'William is signing a pact with Count Fulk of Anjou; this is more than the usual truce', he announced.

'Yes, I know; Morvan warned me it would happen,' said Luc, shrugging with resignation. Gerard gripped the fence in anger and shook his head, 'There is more; he is giving the province of Maine back into the Overlordship of Anjou, and back to Fulk.' He spat in disgust.

There was a stunned silence as Luc absorbed this information. They had spent three long years with the Horse Warriors fighting on the borders of Brittany, Maine and Anjou to keep the Angevin raiders out, now Maine, which they had fought to protect and hold was to be handed back to Count Fulk, William's lifelong enemy. Luc pondered this decision. He had spent time with King William at the siege of La Fleche when he defeated Fulk; William had seemed full of vigour and energy. Why then was he conceding Maine and at the same time allowing Philip of France to annexe half of the Vexin in the Northeast? It made no sense.

Morvan had handed the mare back to the apprehensive squires who kept a tight grip on her as they took her back to her stall. The sides were covered in padded sacking to stop her from destroying the wooden panels, but she had already bitten chunks out of it. He walked over to his brother and Gerard in high spirits. 'That went well; I think we are getting through to her; I intend to try and back her by the end of the week before I leave,' he said enthusiastically.

Luc snorted with laughter, 'Are you mad? She has not been ridden for more than three years. You will break your neck.'

'No, I think she remembers me,' he said in a confident voice. 'Yes, and she hated you back then as well,' added Gerard shaking his head. Morvan pulled off his leather gauntlets, ignoring the derisive comments, 'so what has you two looking so serious?' he asked.

'Is it true that William is handing Maine back to Fulk?' Luc asked incredulously?

Morvan looked surprised that they knew this as it was initially a confidential part of the pact. 'William is short of significant allies at present, and he has a range of enemies forming up against him. In addition, constantly fighting on your borders is both time and resource consuming. William suffered financially far harder than anyone realised by the rout and retreat at Dol. It also bolstered his enemies as they realised that they could beat him when they formed into an alliance together,' answered Morvan staring speculatively across the paddocks.

'I believe he is keeping the Norman right to administration in Maine, although I am not sure how that will work if they answer to Fulk as their Overlord,' stated Gerard.

'It means that Norman systems will be in place, a clear feudal hierarchy, tax collection and justice. It is also a sop to his eldest son Robert Curthose who was furious about this when I left Caen as it means he loses his title as the Count of Maine,' explained Morvan.

'Robert Curthose, King William's eldest, a wild and volatile young man by all accounts I believe,' said Gerard.

'I have spent a great deal of time with Robert and his friends; he has quite a following of young nobles. He was betrothed to Margaret of Maine, but unfortunately, she died just before the wedding, so the claim to Maine returned to Count Fulk. Robert was raging at his father when I left Caen, demanding that his father give him Normandy now and not just as his heir,' explained Morvan.

Luc and Gerard stood, thinking through the implications of what Morvan had just imparted. Relations were fragile in this region, and drastic leadership changes could often have devastating results. 'What of his other sons?' asked Gerard?

'When William dies, his second son William Rufus will get the English throne, Henry is still relatively young and I believe he will get some land and monetary gain.'

'It sounds as if you are going back into a wasp's nest at Caen,' said Gerard, concern evident in his voice; the Malvais brothers were like sons to him. Morvan shook his head, 'I tend to steer clear of all the politics and let the brothers argue amongst themselves. I am leaving early on Saturday; I have to be back in Caen for the dedication of the Abbey of St Etienne on Sunday. The Horse Warriors will be on show,' he grinned.

While watching his brother, Luc was pleased that he had made this move to the King's court; he had carved out a role for himself in Caen. It was not easy being a second son, and although Luc had awarded him a large part of his estates at Vannes, Morvan still had to make his own way and build his own reputation out of the shadow of his famous older brother. Luc just hoped that the fame and prestige he might win in the future would assuage the loss of Constance, as it was inevitable that she would be betrothed to some Duke or Count as William used her as a pawn in building his alliances.

Just then, they heard a considerable uproar from the stables, and Midnight emerged running towards the three men. She was still wearing the halter but had chewed through the leather strap that had secured her in the stall. Fortunately, there was nowhere for her to go as the high wattle gates were closed, so she ended up surrounded by about ten men, all waving their arms until Morvan leapt to grab the halter, and two brave squires managed to get some ropes on her.

'He will be riding her by the end of the week, will he,' snorted Gerard in derision as they pulled her, kicking and squealing in rage, back into the stable.

Chapter Four

Constance had spent the early morning at prayer with her mother, the court ladies and her young brother Henry, preparing for the ceremony in the cathedral. Then they had broken their fast and retired to the solar, waiting for her father and older brothers to join them. William arrived with his son William Rufus. He went straight to his wife Matilda, and, pulling her to her feet, he gave her a resounding kiss, which made her children smile as she laughed and slapped him away. Constance watched with satisfaction; her parents were a love match, often rare in arranged marriages. However, the tale of their courtship was well known throughout Western Europe.

Matilda was the proud daughter of the Count of Flanders, and when William, this illegitimate son of Robert of Normandy, had asked for her hand, she had turned him down flat because of his birth. However, being William, he did not give up; he was angry at her treatment and her mockery of him as the 'Bastard of Normandy'. Therefore, he had lain in wait and when she appeared outside the castle, he had grabbed her by her long braids and pulled her off her horse into the street before turning and walking away. After that manly demonstration, she declared that she would marry no one else but him. This endearing tale and seeing the proof of a successful arranged marriage before her inspired Constance that she might find the same one day. Then she had met and fallen in love with Morvan De Malvais.

Her father was impatiently striding up and down the room when the Abbey bells for Terce began to ring out. They were to walk down to the cathedral in procession; they would have to be in place inside when the canonical bell would ring.

'Where is he? Asked an exasperated William to his wife.

Matilda calmly placed her embroidery to one side and indicated to one of her ladies to go and find her errant eldest son. Relations between Robert and his father had been strained recently because of the imminent loss of the province of Maine, and she would not put it past her son to be late on purpose. However, the door opened, and Robert appeared dressed in full splendour and purposefully wearing the gold chain that denoted his position as Count of Maine, which he would only hold for another month.

Constance glanced at her mother, who was shaking her head in exasperation at her son as he greeted them all with 'Good morrow'. William scowled at him and went to stand with his other son at the narrow window to survey the milling crowds below. Matilda quietly stood and accepted the over-mantle from one of her ladies, telling Constance to do the same, as it would probably be chill in the vast cathedral church of the Abbey.

'Come let us go; the people will be waiting to see their King and his family. We must not disappoint them, she said, glancing meaningfully at her husband and sons. Robert grinned and nodded in acquiescence, offering his arm to his sister as they made their way down to the cobbled courtyard and inner Bailey beyond. A large troop of William's men, Knights and squires awaited them as they all moved into position behind Abbot Lanfranc and his priests, one of whom carried a huge cross to lead the way down to the Abbey. Two other priests flanked them with swinging incense burners, and the Knights and courtiers in all their splendour fell in behind. Hundreds of people had gathered in the outer Bailey, men at arms held them back, but they would be allowed to follow the procession down to cram into the far aisles of the cathedral for the ceremony. As the procession emerged through the arch into the vast area, the priests started the loud Latin intonation interspersed with the singing of Kyrie eleison. William's flags and pennants were held and displayed on all sides of the fortress so that it was a sea of colour; booths were set around the sides, some selling food and some selling religious reliquaries.

There was almost a carnival or holy day atmosphere to this celebration and dedication of the Abbey of Saint Etienne. Constance found it a heady mix, the singing, the incense, the crowds, as she walked beside Robert, her hand resting on his arm. She looked ahead and saw that where the Bailey narrowed to go through the large gatehouse into the streets beyond, the Horse Warriors were arrayed on either side in perfect rows to hold the crowds back. Their tack and kit polished to perfection, the long manes of the huge Destriers brushed until they shone; they were an impressive sight. Her heart stopped for a second as they reached the first riders, for she saw that he was back in Caen. Morvan De Malvais had returned for the dedication. As she looked at him, she suddenly found it was not easy to get to the end of a breath. He was as handsome as his legendary brother was, although they were different. Morvan had thick, rich shoulder-length brown hair and the brown gold-flecked eyes of his father. He had the tall, powerful physique of his brother; there was no doubt that he was a warrior, but she also knew that he was more sensitive than Luc. He was just as well educated, but whereas Luc's presence could intimidate and his steel-blue eyes could chill when they turned on you, Morvan's were more measured as he considered and weighed you up.

She had fallen in love with him the first time she saw him in Dinan after the siege of Dol, and shortly afterwards, he had moved to Caen at her father's request to establish a troop of Horse Warriors. She now saw him almost every day, a deep friendship and far more had developed between them under her mother's wary eye. However, Constance was not naïve; she knew that Matilda saw this as just a light flirtation. They had now drawn level, and she met his eyes, the look between them and the slight smile he gave her told her everything that she needed to know. They were in love, a requited love, but she knew it was a love that could not last, making it doubly poignant. She was conscious of her position in the procession and the hundreds of eyes on her, but she had to glance back so that she could see him dismounting and joining the other Knights in the procession. The bells of St Etienne were now tolling loudly as the chanting priests entered the substantial carved doors of the cathedral ahead of them, but all she could think of was the Horse Warrior several paces behind her.

Morvan stood in the nave of the new Abbey and resting his palm on the cool marble pillar; he lifted his eyes to gaze in wonder at the splendour of the building. The roof had unusual ribbed stone vaulting the likes of which had rarely been seen before. Having talked to the master masons over the last year, Morvan knew that this allowed the beautiful arching stone panels between the ribs. It was breath taking.

William and Matilda had founded two Abbeys; the other one in the east was the Abbey of Saint Trinite. At a significant cost, the building of these vast Abbeys was part of the penance and reconciliation between William and Pope Leo IX. When William married Matilda in 1052, he was a third cousin, and this was against the Pope's orders as it broke the strict rules of consanguinity or kinship, so at first, the Pope had forbidden such a match. However, William forged ahead, and there were strained relations between the Vatican and the Duke of Normandy for many years.

Morvan's attention was brought back to the ceremony as the choir of monks launched into the cadences of a haunting Gregorian chant. The hundreds of candles, the incense, the King and his nobles it was a heady mix for a young Knight, never mind for the wide-eyed townsfolk and peasants crammed into the stone-pillared aisles. Morvan immediately picked out the auburn head of Constance a few rows ahead of him, and as he looked, she half turned, and their eyes met again. His stomach knotted; she was so beautiful inside and out. He knew that Luc was right and she was not for him, but he clenched his fists at the thought of losing her.

Finally, the long Mass and dedication finished and with the choirs singing the Credo and the Kyrie eleison, so ended the blessings of the Abbey and the congregation. Morvan and the senior Knights stood to one side to let Abbot Lanfranc, with the King and Queen, lead the way up through the nave, following the sturdy monk who was triumphantly holding the large cross aloft. Morvan watched Constance walk past, only feet away from him, her eyes modestly lowered, her hand on the arm of her brother Robert. As he watched her gracefully glide by, he suddenly caught a movement in the far aisle; a young man was violently pushing others aside to get to the front. He was thin and tall with long dark hair, and he glared at the royal party as they slowly walked in procession towards the large carved wooden doors.

Morvan kept his eye on the young man as he moved to step between the senior Knights and earls who followed the King, pushing his way through despite their grumbled complaints to the far side to find him. However, when he emerged, there was no sign of him.

Being tall, he scanned over the heads of the large crowd until he spotted a dark head moving rapidly on the far side of the crowds up towards the doors. Ignoring the men at arms shadowing the King's party, Morvan pushed up until he was level with the King's sons, who looked at him in surprise. Robert immediately grasped the concern he saw on Morvan's face and handed his sister to his brother William Rufus.

'What is it?' he hissed at Morvan as the King turned and frowned at them before continuing into the long rays of sunlight streaming in through the open doors.

'It may be nothing, but there is an angry young man in the crowd, heading this way, and I think he means the King harm.' Morvan explained, he pointed out the head of the man. Robert grasped the danger immediately and drew the long ceremonial dagger from his belt.

'You stay with the King; I will break through the crowds and follow him.'

Morvan nodded, moving closer to shadow the King, who glanced apprehensively at the sudden appearance of the frowning Horse Warrior at his side. William was unarmed and in full ceremonial splendour; Matilda's hand was resting on his arm. They were only a short distance from the bottleneck near the doors when the young man, sword drawn, burst from the crowd, pushed through the startled guards and ran straight at the King.

In a split second, Morvan had reached up and drawn his sword, bringing the full force of it down onto the young man's raised blade. The youth cried out with fury, dropping the sword as the force of the blow reverberated through his hand and arm, and then he threw himself at William. Morvan leapt on him and wrestled him to the ground just as Robert pushed out of the crowd to hold a dagger to the attacker's throat, drawing blood. The royal party had jumped back, and now William grasping a sword from one of the guards, put himself in front of Matilda as another man rushed out of the crowd shouting, 'Sire, do not kill my son.' The older man turned to Lanfranc pleading, 'My Lord Abbot help us.' William could see that the older man was unarmed, and he reluctantly relinquished the sword to walk over to the man and his son, who was still pinned to the ground.

'Who are you, and why does your son wish to kill me?' he demanded in his booming voice, eyes blazing with anger at this threat to himself and to his family on this holy day in the house of God.

The man drew himself up to his full height, 'I am Hugh d'Airelle Sire. You built this Abbey on our home and lands; you demolished our home, took everything from us and left us penniless. My wife, the boy's mother, died a pauper's death of a fever last week. This is why my son is so angry. We have appealed several times to the Lord Abbot and to your Steward to have our case heard but to no avail,' he finished wringing his hands. William turned and raised an eyebrow at Lanfranc, who shrugged. 'There are so many cases Sire, I will look into it.'

'Let him up,' said William.

Morvan and Robert reluctantly stepped back, pulling the young man to his feet; Toki, a Saxon Knight and retainer of the King, stepped forward and harshly pulled the young man's arms behind him, quickly tying them. Now that he had time to look at him, Morvan realised that the boy was relatively young, a hotheaded young man of seventeen or eighteen who was out to get revenge for his parents and the loss of his home in the only way he knew. William studied him for a few seconds. 'What is your name?' he asked. The young man gave a surly unrepentant glance at the King, 'Gerotin,' he said.

'Well, Gerotin, you have despoiled the dedication of the Abbey of Saint Etienne, and you have threatened both my family and me. What punishment shall I give you?' he asked, glancing around at his assembled Knights.

'He should pay with his life; he could have killed you and my mother,' shouted Robert.

William still looked pensive; Morvan wondered if he was swayed by the age of the youth or by the wrong done to this family. At that moment, Abbot Lanfranc intervened. 'I think it is appropriate on this holy day, Sire, to show an act of mercy, to manumit a death sentence perhaps?' He suggested.

Morvan glanced around the Abbey, still packed with people; many were now aware of what had happened, some pushing themselves upon others shoulders to see and hear the King. William sighed, 'Yes, Lanfranc, you are as usual in the right, but,' he paused... 'This young man brought a weapon into our Abbey and raised it in anger, intending to do me harm, so he will be punished.' He turned to the Captain of the guard, 'No blood must be spilt in the Abbey, remove him outside to the marketplace and take off the hand that raised the sword.' The guards roughly pulled the white-faced young man out of the

Abbey doors, his weeping father following behind. The King glanced across at Morvan and waved him over; he slapped him heartily on the shoulder. 'Again, my Horse Warrior has stepped in to save my life. I give thanks to you and my son Robert for being so vigilant and acting so promptly.' Turning to his shaken Queen, he smiled at her as he firmly placed her hand back on his arm, continuing unperturbed to greet the cheering crowds who waited in the square outside the Abbey cathedral.

Robert looked only slightly mollified as he walked up to Morvan and grasped his arm in a warrior clasp. 'Well done, Malvais, but we should have killed him,' he muttered, waving his siblings on to follow the King and Queen. Morvan was troubled; his parents had brought him up to be a fair and just Knight. There was no doubt that young Gerotin, hardly more than a boy, should be punished for an act in the heat of the moment. However, for a family that had unjustly lost everything, with no compensation, was taking off a fit young man's hand the answer. He glanced behind and saw the shocked white face of Constance; she may have been brought up in the political turmoil and violence of William's court, but she was still a sensitive soul, so he smiled at her. She blinked rapidly and gazed back at him, her heart in her tear-filled eyes. Morvan turned away but not before, he had caught the look of suspicion and disapproval on her brother William's face.

Chapter Five

Morvan pushed open the well-worn faded blue door of the Boars Head, a large hostelry on one of the narrow streets of Caen that was popular with the young Knights of the King's court. The noise and smell of the tavern assailed him as he stepped into the dark smoky interior with his Saxon friend Toki. It was crowded after the festival day in Caen. He made his way to the large tables at the back. People moved out of the way at the sight of this tall muscled Horse Warrior, his signature crossed swords on his back, a tall blonde Saxon Knight following in his wake. Cheers and approbation greeted him from the considerable crowd of young men gathered around Robert. A large goblet of wine was pushed into his hand.

'All hail Malvais, the hero of the moment,' laughed Robert. It was good-natured, and Morvan gave a mock bow to much laughter. He could see that they were several drinks ahead of him, but he had to see to his men and horses; duty always came first.

'I think you were as much a hero as I was, Sire, the speed with which you had that dagger at his neck,' replied Morvan. Robert raised his cup to him in thanks while shouting, 'I should have cut the bastards throat,' to many cheers and much table banging.

Morvan pulled up a stool and, sitting down beside Toki, and his friends glanced around to see who was there. He was popular with the crowd that followed the Prince; most of them were either the heirs to notable titles and estates or the second cadet sons of the senior Lords and Earls in William's Anglo-Norman court.

As a second son himself, he had a lot in common with them. He had always lived in the shadow of his famous brother Luc De Malvais and had spent most of his formative years managing the large Malvais estates and lands with his mother Marie during Luc's absence in England. When Luc returned, he rode with and captained the Breton Horse Warriors but still under Luc's direction for the most part. Since Luc's grievous injury at Dol, he had taken on more responsibility, however, he still felt as if he was 'second string', so he was determined to establish his own reputation. King William's orders to develop and train a cohort of Breton Horse Warriors at Caen gave him that opportunity. He had over forty recruits, and he spent every day training both the men and their horses to fight. William and his family respected him and often invited him to the top table as an engaging young Knight who could discuss strategy and politics knowledgeably. He developed several friendships with the young Anglo-Norman nobility. Then there was Constance…. He was in love with the King's daughter.

Morvan took a long draft of his wine and raised a hand to his friends Roger-Fitz-Richard and Gilbert De Sorrell; they were sitting with the young brothers Yves and Aubrey Grandmesnil. The two youths laughed and described the charms and delights of two merchant's daughters they had encountered in the marketplace. However, Richard of a similar age to Morvan came to join him and Toki. 'Women again,' he laughed as he sat down. 'It is all they talk about,' he shook his head in amusement. 'Surely not, I am sure it is horses as well,' suggested Morvan adopting a semi-serious expression. Roger snorted with laughter, 'I am more worried that we were exactly the same at their age; my God, how tedious we must have been.' Morvan cast an affectionate eye in their direction; the two Grandmesnil brothers were the youngest in the group that had attached themselves to William's eldest son Robert Curthose. Although still in their teens, they were both well built, tall in stature, and Morvan had heard that they had been through a rigorous upbringing by their father Hugh to prepare them for Knighthood. Even so, they were carefree, ready for any lark, and they brought light-hearted laughter to the group, much needed at the moment. They all had sympathy for Robert, who had just been deprived of his rightful Overlordship of Maine.

'How is he?' asked Morvan, indicating the young Prince who was engaged in a dice game with Hugh De Chateauneuf.

'Angry but now resigned. I think, it is regrettable that his betrothed Margaret of Maine died just before they were due to be married. It would have given him the stronger claim to Maine and kept Fulk of Anjou at bay,' replied Roger.

'I find it difficult to comprehend that William has kept the Norman administration of Maine but under the overlordship of Fulk,' questioned Morvan. Roger gave a cynical laugh. 'Yes, he intends Robert to be a thorn in Fulk's side still. Maybe he thought it would be a sop to his son as he was no longer the Count of Maine,' he suggested. Morvan glanced over at the Prince, whose forced laughter could not conceal the dissatisfaction and frustration beneath. Gilbert De Sorrell strolled over to join them, 'So Malvais how was your sojourn in the wilds of western Brittany,' he asked.

36

'Hardly the wilds, Gilbert, although we did lead an expedition to the west coast to capture the wild black mare I told you about.' he said, grinning. Both men sat forward with interest.

'Did you succeed?' he asked. Morvan refilled the goblets and excitedly described the tracking, chase and capture of the mare. The tale attracted the attention of the rest of the group, and there was much laughter when Morvan rolled up his sleeve to show the bite marks and bruises. He was just about to roll his sleeve back down when a laconic voice behind him drawled, 'I am ready to bet that it was really a woman who gave you those Malvais; I hear that you are now so well-known and have become such a hero that you have to fight them off.' There was some laughter around the table, but Morvan felt his hackles rise. He would recognise that voice anywhere, Robert De Belleme, Seigneur Viscount of Hiemos and the heir to the powerful Earl of Shrewsbury, the eldest son of a wealthy and influential Anglo-Norman family. Morvan knew there was only one way to respond.

'I do my best, Belleme, but what can a man do when there are so many of them and some of them are very passionate?' He smiled and shrugged while raising his hands in a very Gallic gesture. The table roared with laughter, and Belleme turned away in disgust to order the potboy to bring more wine. 'So Robert, what are the plans for this week? Life in Caen is becoming somewhat tiresome; I need to get the smell of incense out of my clothes,' Belleme exclaimed to more laughter.

Robert laughed. 'Don't worry, Belleme, the court moves to L'aigle for a week on Wednesday, so there will be hunting every day and parties every night.' Morvan raised an eyebrow at the news; having been away, he was not aware of this move. He immediately wondered if Constance was going and if William would want the Horse Warriors as his escort. He was brought out of his reverie by an altercation between the Grandmesnil brothers, which was expected and usually ended with the eldest Yves punching the younger Aubrey. However, the worm had turned, and they were both on their feet exchanging blows until Aubrey picked up a stool and swung it at his brother. Unfortunately, the young gangling potboy had just arrived with a full jug of wine for Belleme. The stool swept the jug from the young man's hands, its contents liberally spraying the table, but most of it covered the sumptuous velvet cloak and clothes of the Seigneur de Belleme.

Conversation stopped; it was well known that Belleme cared about his appearance and spent inordinate amounts of money on expensive fabrics from the East. Only the finest linen was considered for his braies and chausses; every piece of leather and chain mail was polished until it shone. Now he sat staring in astonishment and disgust at the wine dripping from his clothes. He roared with fury, and Aubrey retreated to the shadows as the Knight grabbed the potboy by the throat and dragged him back onto the table.

Belleme had a notorious reputation for cruelty and combined with a vicious temper, not many around the table would remonstrate with him. Robert Curthose and many of his followers just sat back and watched with detachment; after all, it was just Belleme. Morvan, however, had been brought up as a Knight with a sense of justice. With his three friends, he had jumped back as the wine flew across, but now he stepped forward and grasped Belleme's arm. The young man was pinned to the table by the throat, gurgling and gasping for air as the angry viscount gripped his throat. 'It was not the boy's fault Belleme, it was young Aubrey who knocked it out of his hand,' he stated in a calm voice. At first, Belleme looked at him in disbelief that he would dare to interfere, then his face suffused with anger. He spat at Morvan. 'Get your hand off my arm, or it will be your throat I will be holding.' The silence and tension that hung in the air at these words were tangible. Malvais was no young Knight fresh from the countryside; he was a hardened Horse Warrior with a formidable reputation as a swordsman. Morvan's companions Toki, Roger-Fitz-Richard and Gilbert De Sorrell stepped up beside their friend.

'You could try Belleme,' smiled Morvan. 'What you are doing is still wrong; some of us live by a code of duty and honour to our family name and to that of our overlords,' he said, indicating the Prince. Robert Curthose smiled at the cleverness of the response, calm but delivering a slap in the face without unsheathing his sword; Malvais was becoming a diplomat. 'Let the boy go Belleme,' he said. Reluctantly the angry Knight let the potboy go glaring at Morvan and his friends, who returned to their stools. However, Belleme grabbed the boy by the arm at the last minute and pulled him back to the table. 'At the very least, he can provide us with some entertainment in recompense,' he said, grinning at Robert with his hands outstretched. Belleme was difficult to resist at times. The Prince laughed and nodded his approval; Morvan felt exasperated he knew that Belleme had an unhealthy influence over Robert Curthose.

'Put your hand flat on the table and spread your fingers, he ordered the terrified boy. Do not move a muscle if you do not want to lose your fingers,' he said, keeping a death grip on the boy's wrist with his left hand. 'The game is Vingt-et-un, place your bets, gentleman, twenty one points for each round, I will award ten pieces of silver to the winner, but you will give me five if you draw blood,' he announced. There was a buzz of excitement as they were all inveterate gamblers and loved a challenge. 'Aubrey, as you apparently caused this upset, you can follow me. William de Breteuil, you can do the count and be the judge of who is the fastest. Belleme had drawn a long stiletto style dagger in a flash, and he stabbed it down into the table where it quivered beside the young boy's hand. Morvan could see the terror in the boy's eyes, but he knew that Belleme had been clever; he could not interfere in a game with wagers such as this. At that moment, the Seigneur turned and sneered in triumph at Morvan. 'Want to try your luck Malvais,' Morvan stayed silent and just shook his head.

Silver was laid down, and the crowd gathered around with men from other tables even standing on stools to see the wagers. Belleme had played this many times; within seconds, his dagger stabbed downwards between the boys fingers moving from left to right and back again to twenty one stabs of the blade into the wood at what seemed like lightning speed. Cheers went up, and further bets were placed on who could equal the fast time as no blood was drawn.

The younger Grandesmil brother was pushed forward. He had consumed a lot of wine, but he wanted to win. He began well, but he became overconfident on the third return, and he sliced the young man's finger, who squealed in pain and bled profusely. 'Pay your silver Aubrey,' growled Belleme as the young man hurriedly searched for his pouch. Several other young men followed, but no one equalled the time set by Belleme until Robert Curthose stepped forward and laughing, took the handle of the offered dagger. Betting became more feverish as he raised it above the boy's hand. He raced the dagger across the fingers and back without touching the skin, and then he stabbed the dagger into the table and gave a bow. Everyone looked at William De Breteuil, who was in charge of the count. The quiet, studious young Knight was in a quandary, he knew he could not favour the Prince as he should, and to give Robert his due, he would expect the truth. 'I declare a draw,' he announced as groans and cheers followed, and final dues were paid to the clink of coins.

The crowd began to disperse, and Morvan drained his drink. 'I must go, duty calls,' he said to his friends. He glanced over at the main table to see that Belleme was still holding the wrist of the terrified boy, eyes glittering. The Knight was muttering something to him. Belleme picked up the engraved dagger, and without warning, slammed it down into the boy's hand, pinning him to the table. The boy screamed as Belleme turned away, and, bowing to Robert and his assembled companions, he strode towards the door.

Morvan leapt forward. He pulled the dagger from the boy's hand, and he, without hesitation, threw it expertly and with force the entire length of the room to embed quivering in the doorframe inches from Belleme's head. The Seigneur initially flinched and froze but then turned calmly to glare back at the group. 'I think you may have forgotten something, my Lord,' said Morvan in an ice-cold voice. Recovering his composure Belleme smiled and nodded. 'Be aware, Malvais, that I will never forget this, we will have our day,' he said, pulling the dagger from the woodwork and leaving.

'That may have been somewhat foolish, Malvais; he is not a man you want as your enemy,' commented Gilbert, his friend Toki just shook his head at Morvan's foolishness.

'Don't worry, I am well able to deal with Belleme, and I will watch my back,' he grinned as he headed for the door.

Chapter Six

Morvan rode through the gates at L'aigle. At the head of the Horse Warriors, his stallion Shadow was dancing on the spot with impatience anticipating a warm stable and oats after the long ride. King William rode beside him, followed by several of the King's Knights. Morvan had never been to the castle before, but he knew it was a significant border fortress that William liked to visit regularly; it was a favourite of the family. He glanced back at the cavalcade behind him. The rest of the royal family, almost a hundred courtiers, and servants and then the men at arms followed on stretching back almost a mile in a sea of dust, despite the colder weather. Robert and his brothers had ridden on ahead, frustrated by the slow pace that had been set to match the Queen's carriage.

As they entered the Bailey, Morvan directed his men to the vast stables built along the inner wall, and then he rode to ensure that the royal party were set down safely at the main donjon. He glanced around as he rode under the impressive arch into the inner Bailey. He was surprised at the quality of the stone carvings; master masons had obviously been employed here for some time. King William was waiting on the broad steps with his Castellan, who bowed deeply as the Queen and her party alighted. Constance followed her parents, but she turned and smiled at Morvan at the top of the steps. Gilbert De Sorrell had just pulled alongside his friend and saw the smile.

'Ah young love, what a sweet fruit it is when we take the first bite, but as the apple, in the Garden of Eden, it can have painful consequences. Be very careful, my friend, you are in dangerous waters there,' he advised, with a knowing smile as he turned away.

His friend's comment unsettled Morvan as he made his way to join the lively party in the Great Hall; he knew he was playing with fire, but he could not help himself. As he walked down the central aisle, his eyes travelled up to the vast wooden vaulted roof; it was elaborately carved and decorated. The Hall's design was unique in that it had beautiful wooden carved staircases to wooden balconies and galleries along the upper floors on three sides, all leading to additional rooms. Flags and pennants hung from their sides, making it a warm and colourful scene. Above the balconies were several larger-than-usual windows, so a great deal of light shone down onto the tables from above. The Hall was full of people, bustling servants, barking dogs and men at arms. The mixed smell of fresh rushes and wood smoke from the massive fireplaces assailed his nostrils as he made his way to join the young men around the fire.

Roger slapped him on the back. 'Well met, Malvais. Did you not find the slow pace frustrating? We had a great gallop through the forests and lifted two hinds that sprang away; there will be good hunting tomorrow.' Morvan smiled.

Roger-Fitz-Richard de Clare was good company, an open-faced pleasant young man and exceptionally well educated; his father was the wealthy Earl of Clare.

The King spotted Morvan and called him over. 'Malvais,

young Aubrey here, has been telling us of your wild black mare. Is it true?'

Morvan grinned and retold the tale, enlivening it with descriptions of the young men being pulled along the surf by the plunging, maddened horse when the weighted ropes were removed. Constance smiled as she listened to him, her Horse Warrior. She watched as he used his long powerful hands to describe the ordeal, hands that she wanted to hold her face when he kissed her. His golden-brown eyes lit with amusement as he described his repeated failed attempts to back the wild horse.

William listened in rapt attention; it was the type of story that he loved, man pitted against beast, a war of wills that the strongest must win. 'I would like one of those older male colts or yearlings of hers. Send a message to your brother. I will pay a good price; you can train him for me,' he added with a grin.

Morvan smiled; he knew that Luc would never take a penny from the King but would gladly gift one of the colts. 'With pleasure, Sire, I will send it tomorrow,' he answered.

Only one man stood unaffected by the tale; Robert De Belleme stood, arms folded leaning against a pillar, a sour expression on his face. He had more or less ignored the upstart Breton Knight initially, but now he found him irritating. As the King and his family moved to retire upstairs to the solar, Belleme put a friendly arm across Robert's shoulder. 'Come, let us find some amusement elsewhere for the afternoon, I believe the local tavern has a buxom serving girl or two if memory serves me correctly, and we could lay some bets on the local cockroaches.' The crowd of young men laughed as they followed him out.

Roger-Fitz-Richard beckoned Morvan to come with them, but he ruefully shook his head. 'Duty calls, Roger; I have men and horses to check on.' Roger grimaced in sympathy and raised a hand in farewell.

It was quite a drunken crowd of Robert's supporters that returned in time for dinner. Matilda was displeased and asked her son, William, to tell some of the worse for wear young Knights to go to their rooms. William Rufus was quietly satisfied, anything to put a spoke in his elder brothers wheel; he knew that he was firmly in his father's favour and was assured that he was his father's heir to the English crown. In a month or two, he would be returning to the court in England. He intended to make his life there now away from his annoying brothers, and he was ready to step into his father's shoes. The King was a large, fit and robust man, but he was now in his fiftieth year, and William Rufus was well aware that anything could happen, especially to such a warlike King.

With a jaundiced eye, Robert watched his brother sending his friends to bed; he had seen his mother's speaking look when they came in. However, he had also seen the grin on his bellicose brother's face. He had a strained relationship with William Rufus at the best of times. He also found Henry, who was coming up to eleven years, more and more irritating. He applied himself to his food until his father addressed him. 'I hope your friends are not going to be disporting themselves like this every night, Robert or they will find themselves back on the road to Caen.' Robert shook his head to clear it; he had not forgiven his father for losing Maine to Fulk of Anjou.

'Of course, father, you never caroused into the early hours or kissed serving girls when you were young,' he replied in a cynical tone.

William regarded his son for a few moments; he knew that he had a problematic relationship with him. Too volatile and too carefree, Robert needed to shoulder more responsibility and better understand the political situation, or he would never succeed as the next Duke of Normandy.

'No, Robert, I was too busy trying to stay alive as all of the different factions, so-called guardians and even my father's friends in Normandy, tried to have me killed. So, time for carousing? No, I don't think I did, and there was only one buxom wench I was interested in.' He turned and kissed his blushing wife.

Robert was only slightly mollified, although he did take pleasure in the relationship that his parents had. Most arranged marriages ended in tolerance at best, sometimes loathing and often the most you could hope for was affection. However, his parents blatantly adored each other, and he had never known his father to stray. His mother was a consummate diplomat and administrator; she often ruled Normandy for long periods while the King was away. He had to admit that she also took the time to teach him how to rule justly but effectively, and he knew he was now ready to step up as Duke of Normandy while his father returned to England.

Morvan watched this interplay with interest. He knew the relationship between the brothers was fractious at best; he treated William Rufus with respect but found he could not like the man. His gestures were flamboyant but empty, he would often pick a fight for no reason, and few of the serving maids were safe from his advances. There was also a lot of rivalry between the supporters of the two brothers, so Morvan tended not to get involved.

Henry was very young and impressionable; he often came to sit on the fence and watch them train the big war Destriers. Morvan had invited him to bring his friends and join in the sword practice, and he could see the improvement in the young Prince, but he also found that the intelligent young man could be manipulative when he played one older brother off against the other.

William and Matilda rose to retire; Robert went to play dice with Belleme and his remaining friends, so Morvan indicated to Constance that they should sit on either side of the fire to have a quiet conversation without fear of being overheard.

'You must have enjoyed being back in Brittany,' she said wistfully.

'I enjoyed the visit to see my family, but I have missed you, Constance,' he said, gazing across at her in the firelight.

She smiled, 'I counted every day you were away, Morvan. Let us rise early in the morning, and we will ride down by the river if you can get away.'

Morvan grinned, 'I will make sure I do. Walk down to Shadow's stall when you are ready; I will be there waiting for you. I will arrange for a discrete groom to accompany us. Now… your maidservant is waiting.' He stood and indicated the young girl at the bottom of the staircase. Constance gracefully rose, but as she passed him, she reached out and gently trailed her fingers through his as he smiled down into her eyes.

He watched her go and then turned to find William Rufus glowering at him. He was still sitting at the top table with two of his entourage, but he had watched the exchange between his sister and the Horse Warrior. Morvan quickly bowed his head to the Prince and strode from the Hall, a slight fluttering of concern in his breast.

He was up and waiting for Constance at dawn the following day. It was not long before she appeared smiling at the stable door. He had already tacked up the two horses, and with few words, he helped her mount. He waved the young groom to follow behind as they rode out into the outer Bailey. The yawning guards were just opening the main gates as they rode down through them and on into the forest. For the first part of the ride, they chatted happily about inconsequential things, his family and the breeding programme they had put in place at Morlaix to produce more of these impressive and intelligent warhorses.

When they reached the meadow by the River Risle, they left the horses with the groom and walked some way along the riverbanks. The trees were all sporting their beautiful autumn foliage as they walked through a carpet of coloured leaves. It was a crisp, dry morning, and before long, they reached a large flat boulder where Morvan laid down his cloak so that they could be seated. They sat in silence for a while watching the deep brown peaty water swirl past them.

Morvan took her hand and looked into her clear blue eyes. 'You do know that I have fallen in love with you, Constance, and what man wouldn't?' he admitted. For a second, she hung her head, her beautiful long deep auburn curls shining in the early morning light that filtered through the birch trees. Then she looked up at him and daringly but gently traced her fingers along the firm line of his jaw and down onto his muscular neck. He smiled, and taking her hand, he kissed the tips of her fingers. She gazed into his golden-brown eyes; this dark Breton Knight entranced her.

'I am in love with you too, Morvan de Malvais, but we know it is to no avail; my father would never consent.' Morvan sighed, and then leaning forward, he tipped her chin towards him, and he gently but lingeringly kissed her mouth. Constance gave an 'oh' of surprise as he released her. Her eyes wide, she raised her fingers to touch his lips. She did this almost forlornly as if she would not get the chance again. Witnessing the naked emotion on her face like this and the sadness in her eyes tugged at Morvan's heart, so he kissed her again, pulling her into his arms and running his fingers through her hair to hold her head and bring her lips to his. He released her, and she was almost breathless with pleasure and excitement.

'Let us bide and enjoy our time together, Constance. If anyone asks, we can tell them we are just friends and riding companions. We will think this through, and somehow we will find a way to be together if that is what you wish?' he asked.

Her blue eyes flew to his. 'I want nothing more, Morvan,' she whispered.

He pulled her to him, enfolding her in his arms, her head resting beneath his chin. They stayed like that for quite some time, not talking, just enjoying the closeness and warmth of their embrace. Constance breathed in the warm, masculine smell of his skin, which mingled with the tang of polished leather. She was enjoying every moment of this embrace, the freedom to have her arms wrapped around his waist, to daringly trail her fingers across the muscles in his back when unexpectedly, he released her. Standing with an almost wistful expression on his face, he held her at arm's length and then gently kissed her forehead, 'we must go back.' He held out his hand, pulling her to her feet to take her back to the horses and back to her life as the King's daughter. As he helped her into the saddle, she put her small white hand on top of his large tanned one. He looked up, and as their eyes met, they both knew that with their declarations and embrace, things had changed forever between them; there was no going back.

Chapter Seven

The next few days were similarly pleasant. Morvan and Constance rode out very early each morning, before the other occupants of the castle were stirring, to enjoy each other's company and steal the odd kiss or embrace. The weather was bright and dry, and the young men accompanied by William and his Knights hunted each day in the verdant forests surrounding L'aigle, bringing back deer and a large wild boar tusker that Belleme had bravely cornered and killed. Each evening there was laughter and song as the young cadets set out to entertain the royal party, and relations between Robert and his father seemed to be on the mend.

However, on Saturday, the weather broke with high winds and a deluge of rain. Not only were Constance and Morvan's daily trysts curtailed, but also the young men were confined within the castle as well and soon became restless and bored.

The King spent his time in his solar in deep discussions with his senior advisors about the forthcoming pacts with Fulk and Philip of France. The thought of conceding any territory was anathema to him, but he knew that, without any significant alliances, he had no choice. He became short-tempered and surly as he tried to draw up terms that would not be detrimental to Normandy.

During nuncheon, Robert and William Rufus constantly bickered and argued until their father told them to shut up or get out. Robert and his cronies, including Morvan, retreated to a large table at the side of the Hall to play dice. Henry attached himself to his brother William and his followers, and they decided to play boules along the long gallery on one of the balconies. This produced so much noise from the shouting and betting that William and the ladies retreated up to the Queen's solar.

The dice game became very competitive, Belleme betting with all takers that Robert would win in the best of three throws against Gilbert De Sorrell. Even Morvan, who infrequently gambled, bet on the Prince to the disgust of his friend Gilbert. There was now a considerable pot of money in front of William De Breteuil, who was always chosen as the banker. Robert won the first two throws and was just about to take the third when the entire contents of a chamber pot were poured from the balcony above down onto his head. Robert jumped up in a fury, overturning the table so that coins and dice went in every direction. Anyone sitting near him had been splattered as well, and they all looked up in anger when the raucous laughter of the two younger brothers and Prince William's cronies came from the balcony above. Within seconds, Robert had whirled and drawn his sword. He raced across the Hall to the staircase shouting 'On Me' loudly to his friends, who scrambled to their feet and, drawing their swords, ran after him.

Morvan and a few others did not follow; they stood in the centre of the Hall and watched in dismay as the rest raced up the stairs after Robert. William Rufus and his friends had stopped laughing, and now watched in concern as the large group of older young Knights ran along the balconies to get to them; the light from the windows above flashed on the drawn blades, and young Henry, fear on his face fled through one of the doorways to escape and hide.

Morvan yelled at the astounded men at arms to get up there and stop them. Robert had reached his brother by now, charging along the balcony at him. William Rufus had also drawn his sword, and the two blades clashed while skirmishes broke out all around them between both groups. There had always been intense rivalry between the supporters of both princes, and now they were prepared to dish out punishment. Robert's supporters had the upper hand; as older, more experienced fighters, they concentrated on disarming or punching their opponents in the face with the hilt of their swords.

The guards tried to intervene, but they were reluctant to draw their weapons against the nobility, and the King's sons and they were pushed back. Morvan shook his head in despair at the melee on the balcony. As he watched, one man at arms who attempted to stop them was pushed out of the way by Belleme, and he toppled over the balcony rails slamming down onto the table below. Morvan, horrified, noticed that Belleme hardly glanced at the fallen man. He ran towards the soldier to see if he was severely injured.

Suddenly, there was a loud bellow of rage. William, alerted by the noise, had emerged just in time to see one of his guards slam onto a table below. He strode swiftly along the gallery shouting in his stentorian tone for them to desist and lay down their weapons. He unceremoniously pulled them back by their hair and delivered a punishing punch to their faces when reaching any men still fighting. Finally, he stood in front of his two sons, who stood panting, swords still drawn facing each other. William ordered them to sheath their swords, which they reluctantly did. He delivered a stinging blow to the head of each in turn. Henry, who had just emerged at his father's bellow, ducked back to avoid a similar punishment.

Robert immediately launched into a tirade against his brothers, telling his father what William had done and how he was shamed in front of the other Knights. Watching from below, Morvan could see Robert's face contorted with fury. The King, however, was not appeased by this catalogue of woe.

'Robert Curthose, you are my eldest son, you may rightly think you are wronged, but you do not react in such a violent way inside one of our homes, endangering the life of your family and my men,' he said, indicating the groaning guard below. Robert had flinched at his father's derisive use of his nickname; his father had bestowed that name on him as a young boy because he had short legs, and he hated it. However, the name had stuck, and now, to add insult to injury, his father was blaming him and not William Rufus and Henry. He shook his head in disbelief as his father roared at them, 'Get out of my sight, the three of you.'

Robert stormed downstairs, followed by his subdued supporters. As he passed Morvan, he shouted at him, 'Join us at the Inn.' Morvan nodded while glancing up at the balcony. Matilda and Constance had also been drawn out of the solar by the noise of the altercation, and they stood white-faced in dismay at the scene. At the same time, the King, red-faced and angry, ignored the raised hand and pleas from his wife and stomped down the gallery towards the Steward's room where he knew he would be undisturbed.

Morvan stood back and watched for a while as they tended

to the fallen man at arms; fortunately, he had not broken his back, but he had broken an arm, and the Steward sent for the bonesetter. Morvan's thoughts were in turmoil; he had watched the royal brothers argue and bicker as they usually did, but this was different; swords had been drawn, brother against brother. Morvan found it difficult to see a way through this. He decided to follow Robert and his friends to the Inn to see if Robert had calmed down and, if not to add some words of wisdom.

Chapter Eight

As he entered the low-ceilinged Inn, Morvan could hear Robert even though he was through the back in the taproom. He was striding back and forth, clearly still full of rage. As he reached the group, Roger-Fitz-Richard greeted him and then rolled his eyes. 'We need to calm him down; Belleme, as usual, is stirring the pot.' Morvan looked over at the arrogant nobleman who was standing with one foot on a stool, encouraging Robert's anger.

'They have disrespected you for too long Robert, insult after insult, you cannot let this lie,' he spat at the grim-faced prince.

Morvan stepped forward directly into the line of Robert's strides which brought him to a halt. 'So what do you want, Belleme, for Robert to raise his sword against his brothers again? That way, madness lies and the consequences would be unthinkable.'

Belleme drew his lips back in a sneer at Malvais, but Robert paused, breast heaving with pent up anger. 'I cannot let this go unpunished, Malvais,' he growled.

Morvan nodded and placed a hand on his arm. 'I understand, Sire, but you are the future Duke of Normandy, and there are other ways of dealing with this than a brawl in your father's house. Let things calm down, then go and talk to your father. Be repentant for your rash actions but demand reparation from your brothers.'

Robert looked at Morvan thoughtfully; a few others were now nodding in agreement at this sage council. However, not Belleme, 'The King should have taken the part of his eldest son; it is Robert's right. Instead, he has lost the title and prestige of being the Count of Maine. He is the true Duke of Normandy and should have that position now and not just as the heir when his father dies. The King should return to England with his other sons and leave Robert to rule here in Normandy,' he argued.

There was an audible gasp from the men standing around the table at these words; nobody openly criticised the King in this way. The King had eyes and ears everywhere, and nervous glances were exchanged as they glanced over their shoulders. Morvan glared at Belleme, who drew himself up to his full height and gave a triumphant smile.

Just then, a hand descended on Morvan's arm, and Toki stood behind him. 'Malvais, the Queen desires your presence.' Morvan reluctantly turned to leave; he did not trust Belleme, who seemed to have his own agenda and enjoyed spreading discontent. With Robert in this angry and volatile mood, he was easy prey for the Seigneur. However, Morvan had no choice and, nodding a farewell to his two friends; he followed the young Saxon back to the fortress at L'aigle.

Morvan entered the solar to find Queen Matilda standing in front of the fire, a worried expression on her face. He had spent some time in the Queen's presence over the last few years, and he knew her to be a calm, intelligent woman with great presence. She administered the Duchy of Normandy exceptionally well during William's long absences. However, now he had hardly bowed before she beckoned him in.

'You have been with Robert?' she asked in concern for her eldest son. 'How is he?' Morvan glanced at Constance, who sat quietly on the settle, but he could see that her hands were tightly clasped as she gave him a speaking glance of affection.

'He is still angry, your Grace. Robert did not see this as a harmless prank; he saw it as another affront to his dignity and prestige, especially in front of his followers.'

She nodded and wrung her hands. 'William is furious; we are to return to Caen tomorrow. He could not believe that they would draw swords against each other here inside L'aigle.'

Morvan agreed. 'I admit I was surprised, but coming at the same time as the pact with Fulk, I think Robert was already angry, and this pushed him over the edge.' He gave a rueful smile, and the Queen nodded in acknowledgement.

'You are right Malvais, this is a difficult time for him, but things will improve shortly. The problem lies in the fact that he and William are so alike and bull-headed that they find it difficult to talk without arguing. I must go to the King. Malvais, you are a sensible, mature young warrior, do what you can to calm the situation. I have noticed that Robert respects and listens to you,' she exclaimed.

'I have already tried your Grace, but there are those around him who delight in stoking the fires further.'

'Belleme,' she spat; he nodded.

'That young man has always been a hell-raiser; I was hoping he would return to England with his father when he left last month. But no, here he is fomenting trouble, and at times Robert is so naïve that he does not always see through his manipulations,' she said thoughtfully while gazing into the fire.

She turned to leave, 'I am sure you will keep Constance company for a short while; her nerves are as frayed as mine,' she said with an enigmatic smile as she swept out of the room. No sooner had the door closed than Constance flew off the settle and into Morvan's arms; he could feel the tension and agitation in her frame.

'This is terrible, Morvan; my brothers have always fought but not like this. My father is sending William back to England next month, earlier than intended, but he is just as furious with Robert. Please try to prevent my brother from doing or saying something he will regret,' she pleaded.

He held both of her hands in his, seeing the concern in her face. 'They are grown men, Constance, and will hopefully look back on today's events with shame. They will also want to regain their father's goodwill.' She nestled deep into his arms. 'I hope so,' she whispered as he kissed the top of her head.

However, the situation had not calmed down at the Inn. Having been whipped up by Belleme and a few others, Robert decided that this was the time to demand that his father give him control of both Normandy and Maine. His father needed to let him take the war to Fulk of Anjou to reclaim and hold Maine.

Roger-Fitz-Richard and his friend Gilbert watched the developing storm with dismay. They knew that the King would never acquiesce to such demands; it would create a schism in the Anglo-Norman realm especially given the dangerous situation with Fulk of Anjou and Philip of France. Roger-Fitz-Richard tried to talk some sense into Robert to no avail, so he left as the small group began to make plans to confront William the following day.

Chapter Nine

Morvan finished checking on his men and horses and entered the Hall at L'aigle to find the royal family at the high table breaking their fast. The King waved him up to join them, and Morvan was pleased to see that Matilda seemed to have placated her angry husband. William announced the plans to return to Caen. He then launched into a discussion with Morvan and his senior Knights on the advantages of increasing the number of crossbowmen and the effectiveness of that weapon in battle. They were about to rise from the table when the doors burst open, and Robert marched in, followed by at least twenty of his supporters. Toki stood up; ready to protect the King and his family, but William waved him down as he regarded his eldest son with a jaundiced eye.

'You appear to be somewhat late to break your fast, Robert, but I am sure that the Steward can find some food for you and your friends if they will be seated,' he said calmly, waving the crowd of young men towards the benches and tables. Morvan could see the doubt and indecision on their faces; after all, this was a request from their King. Many began to comply, especially as some of their fathers were sitting with the King... until Robert strode forward to the high table.

'I am not here for food, father; I am here to demand and claim what is rightfully mine. I want independent control of Normandy, and I want you to tear up this foolish and shameful pact with Fulk of Anjou.' He looked back confidently at his followers, and many of them nodded in support.

Morvan glanced at the King and Queen. William calmly brushed the crumbs of his breakfast from his hands and stood up. Matilda was white with shock; he could see the muscles working in her cheeks as she regarded her eldest son. Morvan was only pleased that William Rufus had not come down yet, or the consequences might have been worse.

'You may be my son and heir to these lands on my demise Robert but do you think that petulant and ill-thought-out behaviour such as this will convince me that you are fit to rule? I think not,' he said and turning, he left the Hall with his senior Knights without a backward glance. Matilda, taking Constance by the hand, also rose and, giving her son a disappointed shake of the head, walked away.

Left in the Hall with only the servants who stood open-mouthed and Morvan who still standing behind the table, Robert shook with fury. He clenched his fists and cried out with rage. 'Do you see Malvais? Do you see how they treat me?' he shouted. Morvan stayed silent, knowing this was not a time to intercede.

'I will make him regret his lack of support for me, I promise,' he said, turning on his heel and storming out of the Hall. As the young Knights trailed out behind him, Morvan saw Roger-Fitz-Richard waiting at the back near the doors. He shook his head in frustration as Morvan approached.

'I did my best, but he would not listen to Gilbert or me, too many others telling him he was badly done to and pushing him into action. Many of them, like Belleme, are hoping to benefit with position and reward from Robert's ascension to Duke. In the early hours, Belleme stood and demanded that everyone now address Robert as Duke of Normandy, for that is what he is in all but name. You can imagine how that fired them all up again. We left at that point.'

Morvan had some sympathy for Robert, but it could not end well if he kept on this path. 'Stay with them, Roger and keep me informed of their intentions, will you?' he asked. Richard nodded and hurried to catch up with the others leaving a very concerned Morvan on the steps.

Chapter Ten

In the pouring rain, the hurried morning departure for Caen was stressful but uneventful, and it was a subdued party that returned through the gates into William's fortress that evening. The King had hardly spoken a word during the few stops when they had to water and rest the horses. He was obviously both annoyed and frustrated at the actions of his eldest son. Queen Matilda, knowing her husband, wisely left him to his thoughts.

Morvan was tired as he rubbed down and fed Shadow in the gloom of the stable block; he intended to have a much-needed hot meal with his men and then turn in for the night. He brushed the stray wisps of straw from his clothes and headed across the cobbled inner Bailey. However, as he approached the main steps, a horse rider clattered into the courtyard. The young rider flung himself out of the saddle, dropping the reins of his panting, winded horse and ran up to Morvan.

'Is the King here? I need to see the King.' Morvan put his hands on the shoulders of the mud-spattered squire.

'He is but take a deep breath and compose yourself, and I will take you to him; the family will still be at dinner in the Great Hall.' The young squire took a breath, nodded and tried to brush some of the mud from his clothes.

A wave of welcoming warmth, light and noise met them as

Morvan pushed the enormous wooden door open. William was at the top table with his senior Knights around him; the ladies were not in evidence, no doubt eating in the solar after the day's long and tiring ride. Morvan strode up the Hall through the packed benches, stepping up to the dais with the squire behind him.

'Sire, an urgent messenger has arrived for you.' William frowned and waved the boy forward as conversation died around them.

'Your Grace, I have ridden long and hard to bring you this message from your Castellan, Lord D'Ivry. Rouen has been attacked and is under siege,' he announced, handing the King the wet leather pouch. William's senior Knights were on their feet immediately, astonishment evident on their faces,

'Rouen, our old capital of Normandy? Who would dare to cross our borders and attack the city? It must be the bastard French,' declared Robert de Beaumont angrily.

William held up a hand for peace from the clamour as they crowded around. He placed the vellum down on the table and stared sightlessly down the Hall for a few moments before declaring, 'My son, Robert, and his followers have attacked and laid siege to Rouen, hoping to lay claim to Normandy,' he said in a flat voice.

The shock at these words rippled throughout the room. The King's eldest son had raised his banners against his father; there was disbelief and annoyance that Robert would be as foolish as to do this. There was also concern from several Knights who had cadet sons riding with Robert, now in rebellion against their King.

'Malvais ready your Horse Warriors for a dawn departure. You ride for Rouen.'

Morvan stood rooted to the spot. He would be riding out against the King's son and many of his own friends, such as Roger and Gilbert, in the morning. William noticed the grim set of Morvan's face. 'Malvais come with me; we will look at my map of the city and decide on a strategy.'

Morvan bowed in acquiescence as he turned to the messenger. 'Go and see to your horse and then report to the Steward for some food and a bed,' he said, guiding the bemused but exhausted young man towards the doors. Morvan followed William into his solar, which was mainly his business room; he had been here several times. It was very much a male domain, maps and documents on tables around the room, several tomes lay open with markers in them. A welcome fire blazed in the hearth.

'Shut the door, Malvais and sit down,' he said as he settled into his vast carved chair behind the table. 'I saw your face out there. This is a difficult decision for all of us; I do not want to meet my son in battle either. Therefore I need you to hand command of the Horse Warriors to your Captain; his name is Geoffrey, I believe.' Morvan nodded, not at all surprised that the King knew that. William had a prodigious memory and was famous for his common touch with the men, making him very popular.

'I want you on the road on that huge stallion of yours before the sun rises, before our forces leave. Go to Rouen and talk some sense into Robert. Tell him I am sending several hundred men to lift the siege. Make sure he understands that I will give orders to arrest and imprison any of the insurgents, and it is highly likely that if they continue their assault on Rouen, I will confiscate their lands,' he said.

Morvan blinking considered the impact of the King's words

for a few moments; it was apparent that the King wanted the rebels to retreat before his forces arrived, and he knew it would be a difficult task to persuade Robert to do that. He met the King's eyes in understanding. He stood, bowed and turned on his heel to try to get a few hours' sleep before he had to leave. He glanced back as he closed the door to see William, his chin now resting on his fist, frowning at the fire in both frustration and sadness at his son's thoughtless actions.

Chapter Eleven

Her brother's decision to rebel against his father tore at Constance; she was closer to Robert than her other brothers. Her mother was shocked by what Robert was doing, they knew that he was unhappy with recent events, but they never expected him to rise in open rebellion against his father. This threatened the whole stability of Normandy and Maine. Constance had another reason for fear; her natural anxiety was for Morvan, who could find himself riding into battle against her brother and his friends.

She was head over heels in love with Morvan De Malvais. Her tall, dark Horse Warrior was Lord of a large estate in Vannes in Brittany, but she knew that he would never be considered suitable by her parents. Her mother kept a sympathetic but watchful eye on the dalliance between them, but she knew that her parents could put a stop to it at any time; it had happened to two of her other sisters, one of whom had been sent to a nunnery.

Morvan De Malvais was just another Knight to her father, one of many who buzzed around Constance. Her father did not see that her eyes followed the Horse Warrior everywhere or that she felt a deep aching love for him. She had experienced many light flirtations, but she had never felt anything like this, her stomach clenched just watching him stride down the Hall to join them at the top tables. She longed for the time when they could be alone by the river or riding close together in the woods. She could not begin to describe how she felt when he kissed her, the currents that raced down through her body. Despite that, they had never considered taking things further, even though she loved the thought of giving herself to Morvan. It was as if they both accepted that she was intended for someone else, so physical love could not be allowed.

She did know how much he desired her; she had recognised the passion in him and felt the hardness of his manhood pressed against her when they kissed, and they had always reluctantly parted.

Now, sitting in the solar with her mother waiting for news from Rouen, she wished that she were not a royal princess; she would give anything to spend her life with Morvan and bear his children. She raised her eyes to Matilda, who was finding it difficult to settle to anything. Her father had curtly informed them of his actions and his expectation that Robert would come to his senses. Constance stood watching her father's forces leaving for Rouen this morning; she just prayed that Robert would withdraw and make his peace with their father.

Morvan galloped into Rouen at midday. He walked his stallion over the bridges of the River Seine and stopped for a second. Despite Robert's siege, or maybe because of it, the town was bustling with people coming over the bridges towards him and heading south, some carrying their possessions. He glanced up and down the river; Rouen had always had a busy river trade, and it was an important port with laden barges and small cutters going back and forth. Ahead of him to the north, the cathedral of Notre Dame towered impressively over the town. This city had always been the capital of Normandy until William decided to move the capital to Caen, but it still had the feel of a vibrant capital city.

Morvan made his way up the narrow streets towards the castle. It did not take him long to find Robert's forces. He was taken aback by the number of men there as he rode in; there seemed to be far more troops here than Robert could have been expected to assemble. He picked his way through the groups; many sat around campfires, responding to the raised fists and shouted greetings from various compatriots. Finally, he found a significant-looking tent in the centre. He dismounted, handing his reins to a squire, and pushed his way through the crowd assembled outside. It was only a small pavilion, hastily erected, but Robert had established himself here and could be seen inside stood at a table discussing strategy with a small group. Morvan strode into the tent.

'Sire, I need to have speech with you in private,' he said. Robert looked up, and a smile lit his face. 'Malvais have you come to join us?' he exclaimed, opening his arms in a gesture of welcome.

'Unfortunately not, but I do bring a message that is for your ears only.'

Robert looked slightly crestfallen and then told the assembled nobles to leave. Morvan noticed that Belleme was at Robert's right hand and made no move to leave.

His friends Roger and Gilbert slapped him on the back in greeting as they passed him. 'I hope you have come to help us out,' Roger said in a meaningful way as he left the tent.

Morvan smiled. 'I bring a message from the King, but it is

only for his son's ears.'

Belleme still did not move and sneered. 'I think we should all hear this to ensure the Prince is not bullied by his father when we have achieved so much. We are in a strong position here; the castle will be ours in a day or so. Then we will declare Rouen to be once again the capital of Normandy, and Robert will be acclaimed Duke in the cathedral as he should be.'

Morvan looked at Belleme in disbelief. 'So you are advocating civil war in Normandy, are you?, Pitting father against son and brother against brother while we have wolves such as Count Fulk and Philip of France raiding our borders ready to take full advantage of such a schism. You are clearly mad, Belleme,' he ended in a derisive tone.

Robert looked from one man to the other as Belleme clenched his fists and glared at Morvan. 'If we do end up in battle, which I doubt, I will look for you, Malvais,' he spat.

'I will make sure you find me Belleme when you spout treason such as this against the King, and the pleasure I assure you will be all mine.'

Belleme paled at those words; he knew he was walking a fine line encouraging Robert on this path, but no one had yet accused him of treason. His father, the Earl of Shrewsbury, would be furious and likely disown him if he heard those words. 'I am not advocating attacking or deposing the King, just ensuring that Robert gets what is rightly his,' he muttered as finally, with some reluctance, he left them.

'Sit down, Malvais and wash the road from your throat while you tell me what my father has to say,' Robert said in a resigned tone, pouring them both a goblet of wine.

Morvan took a long draught and wiped his mouth. 'Your father is giving you notice to stand down, and by sending me ahead of his forces, he is giving you time to gather your men and leave. He thinks that you are poorly advised, that you made this move at the height of your anger, and you have now had time to reflect on your actions. He has despatched a large force, including the Horse Warriors, to Rouen; they will be here by late afternoon, I imagine. Over five hundred men are led by Eustace De Boulogne, who has orders to arrest all insurgents. If your followers do not accede to the King's demands, he is prepared to seize their lands.' Morvan finished and took another long draught of the watered wine while watching the emotions play across Robert's face.

Robert frowned; he never expected his father to send a force of that size. He leant his elbows on the table and, steepling his fingers, rested his forehead on his hands. The silence continued for some time as Robert closed his eyes and considered what he had just heard.

'Your father is allowing you to back down and return to court Robert. You have made your point to him; it would be no disgrace now for you to return and ask him to consider your demands,' said Morvan in a soft voice.

Robert sat up and took a deep breath as he looked into Morvan's face. 'So I have three options. Firstly, I can stay and fight a far greater force, and no doubt, Sir D'Ivry will sally forth from the castle and attack us from the rear as well. Secondly, I can return like a whipped dog with my tail between my legs to Caen to beg my father's forgiveness while my brothers crow and lord it over me,' he said, his face now white with anger. Morvan shook his head.

'I assure you, Robert, the King does not want that; he wants reconciliation. What you have done puts you in a better position to negotiate with him for an early accession to the Duchy.'

Again, silence descended as Morvan realised that only two options were aired. 'What is the third option Sire?' He asked.

'We can run, Malvais. We take the men who have come to our banners, and we remove ourselves to a distance to demand what we want; I have been patient for too long,' he exclaimed.

Morvan looked at the tight-lipped white face in front of him, and he could see that the prince was torn. He knew he was betraying his family, but his pride and prestige had been injured.

'Think carefully on it, Sire, I beg you. Sometimes when you widen a rift too far, it becomes difficult to heal, and all sides are damaged.'

Robert bit his bottom lip and nodded. 'It is a shame you are not with us, Malvais, you are wise and experienced for your years; I could do with you by my side to give me council.'

Although this was King William's heir, Morvan leant forward and clasped Robert's arm in a warrior's grip as if he was just a comrade. 'Unfortunately, duty and loyalty are my family's motto. I was brought up in the shadow of my brother, Luc De Malvais, one of the greatest Knights in Europe. He always puts duty before everything, even his life and his own family; I have watched him do that repeatedly. I serve your father the King, so I have no option but to support him.'

Robert nodded. 'I know, and I admire you for that, but I wish it could be otherwise,' he said.

Morvan stood to take his leave. 'Think on your father's offer, Robert. Do you have any message for him?' he asked.

Robert slowly shook his head. 'I will consider what he said, and my actions will be my answer.' Morvan held his gaze for a few seconds, but then Robert dropped his eyes, and Morvan bowed and left the tent with a feeling of foreboding.

His friends Roger-Fitz-Richard De Clare and Gilbert De

Sorrell were waiting for him to give them any news outside the tent. 'So tell me, De Clare, how is the siege going for Robert? Will he dislodge them?' Morvan said with a grim smile in greeting while gazing up at the solid walls of the colossal Donjon in the centre of Rouen, the top of which bristled with armed men.

Roger answered, 'D'Ivry, the King's Pincenar, holds the castle against all comers; I cannot see us taking it in all honesty; it would take months. This is more of a token protest by Robert because of the way he has been treated. What happens next depends on the King's response.' Morvan relayed the gist of the King's message to them.

The shocked expression on his friend's face said it all. 'There is no way that we can hold against such forces,' Gilbert said, shaking his head.

Morvan agreed. 'I have advised Robert, so we will see what develops. Go to him and add your wisdom to mine.'

'I think someone is ahead of us,' Roger said, indicating the Seigneur De Belleme, who was entering the pavilion.

Morvan frowned. 'Do what you can, my friends; I must leave to join my men with the King's force, and I do hope that when we return, I will not be raising my sword against you.' He clasped arms and went in a troubled state of mind to find Shadow; he just prayed that Robert Curthose would not decide to stand and fight or many would die unnecessarily.

Later that afternoon, Morvan returned and rode back into Rouen as part of the large force that William had despatched to deal with the insurgents. When they reached Robert's camp, it was deserted; they had gone as Morvan had advised. Morvan sat on his stallion, surveying the scene as Sir D'Ivry came down from the castle with his cheering men to meet the King's commander who had relieved the siege. As Morvan gazed at the empty pavilion, the upturned chairs and scattered maps that spoke of a hasty departure, he wondered which option Robert had chosen, whose advice he had listened to at the end. Had he retreated to then return to court and mend the rift with his father? On the other hand, had they fled elsewhere to regroup? He prayed it was the former as the consequences of the other option filled him with dismay.

Chapter Twelve

It was not long before King William had Robert's answer; his son and most of his supporters had fled from Normandy. They had gone north. Robert Curthose had now established himself at the court of his Uncle Count Robert I at the capital of Ghent in Flanders; he was on a mission to gain more support and followers against his father. Morvan was exasperated; Robert had chosen a path that could only lead to civil war in Normandy or on its borders.

In all events, it meant that Morvan was back in Caen for a while, and he could enjoy more time with Constance while William decided on the next plan of action. They carelessly walked and talked together every day, wrapped up in each other, seemingly unaware of the servants and courtiers who watched and gossiped about them. Queen Matilda certainly became aware when her son William Rufus burst into her chamber one morning. Fortunately, the King was not there.

'Are you aware that bets are now being offered on whether my father will sanction the marriage of Constance to that Horse Warrior?' he asked in an angry voice. Matilda viewed her red-faced son dispassionately for a moment or two before answering.

'I think, William that you have more important things to think about than the light flirtation of your sister. You and your younger brother are responsible for a rift in this family that is not only upsetting both your father and me but may well lead to civil war,' she said. William Rufus stood tight-lipped; he had to admit that things had gone much further than he wanted or expected. 'You are leaving for England next week; try to disport yourself there as a future King. Do not make us ashamed of you again,' she added, indicating that he should leave.

As the door closed behind him, she sighed; she tried to love all of her children equally, but sometimes they made it difficult, and she was painfully aware of all of William Rufus's faults and vices. However, what he said was a concern; she needed to have speech with Constance before her father became aware of the gossip. She knew that he was already looking for further alliances to bolster his situation against Anjou and France. There was no doubt in her mind that he would be prepared to use his unmarried children to secure such alliances. She finished dressing and sent for Constance.

Constance had arranged for an afternoon ride with Morvan, but as she waited for him, she now realised how foolish they had been; she would have to speak with him. Leaving the castle, they followed the River Orne, taking a different route from usual up towards the southwest. She dismissed the groom after a few leagues, and she pushed the pace laughing together and racing each other up through the forested foothills until they came to a small meadow where a few wild goats were grazing. They knotted the reins and dismounted, strolling side by side in the bright autumn sunshine. Unexpectedly, storm clouds began to roll in from the west, and without warning, the heavens opened.

They re-mounted their horses and rode deep into the trees, trying to find shelter from the enormous drops, until they reached a sizeable craggy cliff face. They followed this round to the south until they came to a considerable overhang surrounded closely by trees that provided shelter for them from the downpour. There was a long hollowed-out depression in the rock that went some way back, ideal for shelter but not deep enough to be classed as a cave.

They tied the horses at one end, and Morvan took his rolled saddle blanket, lay it down at the very back close to the wall, and led a shivering Constance to it. 'Sit down; we are out of the wind and the rain here; there is enough shelter from the cliff and the surrounding trees,' he said, draping his cloak around her shoulders.

She did as he bid and watched him as he gathered dry leaves and tinder from the back and sides of the cave. Before long, he had a small fire going. She loved to watch him, his long muscular frame and broad shoulders silhouetted against the sky as he stood and assessed the weather while gathering more twigs and branches. He turned and crouched over the fire, blowing on it to increase the flames until he had quite a blaze, then he looked up into her eyes, and for a few moments, they just stared at each other. Alone in this remote hideaway, Constance wished above all things for a life like this with him, away from her oppressive and suffocating court life.

She sighed and beckoned to him. 'Come and sit here beside me, Morvan,' she said softly. He brushed his hands of leaves and lowered himself onto the rough blanket beside her, taking her hands and pulling his heavy woollen cloak around both of them. Constance steeled herself for what she was about to say. 'I need to talk to you,' she said in a flat, toneless voice, and he noticed that her eyes remained lowered. Morvan's stomach knotted in concern at what she might be about to say.

'My mother has warned me that our friendship has become too open, and our displays of affection to each other have been noticed to the extent that we are now quite the main topic of conversation at court.' Morvan cursed inwardly; it was true that he had become too careless; too engrossed in the woman he loved to keep up the precautions he had initially put in place.

He raised her hand to his lips and nuzzled her fingers. 'It is difficult, Constance; you know how much I love you, how much I want to be with you.'

She raised her large blue eyes to him. 'Yes, Morvan and I return that love tenfold, but if we are to be together at all, we must be more circumspect, or they will ensure that we are separated.' He gently took hold of her chin and turned her head, bringing his lips down on hers. They had kissed several times before, but this time it was different, more intense as he pulled her unresisting into his arms and close against his body under the warm cloak.

Constance was almost light-headed from the rush of emotions and excitement that she felt. She was not naïve; she listened to her brothers, and she knew that Morvan must have had many women. A tall, good-looking warrior like him would attract all the married but bored, beautiful court women. His name had been linked with several of them when he first arrived in Caen, and part of her did not blame him; after all, he was single, and he was not a monk. Moreover, that was the nub of it, that she might be consumed by love for him, but she could never have him, and that thought burned within her.

Perhaps it was that heart-rending thought that suddenly made her reckless as she took his face in both of her hands. She kissed his eyes, his cheekbones, the line of his strong jaw, then she nuzzled her way down his throat, and he groaned. She pulled back and started unlacing the leather ties at the front of his doublet, opening it to the waist. Morvan did not say a word; he watched her, mesmerised as she ran her hands inside his leather doublet and over his soft linen tunic to feel his body beneath. He shrugged off the cloak and the doublet and pulled her down beside him, so they were lying side by side on the blanket. He hooked his right leg over hers, pulling her even closer, then, taking her hands, he slipped them up under his tunic to rest against his warm skin. She closed her eyes in pleasure and followed the hard contours of his muscled torso.

She stopped and opened her eyes. 'They may send me away, Morvan, if my father has heard the gossip,' she whispered.

Morvan stared down at her, his anguish plain to see in his face. 'We will be careful, Constance; I cannot lose you yet.'

'Make love to me, please,' she begged him. 'We may not get another such chance like this.'

Morvan raised himself upon his left elbow so he could look clearly into her face. 'Are you sure, Constance? Kissing is one thing, but there will be no going back if we do this,' he said, torn between joyful desire and the implications of what it would mean for her and him.

She nodded. 'I want to experience genuine lovemaking with the man I love. I have thought long on it. I will be sent to a loveless political marriage to a man who does not know or love me, and he will take me whether I want it or no. He will not be my lover; he will be my keeper. I am a valuable asset to my father, no more than that.' Her voice broke with passion and emotion.

He pulled her tightly against him; his love for her at that

moment was overwhelming. 'If you wish this, then yes, I desire you, and I promise that I will be careful,' he said as his hands firmly stroked the outside of her arms and then moved to cup and caress her breasts. She gasped in pleasure. He pulled his linen tunic over his head and began to slowly remove her clothes. The storm had blown over, the sun was flickering once more through the trees, and she could feel the warmth from the fire on her naked skin as her eyes ranged with interest over his body. She loved the perfect shape of his broad shoulders and narrow waist. She ran her fingers over the white marks and scars from sword practice and the many skirmishes he had carried out on the borders with Anjou.

He pulled her back down beside him, and within moments, he was kissing her deeply and gently stroking the most intimate parts of her body. Excitement raced through her; the feel of his skin against her skin, the heat from his body, the warmth from his hands as he caressed her was almost too much for her as his tongue explored her mouth, his lips so warm and gentle.

She watched with interest as he unlaced his chausses from his braies and then slowly unlacing those, he removed them too so that he was lying naked beside her. She knew what to expect; years spent among the gossiping courtiers had given her all the knowledge she needed about what they were going to do. Despite that, nothing had prepared her for the red-hot desire that consumed her, the passion, the heightened emotions, and the impact of every touch.

Then there was the feeling of pure abandon, the joy of letting him and wanting him to do anything he wished with her.

He pushed her onto her back and moved to lie on top of her. She looked up into his golden-brown eyes, shining with love for her as he moved his knee in between her legs. 'I will be as gentle as possible, Constance, I promise,' he said, his face a mask of passion.

She smiled and took her bottom lip between her teeth in anticipation as she felt his fingers gently probing to position himself between her legs. His lips descended on hers as he moved forward, and she found herself rising up to meet him, wanting him so much. She felt only a moment of resistance, and then he was moving deep inside her; she clung to him, wrapping her legs over his as she entwined her hands in his thick, shoulder-length hair, and she ran her hands over his broad muscled shoulders.

He caressed and kissed her breasts and nipples as he moved within her, and she could feel the excitement building as she suddenly reached a climax that seemed to go on and on; she had never experienced anything like it. As the feeling slowly subsided, she opened her eyes in wonder to gaze at him, but she could see that he was still in the throes of passion, moving now with urgency until, at the very last moment, he suddenly withdrew and cried out in ecstasy.

He lay supine on top of her, still breathing heavily as she stroked his head. A tear rolled down her cheek, expressing the emotion of this moment with the man she loved, but the tear also embodied the sense of loss she felt. She would lose him. She would never bear his children or share his life; some other woman would do that. Even so, she knew that no matter what happened to her, no matter what she might have to endure, inside, she would always belong to Morvan De Malvais. He raised himself onto his elbows, and gazing down into her eyes, he gently kissed her.

'You are mine now, Constance. We will find a way, I promise you.'

Chapter Thirteen

They dressed and reluctantly returned to the fortress at Caen to find the outer Bailey full of horses as they rode in. Constance suddenly remembered part of her mother's conversation that morning. Her father had guests arriving today. She dismounted and, handing her horse to a groom, she stood and bade a lingering farewell to Morvan and then quickly made her way to her chamber to change her dishevelled clothes and rebraid her unruly hair before her mother saw her. She was not aware that anyone who saw them would just know by looking at her what they had been doing. She positively glowed, and her love for Morvan shone out of her eyes as she looked at him.

One person did see and was instantly dismayed. She did not take much notice of the two men deep in conversation outside the Donjon, part of her registering that one of them was a tall, dark warrior. She was still utterly engrossed in what she had just experienced with Morvan as she mounted the steps, a smile playing on her lips.

Morvan had dismounted, and his face lit up as he saw the tall warrior striding towards him. 'Luc,' he cried, grinning. 'What has brought you to Caen?' Luc enveloped his brother in an embrace, but there was no answering grin as he held his brother's shoulders and looked into his face.

'Not here. Let us go into the stables,' he said curtly. Morvan looking perplexed led the way into the stall with Shadow.

Once inside, Luc stood and watched as Morvan untacked the horse and then, checking they were alone, he turned on his younger brother. 'Morvan, what the hell have you done?' he hissed at him.

Morvan's brain whirled; there was no doubt that Luc knew, but how did he know?

'I love her,' he faltered out to his brother.

Luc turned away in disgust. 'You have lain with a royal princess, and it was written all over her face, her hair, and her rumpled clothes as she entered the Donjon. Do you not think her family, the servants, the courtiers in the Hall will not see this?' he asked in a harsh, exasperated voice running his hands through his hair.

'William will kill you for this if he finds out,' he said with a toneless finality as he sat down on the edge of a wooden trough. Morvan stood forlornly, looking down at his brother, who now had his head down in his hands. He knew that Luc was right in some ways; he had not thought this through. He hoped against hope that William would see how much they loved each other and agree to a betrothal.

'We must get you away from here until she is betrothed elsewhere,' said Luc.

'No,' whispered Morvan. 'She is my life, and I cannot lose her. Do you not remember how you felt about Merewyn? That was a forbidden love, a Breton-Norman Lord and a rebel Saxon, but you overcame what appeared to be insurmountable obstacles to marry her.'

Luc looked long and hard at his brother before replying. 'Yes, that is true, and I still feel that way about Merewyn, but she was a Saxon Thegns daughter of similar standing to me. Here we are talking about a royal princess. I have told you repeatedly that this could never be; William has plans for her. I have just left one suitor who is here for the next week.'

Morvan's face registered his shock. 'Who?' he gasped.

Luc looked at his brother's white face. He knew this would hurt, but he needed Morvan to face up to the reality of the situation. 'Alan Fergant. William invited him to discuss a future alliance,' he said.

Morvan felt a wave of hopelessness wash over him; Alan Fergant, known as Iron Glove, was the heir to Hoel, the Duke of Brittany, and a powerful and wealthy young man. He would come into his Dukedom in a few years; there was no way he could compete with that even as a Knight who now held large estates in Vannes.

'Think on what I have said, Morvan. You must leave here and get away from her for a while or at least until she is betrothed or married to some foreign Prince or Duke,' said Luc, standing to depart. 'I have just arrived, so I must go and give my greetings to the King and Queen. I will see you at dinner, no doubt,' he said, taking his leave from his shaken and dismayed brother.

Constance felt no remorse for what she had done; making love with Morvan De Malvais was the most beautiful experience, and she would treasure it and the way she felt about him for the rest of her life. However, she was aware that she was putting Morvan's life at risk; she knew her father, he would enact some terrible retribution on the man who had deflowered his daughter. William had a long history of blinding, maiming or poisoning those opponents or Knights who had dared to challenge or oppose him. She would be careful, and she would follow her mother's wishes and pay attention to other men, flirting and encouraging them. She had to do anything she could do to deflect the court gossip away from her lover.

This was particularly easy that evening as her mother placed her next to Alan Fergant, the heir to Brittany. The Hall was packed with several guests and their retainers, so her father was in his element, his booming voice and laughter echoing around the Hall. As she took her seat and smiled at the company, she automatically turned around to see if Morvan was there. However, further, along the top tables set out in a horseshoe shape, she encountered the hard, steel blue stare of an unsmiling Luc De Malvais with an empty seat beside him. Her stomach flipped. She could see at once that he knew; the way he looked at her, Morvan must have told him. That cold, condemning stare said it all, and a wave of chagrin washed over her. She could feel the colour rush to her face, and she did not dare look in his direction again.

Constance took a long draft of the white wine in front of her. She could not eat; she mechanically picked at her food but left it on her plate. What would the famous Breton Lord do? He was head of the Malvais family, a loyal and courageous supporter of her father. He would not tolerate any scandal attached to his family name; duty and honour were everything to a brave but ruthless warrior Lord like him. Despite these fears, she fixed a smile on her face and set out to entertain and even flirt with her father's guest. She had been raised to be politically astute, and she knew how important it would be to her father to have an alliance with Brittany. Alan was younger than she was, but he was not called 'Alan the strong' and 'iron glove' for nothing. He had an impressive physique and an imposing mature presence. He kept up a stream of witty and intelligent conversation. He was very confident, but she detected a touch of vanity and arrogance as well. She played on this, ensuring his wine cup was filled, hanging on his every word, placing her hand on his sleeve to hear more of his exploits. She saw her parents smiling and nodding at her in satisfaction, but inside, her stomach was in knots; she did not dare look down the table to see if Morvan had arrived.

Luc sat and watched the accomplished performance that Constance was delivering only a few feet away from him. She was an experienced courtier; no one watching her monopolise Alan Fergant would have thought she had spent the afternoon making love to Morvan. His brother had just arrived, and he sat in a sea of misery beside him as he watched Constance monopolise another man. Although astute in many ways, his brother could not yet hide his feelings from others, and his face and demeanour were giving him away. However, watching the faces of some of the courtiers, Luc thought that this was not a bad thing; they would think that Constance had just been amusing herself in a flirtation with his brother. It was clear that she now had a far bigger fish in her net, and it looked as if she meant to catch him.

At that moment, Alan Fergant was engaging in conversation with her father, so Constance risked a glance down the table at Morvan, and Luc caught his breath; the pain in her eyes as she looked at his brother was plain to see and heartrending. She truly loved Morvan, and Luc knew that it was now imperative that he get his brother away from the court here in Caen for a while before anyone else saw those glances.

The following day, an opportunity presented itself; Luc had been summoned to Caen by the King to discuss Fulk's ongoing attacks on the borders despite the pact that was due to be signed with him in a few weeks. William also wanted to discuss the thorny subject of Robert's rebellion with the Breton Lord; he respected Luc's opinion and considered him a shrewd strategist. He also needed someone away from the court and the family to give him a balanced view. William listened to Luc's frustration at the intended transfer of Maine to Fulk; he understood this as Luc had fought the Angevins in Brittany and Maine for years. However, William was becoming weary of constant warfare; it had defined his whole life from a very early age. He hoped that the forthcoming pacts with Fulk and Philip of France would give him the breathing space to build stronger alliances with the likes of Alan Fergant.

Luc listened and was forced to acquiesce; he knew that the terrible defeat at Dol had taken a toll on both of them but particularly for William in terms of cost and reputation. William found he could talk to Luc De Malvais in a way that was often impossible with some of his senior Knights or his sons.

'You will have heard no doubt about my son's attempt to take Rouen?' he asked.

'A sad situation, Sire, and one I hope you will resolve.'

Before he replied, the King sat pensively staring at the rich tapestry on the wall in the solar. 'I was hoping that you would be willing to go and mediate for me with Robert. He is holed up in his uncle's court in Flanders. He may likely listen to someone of your experience and reputation. I cannot send my senior Knights as many of their cadet sons are there with him.'

'Unfortunately, my Lord, Merewyn is due to give birth to our third child in the next month, and I would not like to be as far away as Flanders.' William sighed as he remembered that Malvais had lost his first wife in childbirth, a dangerous time still for many women if they had a difficult birth or contracted childbed fever.

'However, I suggest you send Morvan. He is friendly with Robert and his followers, and I know your son values my brother's council.'

William looked thoughtful for a few moments. They sat in the solar beneath the window, and Luc could see the lines of concern and worry that were etched onto the King's face since he had last seen him at Dinan a few years ago. William agreed, 'Yes, Malvais send Morvan to me; he can leave for Flanders tomorrow. Now I must go; I am riding out with our falcons. Fergant is keen to show me his new bird, a huge gyrfalcon he bought from a Muscovite trader. Do you come with us?'

Luc smiled and shook his head. 'No, Sire, I need to see my brother, and I want to spend the day assessing the troop he has assembled here. I do not lightly let the name 'Breton Horse Warriors' be assigned unless both men and horses are exceptionally well-trained,' he jibed. William gave a burst of laughter at Luc's audacity and slapped him on the back before heading for the door.

Matilda and one of her women had been sitting quietly with their needlework near the fire during this conversation, and now, as Luc picked up his gloves, she hailed him.

'My Lord De Malvais, a moment of your time?'

Luc bowed. 'Your servant, your Grace,' he said as he looked into those beautiful grey but concerned eyes.

'I would like to thank you for sending your brother away on this task; I believe that you are also aware of the affection between him and my daughter Constance.' Luc nodded, unwilling to betray his brother and share any thoughts on how far it had gone.

'A separation for a month or two will do them good. As I am sure you have seen the King has plans for Constance with Alan Fergant and no-one wants his wrath if an illicit love affair stymies those plans.'

Luc gave a tight smile. 'Amen to that, your Grace. I will ensure he leaves first thing tomorrow,' he said and bowing, he left. Matilda watched him go, this exceptionally handsome, tall, dark Breton Knight who had served them so well. She remembered the King singing his praises after the battle of Hastings when Malvais was still very young, one of the most formidable warriors that William had ever seen. He was now in his early thirties, and she knew that he was a diplomat as well as a warrior; his being here just at this time was no accident, and of course, he would protect his brother if he could.

She sat down again with her embroidery in her lap. She had seen the glow and sparkle in her daughter. She had been awakened, and her love for Morvan shone out of her eyes; it was evident to her that they were now probably lovers. She also knew her husband, and although he liked and respected the young Horse Warrior, he would probably kill him in pure rage if he found out. She crossed the room to the prie-dieu in the corner and dropped to her knees in front of the gilded painting of the Virgin Mary to pray that would never happen.

An hour later, she sent for Morvan; she had a task for him in Flanders that was just as important, but William must not know what she was about to do.

Chapter Fourteen

Morvan arrived at the court of Flanders in late September. He travelled with ten of his warriors, as the roads through northern France could be hazardous. However, he had hardly spoken a word to his men for the first day.

He was consumed with both anger and shame from the last meetings he had with his brother and the Queen; it was immediately apparent that they were somehow both aware of what had happened between himself and Constance. The worst part was that he knew that Luc was right and that they were risking everything by continuing their affair, but it had taken every bit of willpower to ride out of there and leave her with Alan Fergant for the next few weeks. He had no chance to say goodbye to Constance as the Queen kept her close, and Luc insisted that he stay with him and the men on his last night. It was a resigned and irritable Morvan that rode into Ghent several days later.

He knew that Robert Curthose was still here in Flanders as he was trying to win support against his father from the powerful Archbishop-elector of Treves visiting his uncle. Morvan was not sure what his reception would be at the court.

Count Robert I of Flanders was still openly hostile to his

sister Matilda and her husband, King William. Count Robert had usurped his nephew Arnulf to seize Flanders, so Philip of France had amassed an army against him. Count Robert had defeated him, and Arnulf was killed, but Robert's own sister Matilda had sent Norman troops to support her nephew Arnulf against him; he had never forgiven this betrayal by his own sister. The court of Flanders had then become a refuge for any of William's enemies, which was why Robert Curthose had fled there following his flight from Rouen.

As they rode through the narrow streets towards the castle, the first people Morvan saw were Roger-Fitz-Richard and Gilbert De Sorrell, who embraced him like a long-lost brother.

'Have you finally come to join us, Malvais?' Roger asked.

Morvan smiled at his friends. 'Unfortunately not. I bring letters for the Count of Flanders and for Robert from his father.'

'Ah... of course, duty, loyalty and honour, the Malvais code,' his friend, Roger, chanted and grinned.

Morvan dismounted and slapped him hard on the back. 'Where are you situated?' he asked.

'We have rooms in the town. Count Robert is with the Court at present; I will take you there,' Roger offered.

Morvan hesitated as he glanced at his tired men and horses. 'Leave them to me; I will take them to the Golden Cock Inn,' offered Gilbert, 'I will see them settled into the stables.'

Morvan nodded in gratitude and, dismounting; he followed Roger up through the narrow bustling streets of the town. Ghent was built on the banks of the River Lieu at the confluence of two rivers. It was a large, prosperous city, home to the Counts of Flanders who had built a castle there on a promontory at Gravensteen. They entered the gates, and Roger took Morvan into an expansive Great Hall with many leaded windows. There was a blaze of colour and light everywhere, rich tapestries, velvet hangings, flags and pennants. It appeared almost opulent after the bleak military fortress that was home to King William in Caen.

The place seemed to be packed with dozens of Knights and courtiers as Morvan made his way apprehensively to approach and present himself to Count Robert. He could see that the Count was engaging in deep conversation with an imposing bishop and several nobles.

At last, Count Robert turned and noticed the young Horse Warrior standing patiently with Roger-Fitz-Richard. He raised an eyebrow in question, and Morvan stepped forward, opening the leather pouch he was carrying. 'I bring you greetings Sire from King William and Queen Matilda of Normandy; I will wait in Ghent for your reply,' he said while proffering the rolled sheet of vellum.

Conversation stopped around them as Count Robert stared down at the missive in Morvan's hand as if it were poisoned. Then he nodded to one of his nobles to take the vellum scroll. He looked Morvan up and down and began to turn away without a word when suddenly; Robert Curthose appeared with a shout.

'Malvais, you are here!' and he grasped Morvan's arm.

Count Robert turned back and reappraised the young man. 'Malvais? I thought you were familiar; you must be the brother of Luc De Malvais. You are a long way from your home in Brittany,' he said.

'Yes, Sire. I am resident in Caen at present, leading and training a troop of Breton Horse Warriors. The Queen asked me to deliver messages both to you and to her son,' he said, indicating Robert and drawing a second scroll from his pouch.

Count Robert nodded. I fought alongside your brother, Luc,

on several occasions. Well, I say alongside, usually we were trying to keep up as he cut his way relentlessly through our enemies. I have never seen a swordsman like him,' said the Count. Morvan smiled; even here, in Ghent, hundreds of leagues from home, he was still living in his brother's shadow. The Count turned back to his companions, and Robert, with an arm around Morvan's shoulder, led him out of the crowded Hall into the late autumn sunshine.

'How is my mother?' he asked.

'The Queen is very well but obviously worried about you and the split with your father. The King is exasperated by the decision you took.'

They walked to the nearby battlements; Robert sat on a nearby wall in the late autumn sunshine and unrolled the missive from his mother. When he had finished, he looked pensive for a while, staring off across the roofs and spires of the growing town sprawling below the castle. 'This is a situation of my own father's making. He needs to give me the recognition that is rightfully mine as Duke of Normandy, recognition that I am already getting here in Flanders.'

Morvan said nothing about that; he did not want to become embroiled in such a discussion. 'It must be difficult, Robert, to be so estranged from your father and sitting in the court of his known enemies,' he said finally.

Robert scowled. 'He left me no choice, and I could not go running back to Caen with my tail between my legs,' he spat. Morvan sighed; he knew when he heard the words of Belleme.

'My mother says you have something for me?' Robert asked.

'Yes, but not here. My men are at the Golden Cock, and there is a small chest there, but she says your father must not know, or her position would be very difficult.'

Robert grinned and nodded, following Morvan back down through the town to the inn, where Morvan handed over a small chest. Robert opened it and whistled as he saw the small red leather bags emblazoned with his mother's crest, each one full of gold coins. 'With this, I can recruit and attract more Knights, men and horses; I will show my father what I am made of,' he laughed.

Morvan shook his head; he hoped the Queen knew what she was doing, or her love and generosity to her favourite son might trigger the very war she wanted to avoid.

Morvan spent a more enjoyable week in Ghent than he expected while he waited for the response from Count Robert. He still had a gnawing pain every time he thought of the loss of Constance, but he was treated with respect by the Count and the Knights and courtiers of the opulent and wealthy Flanders court when they heard who he was. The Malvais name was legendary throughout Europe, and it opened many doors, which brought a rueful smile from Morvan, who was trying to establish his own reputation. It also brought him many beautiful women, and Morvan gave in to their wiles spending several nights in different beds as he tried to lose himself in drink and pure lust to blot out the pain of losing Constance.

With the apparent exception of Belleme, Robert's companions were delighted to have him back with them. However, it did not take Morvan did not take long to pick up the undercurrents; he was aware that Robert was buying horses and weapons. He noticed various shadowy figures appearing and disappearing after meetings with Robert. He also found that conversations would dry up when he entered a room. To a certain extent, he expected this; after all, he was the envoy of King William.

Towards the end of the week, Morvan became unsettled by

two things. Firstly, he interrupted several heated conversations between Belleme and his brother-in-law, Hugh de Chateauneuf. At one point, Belleme was holding Hugh against a wall by his throat, which made Morvan step forward until Belleme, glaring at the Horse Warrior, let go, turned on his heel and left. Morvan received a grateful nod from Hugh, the wealthy Lord of Chateauneuf was about five years or so older than them, but he was a pale, quiet, cultured man. Morvan raised an eyebrow at Roger-Fitz-Richard, who shrugged it off. 'Belleme is a bully; he picks the easiest victims even in his own family. He will get bored with baiting Hugh,' he said, but he did not meet Morvan's eyes.

The second one was the next day, he found Robert sitting at a table with Belleme and a slightly familiar man. He was dark with a narrow face but dressed in the finest clothes. He wore a sword, but looking at his hands, he was obviously a courtier and not a warrior. He gave Morvan a thin smile and then left the Inn. Watching him with Robert for the next few days, Morvan picked up that he was fluent in several languages. He spoke French to Belleme but Italian to his own servant, a large dark man with a pockmarked face who accompanied him everywhere, always standing or sitting at a distance from his master but ever watchful. On several occasions, as he drank with his friends Gilbert and Roger, he would find both the servant's and his master's eyes on him as if they weighed him up.

He asked several of his friends who the wealthy stranger was, but they just shrugged, and Morvan became aware that he was being fobbed off. It was clear that the stranger had a lot of influence as he noticed that Robert's demeanour changed when the man arrived with Belleme.

A thoughtful Morvan went up to his room that night. When he reached the landing, he noticed the chamber door was ajar. It took just a glance in to see that his room had been ransacked. He had brought only two large saddlebags, but now their contents were strewn around the room; even the bed had been turned on its side, the stuffed mattress slit and the bed cover on the floor.

Morvan bellowed for the innkeeper who came puffing up the stairs. He looked with surprise and alarm at the state of the room, apologising profusely; such a thing had never happened in his Inn before he assured Morvan, arranging to have the room set to rights. Morvan cast his mind back to the last few hours in the pot room. He had not noticed any strangers, but the staircase was out of sight. A thought occurred to him; the wealthy stranger had appeared for a short time, but his serving-man had not been in evidence, which was unusual. The courtier never stayed to carouse with Robert or his companions. He drank wine but only sparingly. He usually went to one side of the room, a table apart with Robert and Belleme and then left. He had never initiated any contact or conversation with Morvan or his friends. Morvan was determined to find out exactly who this man was; he decided to follow him the next time he appeared at the Inn.

The next night Morvan watered his own wine and then watched the courtier and his servant surreptitiously while dicing with his friends. When the man left, Morvan downed his drink and, throwing a few coins on the table, followed them out. It was a chilly, damp autumn evening in the lowlands of Flanders, but there was sufficient moonlight as he scanned the narrow streets outside the Inn. He spotted them up ahead, just turning the corner, the manservant a few paces behind his master.

Morvan quietly walked after them for a few streets, clinging closely to the sides of the buildings as they headed down towards the river. He turned another corner, and they had disappeared. He searched up and down the street to no avail; it was dark, and there was no trace of light from any house. He kicked himself for not following more closely when he heard a double knock on a door or shutter. He spun around, back the way he came and spotted a narrow alleyway that he had missed. He could now hear conversation, so he crept forward in the narrow space and peered around the corner.

Light spilt from a doorway, and he could see the courtier, his distinctive velvet chaperon hat draped around his head. He was talking with the house occupant, who seemed delighted to see him. Morvan realised they were speaking French from the odd word he caught. He crept closer still to try to decipher the words as the courtier handed over a flat leather pouch, and then he disappeared inside with the owner.

Morvan was so preoccupied with what was happening ahead that he had not realised the man's servant was not in evidence until he felt a sharp knife blade against his throat, cutting into his skin. He felt blood trickle down his throat as the man's other hand grasped the top of his doublet. A voice spoke in heavily accented northern French. 'Move a muscle, and I will slit your throat; now tell me why you are following us,' he said while pulling Morvan's dagger from his belt with his left hand and throwing it down the alleyway. Morvan did not say a word but the long hours of training with Sir Gerard paid off, so he suddenly dropped to his knees and threw the man forward over his head, dislodging the knife and slamming the man headfirst into the wall. The servant lay crumpled on the floor, groaning as

Morvan picked up the dagger; it was a wicked looking weapon with an unusual long carved ivory handle. He noticed that there were also designs and engravings on the good quality exceptionally sharp blade. This was no servant's dagger. He walked over to the man and, grabbing a handful of his clothes, he dragged him out of the gloom. The faint moonlight shone on the man's face, and it was no pockmarked servant; this was the courtier himself.

Morvan placed his booted foot on the winded man's chest. 'Who are you, and why did you attack me?' he hissed at him.

'You will pay for this Horse Warrior, I promise; I could ask you the same question, following behind to attack and rob us,' the courtier gasped.

Morvan got hold of his rich silk tunic again and yanked him to his feet. 'I am protecting Robert Curthose on the instructions of his father, the King, and somehow I do not think you have his best interests at heart,' Morvan said in an ice-cold voice.

The courtier tried to straighten his rumpled clothing, but Morvan still gripped him by the chest; he spat on the ground at Morvan's feet. 'The only interests you are protecting are King William's; you are the King's man. You do not care about Robert or what is rightfully his, whereas my master does.'

It suddenly dawned on Morvan, who this man may be representing. 'Fulk, Count of Anjou. You are one of his many spies, but I am surprised that Robert tolerates you as Fulk has just taken Maine from him, so are you providing him with money and men to fight against his father? Has Fulk a grander plan than just taking Maine?'

The man pulled himself out of Morvan's grasp. 'My master is supporting Robert Curthose, and for all I knew, you were about to kill me,' he said, watching Morvan as a dog watches a wolf.

Morvan stepped into the street and picked up his own dagger. 'I am proud that I have killed dozens of Angevin raiders; one more Angevin spy will not make a difference,' he said with a grim smile. He walked towards the man who was backing away, his hands raised palm out in supplication, expecting an attack. Instead, Morvan returned the man's dagger, handle first.

The man stared at Morvan in amazement and then took the proffered weapon. 'An imposing and costly weapon,' Morvan said as he relinquished it.

'Yes, a present in gratitude from my master for my many services,' he said. Suddenly the door down the street opened, and the man's servant reappeared and started walking towards them. Morvan watched him approaching with a wary eye.

'I suggest we avoid each other from now on or agree to be serving the will of our different masters. But, I must warn you, Robert is a friend as well, and I will protect him if necessary,' said Morvan.

For some moments, the man stared at him as he took his cloak and chaperon from his looming servant, who was glowering at Morvan. 'Your brother Luc would have killed me without a second thought as soon as he felt the blade at his throat,' he said.

Yes, you are right, but I am not my brother, and although I am just as capable of doing that, I think perhaps you may be of more use to us alive. Sometimes information is a better weapon than a dagger,' Morvan said. The courtier raised his eyebrows, looked thoughtful, and then he turned away. After two or three steps, he stopped and smiled, 'Incidentally, Morvan De Malvais, Breton Horse Warrior, I never agreed my master was Fulk of Anjou. I would not stoop that low,' he said before disappearing with his servant into the gloom of the descending mist. Morvan watched them go, his mind in a whirl. If not Fulk, then who was helping Robert? He needed to find out whom this man was and whom he was working for; the King would need that information.

Morvan was leaving for Caen the next day; he had been away for weeks, and it would take another four or five days to get back. He was desperate to try to see Constance even though she now probably belonged to Alan Fergant. His stomach knotted every time he thought of her, especially as the last time he had seen her, she was entertaining and flirting with another man on her parent's orders.

He took his leave of Count Robert of Flanders; he had no placating message for his sister or brother-in-law William. Morvan was disappointed, he had hoped the Queen's request for help from her brother to persuade Robert Curthose to return would be heeded, but it had obviously fallen on stony ground; Count Robert had not forgiven his sister Matilda or her husband for their betrayal of him. However, he assured Morvan that, as a Breton Knight, he would be welcomed back to his court at any time.

Returning to the Inn, he called first at the large house where Robert had established his court. He found him with Belleme and Hugh De Chateauneuf seated around a table with a large map. Morvan could see that Hugh was uncomfortable, his eyes darting nervously at Belleme, who sneered as soon as he saw Morvan.

'Ah, I thought I could smell the stables,' he joked as Morvan approached.

Morvan shot him a vitriolic glance and then ignored him,

addressing Robert. 'Sire, I am leaving for Caen. Do you have a message or letter for your parents?' Robert reached for two rolls of vellum, which he handed to Morvan.

'This one is for my mother's eyes only,' he said meaningfully. Morvan nodded, glancing down at the map on the table and noticing that several castles were ringed in red ink. 'There is always a place for you here with us, Malvais, if you change your mind,' Robert added with a wistful smile. Morvan smiled back and nodded, but both men knew that the likelihood of that was remote. As he took his leave, he did not notice that Belleme followed him out.

He was about to mount Shadow outside the Inn, and his men lined up behind him when Roger-Fitz-Richard arrived outside with several others. His friend hailed him. 'Back to Normandy, Morvan?' he said. Morvan nodded and clasped arms with his friend. 'Send my greetings to my father and ask him to forgive me,' he said his head on one side with a rueful smile. Morvan grimaced. The peppery and bad-tempered Earl of Clare was furious that his son had joined Robert's rebellion; he did not want to feel his wrath, so he would stay out of the Earl's way. Roger laughed as he saw his expression. 'Do not worry, I will write to him.'

Mounting his stallion, he noticed that Belleme had come out and was leaning on the doorjamb of the Inn, watching him intently and throwing a red leather bag in the air with one hand and catching it; Morvan knew at once it was one of those from the Queen. As Morvan stared at him, he placed it back in his purse with the usual sour expression on his face and folded his arms. Morvan suddenly recalled the incident from the night before, and leaning down; he related what happened to his friend Roger who looked away as he finished the tale until Morvan pointedly asked him in a loud, exasperated tone. 'Who is this man, Roger, who is he working for?'

Roger sighed. 'For your ears only, Morvan,' he said, glancing nervously over his shoulder at Belleme, who was obviously listening and leaning forward he said, 'his name is Piers de Chatillon, not a man to be crossed, exceptionally wealthy and highly influential. That is all I can tell you.' He lifted a hand in farewell and turned into the house. Morvan noticed that Belleme stopped Roger, putting an arm across the doorway as he tried to go through, but he knew that his friend was well able for Belleme.

As he rode away, Morvan was perplexed; he was sure that he had heard the name Chatillon before, but he could not remember in what context. He would relay this information to the King, who would know who he was. At the doorway to the house, Belleme was still tightly grasping Roger's arm as he hissed at him, 'Giving away information to the enemy. Whose side are you on De Clare?

Roger shook him off; 'I could ask that of you at times, Belleme, we need to resolve this rift, not escalate it as you seem intent on doing.' Belleme narrowed his eyes at him, 'That Horse Warrior is trouble; we do not tell him our plans or let him know who is supporting us, that is for William to find out when we are ready, and I think he is in for a shock.' Roger shook his head in frustration, 'I just hope this does not all blow up in your face Belleme. You are playing with fire.' He finally shook Belleme off and went into the house, but Belleme stood there in the autumn sunshine for a few minutes more and then extracted the red leather purse from his belt and set off with a purposeful stride towards the castle. Anyone who knew Belleme would have seen the sardonic smile on his face and shuddered.

Chapter Fifteen

It was a tired Morvan who finally rode through the gates of Caen on the last day of November; he had been away for over six weeks. The journey had proved to be perilous. Crossing through parts of Picardy, one of the outriders had reported that a large group of horsemen was shadowing them. The young outrider thought that they looked like a group of renegades and deserters. Morvan had gone on the attack, circling and coming up behind them.

They had scattered in all directions making it pointless to pursue them, but an hour later, had reappeared again about a league behind, still following. About twenty of them at a guess, Morvan knew his group were outnumbered, but he also knew that each of his trained Horse Warriors was worth about five of these deserters, so he had just watched them warily as they rode south. Then they had disappeared, so he presumed that they had moved out of their territory, or maybe they realised that Morvan's Horse Warriors were not the easy pickings they had thought.

The men in the trees on the hillside watched the Horse Warriors below them, 'No one said they were trained warriors,' said a burly grizzled hooded individual to their leader in a concerned voice.

'We only want one of them; the rest we can chase off or get them to follow us away from the camp. We need to split the group up somehow, and we will have some element of surprise; I have an idea,' the leader said thoughtfully.

The Horse Warriors made camp that night and slept in two shifts so that at least five at a time were on mounted sentry duty.

It was just before dawn when the renegades attacked, and the sentries were at a low ebb, some nodding into sleep on their horses. The attackers came riding down into the camp at a gallop. Fortunately, the five on sentry duty had time to put themselves between the attacking renegades and the Horse Warriors who were just waking, including Morvan. It gave those on the ground time to draw their weapons as the sentries engaged with them. However, before they could do anything, the remaining renegades quickly corralled the Warrior's grazing horses and drove them away. Morvan watched in horror and then yelled at his mounted men to disengage and chase them. There were only half of the men he had seen on the hill in the attack. The others must have given up, but this smaller group had split, and half had made a beeline for the horses, including Shadow.

So they were horse thieves, he thought as he frantically looked around for anything that would help them fight the remaining mounted men, He realised that one horse had been grazing further away remained. In seconds Leo, a young Horse Warrior, had raced to his horse; he was halfway onto its back when he took a spear through the thigh as he tried to mount, and he fell backwards as the horse cantered off in alarm.

Morvan whirled to face the attack drawing his sword, but

what he saw made him lower his sword. At least another twelve men, spears raised, were now emerging from the trees poised to throw at the four men who stood sword in hand around the campfire; Morvan's young Horse Warrior Leo was bleeding and groaning on the ground. 'Drop your weapons, or I swear we will finish him off,' said the hooded leader in a heavily accented voice. They had cleverly divided their group into two for the attack, there were about twenty-five of them, and there was nothing that Morvan could do. He cursed to himself as he signalled to his men to lower their swords and dropped his own. Within seconds, several of the renegades were off their horses; they collected the weapons and bound the hands of each of the five Horse Warriors tightly behind them.

Morvan watched in dismay as his men were led away and forced to sit on the ground under the trees with at least three men guarding them. The three hooded men at the front now rode forward and stared at him. Fury raced through his body as he glared up at the three hooded figures in front of him. The leader removed his hood, and shock registered on Morvan's face. The man was a warrior monk, his tonsure and tattoo of the cross on his dark tanned neck giving him away, as did the heavy gold chain hanging down into his cowled garment. He had not seen the like of men such as these since the wars in Lombardy when he had fought against them as a mercenary alongside Luc for several months. He recovered his composure.

'You are a long way from home, Father,' he said. The man smiled, and Morvan noticed a deep scar running along the side of his face.

'We go where we are summoned to do the work of God by those who need us. We are about his business, Morvan De Malvais.'

104

Morvan immediately felt a shiver of apprehension while he wracked his brain. These were no renegades or horse thieves; they were warrior monks. They had been looking for him, but why? He took a deep breath as he willed himself to remain calm.

'So you have the advantage of knowing my name, but what do you want with us?' he asked in a clear voice.

The monk laughed, 'you are so like your brother, so direct; he gave me this and would have taken my head off if I had not slipped off the cliff edge into the sea,' he said, indicating the scar that wrapped itself along his chin and down his neck.

'Sicily,' said Morvan in a whisper. The monk laughed again. 'Ah yes, you were there for a while, Normans and their paid mercenaries who had no right to be in our lands. However, enough of this, I have been sent to give you a message, you have certainly caused some inconvenience to some very influential people Malvais, and they want you punished.'

He indicated to three of his men who dismounted and came forward, Morvan braced himself for the kicking he was about to receive, but then he saw that they held a noose, and he went stone cold. They meant to kill him; they intended to hang him here and now.

Morvan struggled and kicked out at them as they laid hands on him but to no avail as they dropped the looped rope over his neck and dragged him towards the trees. Two men held him while another threw the rope over a branch, and he pulled it taught. For the first time in his life, Morvan felt a wave of panic as he felt the rope tighten around his neck, and as the rope was pulled, he realised that he did not want to die, not here and not in this way. The warrior monk nodded, and Morvan's feet left the ground, he felt the rope tighten, and he gasped for breath as his weight pulled him downwards, and the pressure on his neck and spine increased. He swung for several long moments, and then suddenly, he was dropped to the ground again, gasping; he felt fingers loosening the rope around his neck. 'We have let you down for a short while to talk to us; my patron wants answers. What do you know, Morvan De Malvais? What information are you taking back to your King? He asked.

Morvan thought frantically for a few seconds and then hoarsely said, 'nothing, I know nothing.' The monk sighed and nodded, and Morvan was pulled off the ground again, this time for longer. He could feel the pressure building in his head and the rope burning and grazing his neck as he fought and kicked for breath.

'We can do this so many times, Malvais, so that you are barely alive and your bowels empty in fear. Just tell us what you know.'

Again, he was dropped to the ground, and he laid gasping and coughing as they loosened the rope. 'I know nothing, I swear, I admit I followed Chatillon, but I found nothing out about him other than he was supporting Robert Curthose,' he gasped.

The monk sat and regarded him for several moments, 'I am disappointed you know so little. Fortunately for you, my Patron did not want you killed; he just wanted you punished and warned off. I would like to have delivered your body to your brother personally but another day perhaps. Keep yourself out of business that does not concern you, Morvan De Malvais,' he said, nodding to his men, who pulled Morvan to his feet and laid into him with their fists.

As the blows landed, Morvan felt a small amount of relief that they would not kill him, but within moments, he was doubled up on the ground as their boots and fists descended on him. Then he heard the sound of hooves and shouts, and suddenly there were horses everywhere. He felt his ropes being undone and the welcome voice of one of his men asking him if he could stand. He nodded and, getting to his feet, surveyed the scene; his Horse Warriors who had gone after the horses were back galloping the horses through the camp. The raiders were taken by surprise and driven off. He still had the noose over his head, and he pulled it off; flinging it away, he gingerly felt his bruised and grazed neck. Then he searched around for Shadow and saw him standing in the trees with two returned horses. He quickly reclaimed his swords from the ground and ran to his mount; within seconds, he was galloping bareback with his men after the raiders despite the bruises and pain from his beating.

It was a tough fight in the mists of the dawn. Morvan turned the full fury of the remaining men and their horses on the attackers. It was clear that these men had never come across horses that attacked and struck out kicking and biting their mounts. Several were taken by surprise and unhorsed very quickly. Morvan singled out the hooded leader who was shouting orders in Italian as he tried to rally his men. He rode his stallion straight at him, and slamming Shadow into the smaller horse, he knocked the monk out of the saddle. In a flash, Morvan was on the ground, sword drawn. He ran at the man who was back on his feet, and he certainly put up a brave fight as a trained warrior. Still, he was no match for Morvan's swordsmanship, and in moments Morvan, without a second of remorse, had plunged his sword through the man's tattooed and scarred throat in a furious thrust that would have delighted his brother.

Having seen their leader killed, the remaining dozen attackers fled, leaving Morvan breathing heavily and leaning on his sword. Back at the camp, two of his men were helping young Leo, the injured Horse Warrior who was bleeding profusely.

Morvan glanced down at the man he had killed and saw the glint of the chain; he reached down and pulled open the man's robe. Morvan pulled out the chain to reveal the expected large gold crucifix worn by the warrior monks. As he pulled it over the man's head, he noticed that there was also a bulging well-worn leather pouch at the man's waist. Using his dagger, he cut it from the belt and opened it...

Inside the pouch was a red leather bag full of gold, one of the same red leather bags he had seen in the chest he had given to Robert Curthose, the same type that he had seen Belleme throwing in the air. It had the Queen's crest on the front. Morvan gazed thoughtfully down at it, fingering the soft red leather.

How had this man come by the Queen's gold? They had been paid to attack Morvan and his Horse Warriors, to warn him off. Who would do that? Surely not Robert Curthose, what would he have to gain? Was it the courtier Chatillon or did this have the hand of Belleme all over it? Who would have the influence to bring in warrior monks for this task? What were they doing here so far away from Italy? The more he thought, the more the questions raced around in his mind.

They had treated the thigh injury of Leo as best they could, but Morvan knew that if he were not to lose the leg, they would have to find a physician. In addition, he needed rest for his bruised body and time for his neck and throat to recover. He had no choice but to detour to Amiens, a few miles to the west. It was to be four days later that they finally got on the road to Caen when Leo and Morvan were able to ride any distance.

Having time to reflect in Amiens had given Morvan even more questions than answers. He had failed to persuade Robert

Curthose to return, what threat did Morvan and his Horse Warriors pose to whoever had arranged this attack? The monk had said it was punishment, but for what?

He gratefully and wearily dismounted in Caen and led Shadow into the stable block, shouting for the stable boys to bring fresh water. He glanced along the stalls in the enormous stone-built building and was surprised to see the vast stables were full and that his brother's stallion, Espirit, was still here, towering above the other horses. Morvan was perplexed; surely, Luc had not been still here in Caen while he was away as he knew that Merewyn, his wife, was due to give birth a month ago?

Sometime later, having washed and changed into a clean tunic, he entered the Great Hall and made his way to the upper dais. The Hall was hot, smoky and noisy as he made his way through the tables, greeting his men. He mentally compared this large stone, austere building with the sumptuous, wealthy court of Flanders. As a warrior, he much preferred the atmosphere here. Count Robert's velvets and expensive carved cedar wood only masked the continuous political intrigue, plotting and machinations as visitors and envoys came and went each day.

As he made his way to the King, he was a trifle apprehensive as he brought no good news and only a missive from his son that may well infuriate him further. However, William welcomed him effusively, 'What news do you bring me, Malvais, of my errant rebel son? Has he reflected on his actions? I have just been informed that he left Ghent and is now plundering my lands in the Norman part of the Vexin.'

This news came as a surprise to Morvan, who had been delayed at Amiens. However, he acknowledged the King's comment with a bow of his head and handed him the vellum sheet from Robert. The conversation amongst the Knights around them dropped to a low hum in the Hall as the King read his son's words. Morvan saw the frown deepen on the King's face, and then he pushed his sizeable carved chair back and stood. The silence that spread across the Hall was palpable.

'From this moment, my son Robert Curthose and his companions are declared outlaw. Their lands are confiscated, and they are subject to arrest and imprisonment,' he shouted.

Dismay registered on Matilda's face and on those of several Knights and nobles whose sons were with Robert. Morvan looked at his brother Luc who was sitting further along the table, shaking his head in exasperation.

The King continued, 'I have summoned Luc De Malvais and over a hundred Breton Horse Warriors to aid us in this; they will hunt down these renegades and bring them to justice,' he announced.

A wave of comment and shock reverberated across the Hall at these words; everyone knew that it was rare for the Breton Horse Leader to give any quarter in battle.

The King turned to go summoning Luc and several of his senior Knights to join him as he stomped out of the Hall. He did not glance once at his wife, Matilda. Morvan was left, trying to take in the implications of those words and what they would mean for him.

The King's announcement meant that the Prince and his friends declared outlaws could also be hunted and killed for reward by any mercenary band. He knew deep down that Luc would not deliberately kill the Prince, but he would set out to capture him and bring him back to Caen, which meant that he would kill anyone who stopped him. Could he warn Gilbert and Roger De Clare? Then he wondered if he did so, would that now be considered treasonable, as he would be acting against the King. He shook his head in confusion until he realised that these young cadet sons would have informers and supporters in this Hall as well as family. He was sure that messengers would be riding out to them after this announcement, leaving him with a clear conscience.

He walked forward to Queen Matilda and bowed. She was now visibly upset, and he handed her a letter from Robert. She looked up at him. 'How was my son, Morvan? Is he well?'

Morvan nodded. 'He is your Grace and was enjoying his uncle's hospitality. But, unfortunately, Count Robert did not show any inclination to accede to your request to council your son Robert to return.'

She clenched her hands. 'Morvan de Malvais, I will still need your loyalty and your help; I will find out where they are at the moment and send you back,' she said decisively.

Morvan felt a wave of dismay as he knew he was being asked to go behind both his brother's and the King's back, but he had no choice; it was essential to have the Queen on his side to have any future with Constance. He sighed and nodded and then turned and looked at Constance for the first time. The noise in the Hall behind him seeming to disappear as he gazed at her. She looked as aggrieved as her mother did. She raised tear-filled eyes to him. 'You must try to persuade my brother to desist in this folly,' she pleaded.

'I will try Constance, but he is surrounded by others who are encouraging him to defy his father on this matter.'

'Belleme again!' said the Queen. 'A cruel and selfish young man. He is at Robert's side no doubt egging him on. He was always a bad influence, always pursuing his own agenda despite the cost to others.'

111

Morvan nodded in agreement, and she shook her head in dismay as she rose to leave. Morvan bowed, and Constance cast a grateful but longing smile in his direction as she followed her mother up to the solar.

Morvan did not see Luc again until the following afternoon; he found him leaning on a fence at the training ground, watching his experienced Breton Horse Warriors putting Morvan's new recruits through their paces. Finally, Luc turned and embraced his younger brother.

'This is a bad business Morvan, blood against blood can leave deep scars.'

Morvan sighed. 'I did everything I could Luc to try and turn him from this path, hours of talking with his followers, showing them where this would lead to no avail. He has too many powerful dissenting voices around him urging him to fight for the title that is his.' Luc stared off into the paddock, stern-faced, his hard steel-blue eyes focussed on the young Normans. Suddenly a messenger came galloping in; it was one of Luc's many vedettes. He saw the Malvais brothers and pulled his horse to a sudden standstill so that it reared up on its hind legs. He leapt from the saddle and ran towards them.

'We have found them, Sire; we know where they are hiding. They have a small force of about eighty men at the castle of Remalard,' he gasped. Luc thanked the young rider. 'Of course, one of Hugh's many estates. I must go to the King,' he said, turning away.

'Hugh de Chateauneuf?' questioned Morvan.

'Yes, Belleme's brother-in-law,' answered Luc, raising an eyebrow.

'I saw Belleme threatening and browbeating him in the inn in Ghent. He looked afraid; Belleme must have been forcing him to use the chateau as a base. It's right on the borders of Normandy and Maine, ideally placed for their raids,' he said.

'And now we need to drive these insurgents out of there. You will not be riding with us against them, Morvan; I know you have friends there,' he added. He turned to the vedette. 'Tell the men we leave at dawn, and make sure the horses are well watered and fed tonight.'

As he strode away towards the vast stone donjon, Morvan raced after him, 'Luc wait, there is something else,' he said, as his brother stopped, one foot on the steps. Morvan described the attack on him and his men on the way back to Caen, but he omitted the Queen's red pouch of gold. This was the first time he had kept anything from his brother, and he felt guilty.

Luc frowned as he considered this information. 'Warrior monks here in Picardy attacking the King's envoy to Flanders? Why would they do that? William needs to know this.'

'There is more Luc; a dark, wealthy foreigner, perhaps French, perhaps Italian, is advising Robert,' added Morvan. He described the man and his unusual dagger and watched as Luc's eyes narrowed.

'Piers de Chatillon,' Luc said in an ice-cold tone. 'Everything falls into place now, and he is one of the few people who could call on and command the warrior monks; they are at the disposal of the Vatican and the Cardinals of the Holy See.'

'Who is he, Luc? Who is this man?' asked Morvan in an exasperated voice.

Luc turned to face his brother. 'He is the rich nephew of Odo of Chatillon, the Cardinal and Prior of Cluny, one of the wealthy and powerful favourites to become the next Pope. Piers de Chatillon is also a spy, a master of intrigue, a papal envoy and a ruthless assassin depending on need; he has killed hundreds of men in his time. He has no moral compass and no compassion. I have had a few brushes with him in the past; in some, he came off badly, and he still has the scars; he would take delight in punishing you to get to me. This means that the Holy See is yet again stirring the pot of politics in Western Europe. I must go to the King.' He turned and raced up the steps.

Morvan stood rooted to the spot for a moment. So that was where he had heard the name before. Odo, the Cardinal de Chatillon, had interfered in politics in Brittany before now, especially in the dispute over the archbishop of Dol, which led to the disastrous siege and William's humiliating defeat. However, he was still perplexed by the Queen's gold; how did Chatillon access that and with so much wealth already, why would he need it? He turned and headed to the stables to see to Shadow, and that was where the Queen's Steward found him. Within an hour, Morvan had met with Matilda and was secretly riding out on the road to Remalard with another large pouch of gold and a letter from the Queen to her son Robert Curthose.

Chapter Sixteen

Morvan galloped towards Remalard in the early hours, trying to ignore the misgivings he felt about his task. He had been summoned once more by the Queen, who had yet again given him gold for her son, and asked him to warn Robert that an attack was imminent. Morvan was torn; he acted on the Queen's orders again, but how would the King or Luc view his actions?

Remalard was situated on the southwestern border with Maine. It boasted a small chateau owned by Hugh de Chateauneuf, the brother-in-law of Belleme. The chateau overlooked the River Huisne, but the basic fortifications, which included an encircling wall, did not look as if it would survive a sustained attack by a large force.

Morvan arrived cold, wet and exhausted later that morning; even Shadow was hanging his nodding head as they rode into the busy courtyard. He led his horse into the stables and unpacked the heavy leather pouches. He untacked Shadow and rubbed him down. Then he set off to find Robert. He walked into the vast light entrance hall; Remalard was a large wooden fortified manor house, so it was bright and airy with lots of windows. He asked the Steward for Robert, but apparently, they had ridden out into the forests to hunt. Morvan shook his head in exasperation and sat down to wait. He knew he had six or seven hours start on Luc and William's forces, but he still found himself walking anxiously up and down the bright whitewashed hall as the sun rose in the sky.

Suddenly, there were sounds of arrival and his friend Gilbert De Sorrell appeared; his horse had gone lame, he explained as he greeted him like a brother. Gilbert knew that Morvan would be there with Robert's messages, so he plied him with questions as they shared a jug of wine.

'We have tried repeatedly to persuade Robert to reconcile with his father, but he now believes that as he has come this far, he can force his father's hand.'

Morvan snorted in disbelief. 'I was surprised to hear that you had left Ghent so suddenly. Was that because Robert had gained the support that he needed?'

Gilbert laughed. 'Yes, he had significant support, but we had to leave because of Belleme; he caused problems. He became embroiled in fights and duels repeatedly. Count Robert found him entertaining at first, but then Belleme went too far.' Morvan raised a questioning eyebrow.

'We were in the marketplace when a group of ladies appeared escorted by two servants; one of them was a very beautiful girl. Belleme was very taken with her because she ignored him. However, it only turned out that she was a rich merchant's daughter. He turned on the full Belleme charm for days, calling at the house, offering to present her at court but still, the girl and her mother would have none of him. They had heard of him, of course, who has not. He then starts laying bets with everyone that he can swive her before the week is out; a lot of gold was laid down at this point. The bets then went much higher as now it looked as if he would fail. Young Aubrey Grandesmil

116

bet his horse that he wouldn't get her.'

Morvan sat in astonishment and shook his head. 'So did he lose the bet?' he asked, knowing how Belleme would hate to lose.

'No, that was the problem; the next day, he followed her into the market, he broke her manservant's nose, then dragged the young girl off the street and took her kicking and screaming to his room at the Inn. He sent a potboy from the Inn to come and get us all so we could see that he had won the bet. When we arrived, he was swiving her face down on the bed, her skirts pinned over her head. The girl's father, summoned by the people in the market, burst into the room, but Belleme did not even stop; he just kept swiving her while she was still squealing. He told the father to go away, or he would do the same to him.

About a dozen of us watched while Belleme was shouting that he had won the bet. The Grandesmil boys laughed uproariously, and huge debts were paid to William de Breteuil to hold for Belleme. This further incensed the red-faced merchant, who was now so angry that he drew his dagger and threatened to kill Belleme, his dagger held high, despite being surrounded by Norman Knights. We held him back because Belleme would have killed him and claimed self-defence, but Belleme just ignored us all, calmly finished with her, refastened his braies, threw a gold coin on the bed in payment then turning swiftly; he knocked the dagger-wielding merchant out cold with one blow.'

Morvan listened wide-eyed to this; it was shocking, but nothing would surprise him about Belleme, who lived for extremes of pleasure and cruelty, and nothing seemed out of limits. 'So what happened then?'

Gilbert rolled his eyes. 'Well, it only turned out that this merchant was a wealthy official or Alderman of Ghent; he went straight to Count Robert asking for recompense and demanded that the Seigneur Belleme be arrested and imprisoned. The Count had no choice but to tell his nephew to send Belleme away immediately. However, rather than being exiled, the smooth-tongued Belleme persuaded Robert that it was now time to move everyone to Remalard, the perfect spot to begin our campaign. Therefore, we left immediately, and here we are, awaiting further men to flock to Robert's banners while he plans his next move. Several Breton Lords have sent messages of support and say they may join us,' he added.

Morvan looked at his friend in dismay; this news about rebel Breton Lords might mean the old alliance against King William was reforming. His friends seemed to think that this was a game they were playing, but it was a game that became more deadly with over a hundred Horse Warriors galloping towards them. In addition, Gilbert was a good friend; what is more he also knew that the young nobleman had a beautiful young wife and was shortly about to become a father for the first time.

'You have to get out of here Gilbert, the King has called for my brother, and he is riding to attack Remalard as we speak. You have also been declared outlaw; you will be hunted by any mercenary wishing to claim the reward, and many could die. What you are doing is madness,' he cried, running his hands through his long hair in exasperation.

Gilbert de Sorrell shot to his feet, knocking over the wine. 'Mon Dieu, we must tell the others immediately,' he cried, grasping Morvan's arm.

'My horse is exhausted and needs a few hours' rest. How far out are Robert and the others?' he asked.

'They were after wild boar, deep in the forest, but they were returning for a nuncheon,' Gilbert replied, his voice faltering.

Morvan strode up and down in agitation. 'How many men do you have here?'

'Only about sixty or so now. Robert sent many to their homes to wait until we had finished the raids on the Vexin,' he explained.

'So with the group with Robert, you will have eighty or ninety against over a hundred Horse Warriors led by Luc De Malvais!' exclaimed Morvan.

Gilbert paled. 'We have to run,' he cried.

Morvan sighed. 'They may get here before Robert and the others return; I was only six or so hours ahead of them, and I am on the Queen's business; I cannot be caught here by my brother under any circumstances.'

'Go, Morvan; I will organise the defence here; I will place the men here on the walls in readiness.'

Morvan agreed. 'Yes, get them to hold the wall and gates; flimsy though they are, if you try to face them outside, they will cut you down.'

Gilbert stood white-faced and, turning on his heel, raced off shouting for the Serjeants. It was nearly two hours later when Robert and his followers arrived, triumphantly bearing a large tusker into the courtyard. Morvan was pacing the Hall by that time, and Gilbert was fraught with anxiety waiting for his outriders to return with news of their attackers.

Robert was surprised but pleased to see the young Horse Warrior, as were nearly all of his companions. Morvan was surprised to note that Piers De Chatillon was still with them; he was at Belleme's side as usual. He inclined his head in a sardonic greeting when he saw Morvan, while Belleme looked surprised but then glared at him as usual; Morvan took Robert Curthose to one side to talk to him privately. He repeated the Queen's warning and handed him the pouches of gold.

'I cannot thank you enough for risking everything to come here, Malvais,' he said, grasping his arm. Then, without warning, one of Gilbert's young outriders burst into the Hall.

'My Lord, they are no more than a few miles behind me; there seem to be hundreds of mounted warriors on huge horses. I cut across the river and fields, but they are on my heels,' he gasped. Robert's followers, who had not been told yet of the imminent attack, looked at Robert in alarm.

'You cannot fight them, Robert. They will give no quarter if you attack them,' cried Morvan.

Belleme jumped in. 'Don't listen to him, Sire; we should not be running again. Surely we are in a strong position here to keep the King's forces out.'

Morvan snorted in derisive laughter. 'So you expect to keep my brother, Luc De Malvais, out while you are holed up in what is a country manor house?' he said waving his hand at the large windows and the low walls of the chateau outside that had no walkways or hoardings.

Belleme paled. 'Your brother? Has the King sent your brother against his own son? Does he want to kill Robert?' he asked in scorn.

Morvan looked at Belleme in disbelief. 'You of all people have pushed Robert into this situation to rebel against his father, one of the most warlike Kings in Europe. What did you expect him to do, roll over and give in to you?'

Piers De Chatillon put a hand on Belleme's arm and gave him a significant look that did not go unnoticed by Morvan. The papal spy held up his hands in supplication to Robert.

'We must leave Sire; we have no choice. Morvan de Malvais

120

is right, we must listen to him. He is also a Horse Warrior, and all of us here know what his brother is capable of,' he said while glancing around at Robert's grim-faced followers, who were nodding in agreement. 'What do you say we should do, Malvais?' he said, his large, dark, almost black eyes never leaving Morvan's face.

Morvan found himself in a difficult situation. He had to leave now, but he could not abandon them; they were his friends and comrades. 'Divide your force into three, put your strongest fighting men in the rear-guard; the other two groups need to split up and get over the border taking different routes, but go now.'

They sprang into action, and Gilbert shouted over the rush that he would command the rear-guard and empty the chateau of men and servants. 'I will try to give you time to get away, Sire,' he said, bowing his head to Robert, who stepped forward and clasped him by the shoulders in gratitude.

Robert turned to his friends. 'I will lead the first group with Hugh; Belleme takes the second group and gets the Grandesmil boys to safety. However, Malvais, you need to go. You cannot be caught here, or you and my mother will be undone.' He raced out of the Hall after his fleeing comrades. At the door, he turned and gave Morvan a boyish grin and a wave of the hand.

Morvan smiled and shook his head as he picked up the large leather pouch and placed the vellum sheet from the Queen on the fire. He turned to find Chatillon still standing at the door, watching him. 'You are a courageous man, Morvan De Malvais, but I find myself asking why you are risking so much. Why are you working against your King and your brother?' he asked.

Morvan did not answer the question. 'You need to go as well, Chatillon. You do not want to be caught here either; my brother remembers you far too well, and now he knows about your attack on me and my men, he is out for revenge,' he said.

Chatillon looked puzzled for several moments but then bowed his head in acquiescence. 'I go, but I have nothing to fear. I carry the Pope's seal; no man will touch me, not even Luc De Malvais. But you, Morvan, are playing a dangerous game,' he said, and with a swirl of his long black cloak, he was gone.

Morvan ran out into the courtyard where Gilbert was mounted on his horse with William de Breteuil at his side. Morvan reached up and took his arm. 'Do not engage with them, Gilbert, use the feinting 'retraite en echiquier' tactics, pretend to attack and then turn and retreat a little further each time; I do not expect them to follow. Finally, melt into the trees and then gallop away to safety.'

Gilbert smiled. 'I will do my best, Malvais. Now be gone; your brother cannot find you here.'

Morvan waved him off and ran to the stable, where he found that Shadow had been tacked up and was tied to a metal hoop in the wall outside. He vaulted into the saddle and cantered out of the yard. He knew that he had to ride east first, away from the attacking force, and then go north to come round in a large loop to head back to Caen. It was only after he had galloped for five or six miles that he realised Shadow had the wrong bridle. The stallion was now shaking his head repeatedly because of the cruel bit that had been put in his mouth. Morvan pulled up, unhooked the metal band, and threw it away; he knew that Shadow, although frisky and bad-tempered at times, would present him with no problems in a bridle halter. However, as he turned west and headed for home, he hoped that Shadow's distinctive plaited bridle was on the head of another horse galloping away from Remalard.

Chapter Seventeen

Luc purposefully slowed his Horse Warriors as they approached Remalard from the south. He had seen their outriders, and he was hoping that they would flee. The last thing he wanted was for the cadet sons of Anglo-Norman nobility to die or be mortally wounded in a pitched battle at Remalard. However, the King hoped that he would teach them a lesson, so he was prepared to pursue them for some distance. They stood in the trees gazing down onto Remalard. All looked quiet, although his vedettes reported a group of rebels in the trees to the west. They rode down and through the open gates of the chateau. There were signs of a hasty departure everywhere.

He stayed outside the gates while a dozen of his men searched the house and outbuildings; the first of his vedettes riding back found him there.

'My lord, the force was not large; we estimated about eighty men on horseback. They split off into different directions. Cedric is coming in now. He followed them for some miles, and there is a force of about twenty-five hidden in the copse of trees to the west.'

Young Cedric arrived and confirmed that the first two groups had escaped. Luc turned away when the young man coughed.

'My Lord, there is something else!'

Luc regarded the young man. He was a blonde Saxon boy who had come with them as a groom from Ravensworth in England, a pleasant open-faced young man. He could ride any horse; he had a particular way with them, even with Morvan's wild black mare. 'There was a lone horseman, my Lord, on a large black horse that galloped away to the east.' Luc waited for him to go on, but the young man just stared at the ground.

Luc felt a cold knot in his stomach. 'Could you see the rider?' he asked.

Cedric kept his eyes on the ground as he said, 'No, my Lord, he was galloping at speed and hanging down over one side of the horse's neck.' Luc thanked the young man and turned to observe the group in the trees on the far hill, obviously a sacrificial rear-guard of some description. Then, he turned to the large troop behind him, 'On Y Va, let us chase the rebels from the hill, but try not to kill any unless they attack you.'

As they cantered in perfect formation towards the trees, Luc was preoccupied; he was sure Cedric had recognised the horse and the distinctive style of the rider. He just prayed that it was not Morvan and Midnight Shadow.

Gilbert De Sorrell had watched the immense force of Horse Warriors arrive, encircle and then enter the chateau at Remalard. He knew that he should already have left, but he had seen the vedettes ride out, and he had to give Robert more time. He watched in dismay as at least a hundred of them formed up into a fan shape behind their leader, every horse held in position as they cantered in a perfect formation effortlessly towards his copse of trees.

He turned and encouraged his men, explaining the tactics they would use to delay and slow the attackers. He split his men into two groups, and they galloped out as if they were going to attack. The Horse warriors slowed and closed ranks just as Gilbert De Sorrell's forces wheeled and dashed away again, through the copse and down into the meadow beyond. However, the big Destriers did not pause in the wood as he thought they would. Instead, they came hard on their heels, giving Gilbert less room to recharge and repeat the manoeuvre.

However, they pulled it off again; there were large banks to the left, so Gilbert led his men at a gallop across the meadow and down the hill. Unfortunately, he did not know this countryside well, and they suddenly found themselves up against a loop of the broad and deep River Huisne. The Breton Horse Warriors now streamed into the meadow behind them in a broad sweep. This left Gilbert with nowhere to go; they either had to swim the river and risk losing men and horses, attack or surrender. Gilbert sat on his horse gazing at the intimidating array of Horse Warriors in front of him, their crossed double swords on their backs, their determined faces. These were seasoned troops. Many had ridden with Luc De Malvais for years. He found his hands were wet with sweat on the reins, and he wiped them on his horse's neck as he tried to work out what to do. He thought of his young wife waiting at home about to give birth to their first child; he did not want to die. He was only twenty-six years old, and he hoped to be alive to step into his father's shoes to run their vast estates.

Nevertheless, for his family honour, he knew that he could not face the ignominy of surrender. Therefore, he decided to attack, pretend to whirl away but in fact, race round the slight gap on their eastern flank; if they moved fast enough and took them by surprise, they might just do it. He shared the tactics with his men, shortened his reins and leant slightly forward, feeling the big horse bunching its muscles beneath him gathering itself to go...

Luc De Malvais looked on in dismay at the rebels' position with their backs to the river; they were trapped. He hoped that they were preparing to surrender, and he was about to go forward and parley; however, they were suddenly charging towards them without warning. Luc turned to his Captain, Benedot, 'Are they mad?' he said as they prepared to meet them head-on.

Luc heard Benedot shouting, 'Prepare to defend!'

The rebels suddenly swirled at the last minute and raced for the right wing. Soon, there was a melee of horses and men, the clash of swords, and warhorses' angry screams in battle. It proved almost impossible to keep a defensive stance when nearly thirty men were determined to do you harm, and Luc suddenly found himself in the thick of the fighting. He watched, as several rebels were unhorsed; they were no match for the big war Destriers.

Luc used Espirit to attack and knock the other horses over. He delivered several flat-bladed but vicious blows to helms that resulted in men falling from the saddle. He locked his knees with one man who tried to thrust his sword in his face. Luc ducked it and punched the man hard in the throat with his sword hilt, and he fell to the ground, clutching his throat and gasping for breath.

He noticed that a small group had made it past them. He recognised young William De Breteil, who raced away with half a dozen others with only a backwards glance. Luc was pleased they had escaped; he just needed the others to surrender as only a few were left fighting. He noticed that Benedot was engaged in a ferocious fight on the ground with their leader, and the man was giving no quarter as he attacked the young Captain, driving him backwards. He was a good swordsman, whoever he was, as Luc watched Benedot parry and bar his opponent's blade with skill. All of his men were trained by Gerard to a high level of skill in swordsmanship, and he was not too worried, but he needed to bring it to a halt. He pushed Espirit towards them when the rebel slipped on the grass, and a downswing sword swipe from Benedot caught him across the throat. The man went down, and Benedot stood back, sword still in hand, panting with exertion.

Luc shouted the order to 'Stand!' the Horse Warriors disengaged as quickly as they could and stood back; only six of the rebel soldiers were left unharmed, standing in the centre, swords in hand. Luc could see from their livery that these men were Robert's armed escort.

'You have fought well and bravely, but now I ask you to lay down your weapons and see to any of your injured comrades. I will ensure that the King knows that you were following orders to protect the Prince and his followers.' The men looked at each other for only a few seconds before the swords and spears clattered to the ground. They all knew the reputation of Luc De Malvais; many had fought with him in the past. They did not doubt that he was ruthless and would kill them if they kept fighting, but they trusted his word.

Luc dismounted, dropping Espirit's reins and walked over to Benedot. 'Are you unharmed?' he asked him.

'My Lord, I did ask him repeatedly to cease and surrender, but I could see that the red battle mist had descended. I did not mean to kill him, but it was impossible to stop the blow when he fell; I expected him to parry it.' Luc put a reassuring hand on the young man's shoulder and walked over to the young Knight on the ground; he was still alive, but his lifeblood covered the ground. Luc knelt beside him and grasped his hand. 'You fought well, but you should have surrendered.' The handsome young Knight gave a sad smile, but his eyes were clouding as Luc remembered his name, Gilbert De Sorrell, one of Robert's close circle of young cadet Knights.

He leaned forward to close his eyes as Gilbert suddenly whispered, 'Tell Robert and Morvan that I did what I could for them.'

Luc assured him that he would as the young man let out a last breath. He stood for a moment looking down on him and sighed with exasperation. 'It was not your fault Benedot. We did our best in this messy business,' he said as he walked back to his horse.

An hour later, he rode back into the chateau of Remalard; they would stay here for the night and then head back to Caen with the injured and dead rebels. As Luc untacked Espirit in the large stable, he suddenly found himself full of anger. 'What a waste of life over what should have stayed and been treated immediately as a family argument. Instead, it has escalated into this!' he said in a frustrated voice as he leant his forehead against the neck of Espirit. He prayed that they would resolve it soon; it was never good finding yourself riding against men who had fought by your side.

What is more, he now had to deliver the news and the body of his eldest son to Lord De Sorrell. He wearily lifted his saddle onto the wooden partition of the roomy horsebox and went to hang the bridle on the hook beside the door when he realised that there was already a bridle hanging there.

It was a very expensive bridle, made from the best Italian leather with tight plaited reins and chased silver medallions down the cheek and nose straps. He lifted it down and thoughtfully ran his hands over it; he recognised it immediately. He had given it to Morvan as a gift after his attempted rescue of Merewyn from the rebel fortress at Gael, a rescue that had almost cost Morvan his life. Luc knew that this bridle had been hanging in the stable back at Caen two days earlier. As he feared, Morvan had been here. He had ridden out to warn Robert and friends; that was why the birds had flown.

Luc stood for several moments with the elaborate bridle in his hands, while asking himself what game Morvan was playing. Was his brother running with the hare and hunting with the hounds, and if so, why? More importantly, should he tell the King? Could he tell the King and betray his own brother? What price loyalty and duty then to his liege Lords? He swore long and loudly as he headed to the chateau of Remalard, his brow furrowed, his mouth in a grim white line, the bridle tightly clasped in his hand.

Chapter Eighteen

Luc returned to Caen just as his brother had mounted Shadow to ride out with Constance. Luc pulled Espirit up beside his brother and bowed his head to greet William's daughter beside him. He reached into his saddle pouch and pulled out the silver decorated bridle. He held it in the air for a few moments, and the light caught on the many silver discs as he stared at his brother. Morvan could not meet that steel blue stare for long and looked away.

'I thought you might like this back; I was obviously mistaken when I thought it might mean something to you,' he said in an icy tone. 'I will hang it on its usual hook in this stable, shall I?'

Morvan nodded his head in embarrassed acquiescence and tried to control Shadow, who was sidling nervously away from his father, Espirit. Luc glanced at Constance and her groom, who had moved away, and he turned Espirit closer to Morvan. He reached over to Shadow's head collar and pulled the horse's head tight to his knee so that Morvan could go nowhere. 'We will talk as soon as you get back. Do not delay on this ride as I intend to have speech with you before I see the King,' he said sternly as he released the head collar. Morvan was white-faced, and he visibly swallowed and bowed his head as he turned away to follow Constance.

The couple dismissed their groom as usual and rode to their overhanging cliff. It was a cold late autumn day, and Morvan had rolled up a much thicker blanket to cover them. Morvan was visibly preoccupied as he lifted Constance down from the saddle and pulled her tightly into his arms. She slid her hands up under his thick woollen cloak and round to his back, reaching up to run her hands over his shoulder blades as he kissed her deeply. She could feel the tension in him as he looked down into her eyes. 'I thought I had lost you,' he whispered as he ran his fingers through the waves of her deep auburn hair.

'My mother persuaded my father to leave me at court for another year or two; if a betrothal does go ahead, then a marriage will be delayed.' Morvan breathed a sigh of relief and held her even tighter.

'That gives us time, and we will find a way through this, Constance,' he said, removing his cloak and spreading it on the soft leaf-covered earth at the back of the deep overhang.

She reached up and cradled his face in her hands. 'I will go anywhere with you, Morvan De Malvais; I will not regret leaving this life in any way,' she whispered.

Morvan was overwhelmed by what she would be prepared to lose for him. He pulled her laughingly down with him and pulled the thick blanket over them. He began to loosen her clothes and kiss his way down her soft skin to her breasts. They made love with an intensity that belied her words and his commitment. It was as if this would be the last time they would ever be like this again.

As they lay sated and happily entwined together, Morvan's mind returned unbidden to his brother, whom he loved and admired greatly. He knew that Luc would never deviate from his code of duty and honour. Wrapped in each other, revelling in the feel and warmth of skin on skin, Morvan, tired from his long rides, drifted off; Constance let him sleep and just lay her head on his bare chest watching him breathing, his dark lashes lying on his cheeks, she loved him so much. It was over four hours later when he awoke, when they returned, Luc was nowhere to be found in the stables or barracks.

Having seen to the horses, Morvan walked over the flat bridge, which covered the deep moat into the inner Bailey. The King had constructed a chapel on one side dedicated to St George; it was a temporary stone and wood structure but popular with the men. Morvan noticed that it appeared to be full, and several people were standing outside the door. He wondered if Luc was there, so he pushed his way inside through the courtiers and men at arms.

A bank of candles surrounded a bier in the small centre aisle; the body of a wounded Knight lay upon it. He was covered with his family standard, and Morvan recognised it immediately. The Knight's father and heavily pregnant young wife were on their knees at the front. Morvan found he was holding his breath as he walked forward and looked down on his friend. Gilbert de Sorrell looked as if he were asleep; he had died quickly as his face was relaxed and unmarked. He looked far younger than his twenty-six years.

Morvan wondered how and where he had died. Was he defending the chateau at Remalard, or had Luc killed his friend in a charge with the Horse Warriors? Morvan dropped to his knees beside the family and joined in the reciting of the Misericordia. He found his eyes filling with unshed tears for the loss of a good man who had sacrificed himself so that others could escape. As he left the chapel, a squire found him to say that he was summoned to the King's presence.

Unfortunately, for Constance, her father was with her mother and Luc De Malvais when she returned to the solar. William looked up as she entered. She greeted them all and crossed to sit quietly on the settle beside her mother. William looked at his daughter; she always had been a pretty girl like her mother, but now he realised that she had become a beauty. Her hair was unbraided and held by just a band on her head, the deep auburn curls cascading down her back. However, it was more than that; her skin seemed to glow. He glanced at Luc De Malvais, but to his surprise, he saw not the appreciation he expected to see but a frowning, angry glance at his daughter. Next, he looked at Matilda, who held his eyes for only a moment before dropping them.

William was an astute man; he knew that Constance was ripe for marriage; she would be twenty-two shortly, old by marriageable standards as most girls from noble families went to their husbands at sixteen. He had watched his daughter flirting and laughing with Alan Fergant, and he intended to use her to cement that alliance with Brittany; he could see that Alan had been very taken with her. However, Matilda had asked that they wait until Alan came into his majority and the Dukedom in a few years, then they could marry, and he had agreed, knowing that Matilda wanted to keep her by her side a little longer.

Luc De Malvais brought him back to the business in hand. 'I think I mentioned Sire that Morvan brought disturbing news back from Ghent; Piers De Chatillon has been seen with Robert Curthose on several occasions.'

William gave a harsh bark of laughter. 'Ah yes, Chatillon, that devious assassin and creature of the Vatican. I thought on what you said, but why would he do that? What is his game with Robert? Pope Gregory is a manipulative, cunning man who has alienated several prominent rulers in Europe. Nevertheless, I made my peace with him despite his meddling in Dol, putting his own Archbishop into place and removing my candidate. What advantage would he have in encouraging Robert's rebellion against me?' he asked Luc.

'I am not sure at present, Sire, but I intend to find out. I have sent for Morvan to come here and describe his encounter with the man.'

William was pensive. Like many rulers, he was resigned to the church's interference in secular matters when it suited them. However, this Pope seemed to intercede more than most; Gregory was wealthy and powerful, and William knew he had his own plan to put the Church above the rule of Kings.

With some trepidation, Morvan entered the Donjon. He knew that he had placed his brother in an invidious position because of his actions. He entered the solar and bowed to the company. When requested, he related his encounter with Piers De Chatillon. William listened with interest before adding, 'He may well have been directed by his uncle Odo de Chatillon, but it will be on the orders of the Pope.' He turned a gimlet eye on Morvan. 'Did you see any evidence of him supplying Robert with men or money?' Morvan glanced for a moment at Matilda and then answered truthfully that he had not seen any.

'My informants tell me that he is attracting men to his banner with gold, so someone is funding his rebellion against me,' William growled, his face filling with heightened colour. 'I know that my own court is full of his supporters and paid informers. Is that how they were able to withdraw and leave Remalard so quickly?' he asked in an exasperated tone.

Morvan sent a speaking glance to his brother; he could see that Luc was torn. Unfortunately, William, who was no fool, saw the look that passed between them. 'What do you know?' he asked Morvan in a quiet voice turning his hawk-like stare on the young Horse Warrior. Morvan closed his eyes and took a deep breath as Luc began to answer for him. 'Sire, I found that my brother...' he got no further as the Queen stood and intervened.

'I sent him William. I sent Morvan to Remalard to warn them. He was following my orders, and I did not want you to have the responsibility for killing your own son. I believe that Gilbert De Sorrell, one of our young Knights, only just into his prime, lies dead in our chapel.' The Queen paced in front of the fire while Luc looked at his brother in displeasure.

'So it is true, you have been acting behind our backs, against me and, more importantly, your King. What else have you done? Told them of our plans and betrayed us?' he said, the anger and shock clear to hear in his voice. Again, the Queen intervened.

'I gave him no choice, Malvais. I ordered Morvan to take letters and money to Ghent and then to Remalard to help Robert survive. He is our eldest son, William. I have to remind you that we lost his brother in a hunting accident. How many sons can you afford to lose?'

Despite her passion-filled words, William was not listening; he was on his feet. He stepped forward, his face suffused red with anger. 'Betrayal, here at the heart of my own family and from a Horse Warrior that I thought was loyal to me first and foremost.'

He raised a hand as if to strike Morvan across the face, and without warning, Constance leapt to her feet, screaming, 'No, No!' William looked at her in amazement and then at Morvan; he could see at a glance that his daughter loved this Breton

135

Knight.

He put a hand over his eyes. 'Get out,' he said. Then he shouted. 'Get out! All of you except Malvais,' he said, gesturing at Luc.

Matilda swept Constance up and bundled her out of the door. Morvan stood for a moment looking at Luc, who tight-lipped shook his head and indicated that he should go as the King walked over to stand at the window. 'If he has touched her, I will kill him,' William said in a stone-cold voice.

'I believe that it is just the early days of a dalliance. It is first love for both of them, sad but inconceivable,' said Luc in a matter-of-fact tone that meant he was not openly denying it or lying to the King.

'Did you know he was working for the Queen?' William asked, pinning Luc with an eagle glare.

'No, Sire, not until this moment. I suspected yesterday that he had been at Remalard and intended to confront him today.'

William sat down heavily into the vast carved wooden chair. He ran his hands back and forwards along its arms while staring sightlessly into the distance. 'I am not a heartless man Malvais, I do love my son Robert, and I can see why my wife warned him, but it will take some time for me to forgive the Queen for this. Find out where my son has gone, Malvais. Where have they run to; we need to know their whereabouts and his plans. I have planted one or two informers among the families of his followers, but nothing has come back as yet. And see what more you can find out about Chatillon; I do not like this, I do not like it at all.'

Luc bowed and left, thinking the same; papal interference never boded well. As he closed the solar door behind him, he heard an almighty crash as either the chair or the table hit the wall. Such a fit of anger did not bode well for Matilda or Morvan, he thought as he went to find his brother.

Chapter Nineteen

William's anger continued to simmer unabated for the next week. He did not go near his wife or daughter, who was ordered to eat in their rooms.

When mulling it over, William found that he could have accepted Matilda sending a warning to their son, but he could not understand her sending gold to Robert to continue the war against him. This betrayal was anathema to him. At the end of the week, he suddenly appeared in his wife's chamber. Matilda was pleased but apprehensive; she knew that William loved her, but she did not like the bullish, hurt expression on his face. He had not forgiven her.

'Tonight, you will bring Constance down to the Hall. Dress her in her finery; Alan Fergant will be arriving today, and their betrothal will be announced tonight.

Matilda gasped in shock. 'No,' she whispered, 'you promised me she would not be betrothed yet.'

William turned and faced his wife. 'That was before you went behind my back and betrayed me in favour of your son. In addition, I am not blind; I can see that she loves the Horse Warrior. I will deal with him later, but she is not allowed to be alone with him again. I am told that they take daily rides or walks together. How could you let that happen?' he snapped at her.

'Can you not remember William what it was like to be in love like that?' She asked in a sad voice. William looked away from her beseeching eyes. He loved her dearly, but he was still not prepared to forgive her yet, and he was determined to bring their errant daughter and his son Robert to heel. Therefore, he turned on his heel and left without another word, leaving a distraught Matilda to go and break her daughter's heart.

Luc watched the arrival of Alan Fergant to the court with dismay. Morvan had kept away from the Great Hall on his brother's orders. The King had not summoned Morvan, and William had not appeared at any of the training sessions in the paddock, as he was wont to do. The King usually loved to watch the huge Destriers being put through their paces, to swirl, kick and rear on command. Morvan was apprehensive when Luc appeared in the paddock and stood waiting for him to finish.

He had seen little of Luc since the scene in the solar. Morvan had stayed with his men, eating and sleeping in the barracks in the outer Bailey. The worst part of it was that he knew Luc was right. It was now an unholy mess. He loved a woman he could not have, and he had helped the Queen betray her husband, ruining his own prospects in the process. He told his men to dismount as he went to talk to his brother.

Luc could see the concern on his brother's face. He sighed; as he knew, what he had to tell him would break his heart. Morvan had undoubtedly had many women, but his heart had never been touched before, not in this way. 'I will be leaving tomorrow morning, Morvan; I have been away from Merewyn and my family for too long.'

Morvan smiled. 'How is my new nephew?'

'Young Garrett has a fine set of lungs,' said Luc with a

grin. 'His older brother, Lusian, treats him with contempt, as something loud and annoying. Chantal and my mother love him and spend hours sitting beside his cradle, singing and prattling to him.'

Morvan, hungry for news of the family, laughed. 'And is he a blonde Saxon like his mother or a dark, moody Breton like his father?' he joked.

'He is the image of his namesake, Merewyn's brother Garrett. His hair is a deep dark auburn like….' It was evident that Luc had just stopped in time from saying the name Constance and the pause hung in the air, putting a stop to the light-hearted banter that they had enjoyed of old.

'We are summoned to a feast in the Hall tonight,' said Luc, changing the subject. Morvan was just about to ask why when Alan Fergant strode up to join them.

'I have come to see these famous warhorses I hear so much about, in action,' he said, clasping arms with Luc. He turned to do the same with Morvan, but the young Breton Knight had turned away to return to the riders in the centre of the paddock. Luc knew by the dejected set of his brother's shoulders that he had worked out the implications of the young man's appearance. It did not bode well for tonight.

Constance sat in a sea of misery in the Great Hall, a smile fixed on her face. She listened to the hum of conversation around her and to the exploits and countless tales of the young man sitting beside her. She found it difficult to accept that this was the man she would marry, and shortly her father would announce her betrothal to the packed Hall. She lowered her eyes and risked a sideways glance at Morvan at the end of a side table sitting with Toki, her father's tall blonde Saxon Knight. His brother,

Luc, had been moved to sit close to her father. Following her gaze, her mother Matilda met her eyes and shook her head emphatically at her. It had been a painful interview with her mother. Constance was a loving and obedient daughter, and although she had accepted the betrothal as her lot, inside, she was screaming, No!

She heard her father push his chair back, and he stood and raised his goblet. He toasted Luc De Malvais for his success at Remalard to numerous cheers and banging on the tables. Then he toasted Alan Fergant and the alliance they had formed together. He then put his goblet down and beckoned Constance to her feet. Taking her hand, he placed it in the large hand of Alan Fergant and announced the betrothal. William smiled and told the young man that he could now kiss his betrothed. This announcement brought more cheers and ribald comments from the dozens of men at the tables, all of which William took in good stead.

Without a second's hesitation, Alan pulled Constance into his arms. He held her head in a vice-like grip, and he kissed her long and hard. She felt his tongue go deep into her mouth, and she tried to pull away, but he held her tighter. She could feel as he pressed his body against her that he was aroused. He finally let her go, and she fell backwards into her chair, gasping. She did not look at Alan; she looked straight at Morvan, whose face was full of anger and pain. He was grasping the table tightly with both hands, and she shook her head at him, frightened that he would get to his feet. She noticed that Toki put a hand on his friend's arm to calm him down. Alan Fergant was still on his feet, bowing to the hall and laughing, but he had seen her look, and his eyes travelled fleetingly to Morvan De Malvais. Finally, however, he turned and looked down at her, smiling.

She could see the lust and excitement on his face; her apparent reluctance had excited him.

Constance went to her mother's room that night. She waited impatiently as her mother's serving maid put away jewellery and clothes until finally her mother came and sat on the bed. Even in middle age, her mother was a striking woman with her long braids down her back. She took her mother's hands. Matilda saw the misery in her daughter's face. 'Constance, I know you think your heart is broken, and you think you will never love again like this, but Alan Fergant will love you if you let him. Everyone tonight could see how taken he is with you. He desires you. He is a vigorous young man and will become a strong and successful Duke of Brittany. I am sure you will give him many children.'

Constance raised her stricken, tear-filled eyes to Matilda. 'You may be right, Mother. In normal circumstances, I may have come to care for him, but there is a problem.' She paused and looked away for several moments as she built up the courage to tell her mother. 'I am carrying Morvan's child,' she whispered.

Matilda closed her eyes, her prayers to the Virgin Mary had not been answered, and her worst nightmare had been realised. The silence hung in the room; all that could be heard was the crackling of the logs in the fireplace. Finally, she opened her eyes and looked at her daughter, who had been so careless and disobedient, and she could feel anger building inside her. Without warning, she slapped Constance hard across her face. 'You foolish, foolish girl, you have put your life at risk and condemned that young man to death.' Constance, a hand to her red cheek, sobbed, the tears streaming down her cheeks both at the hopelessness of the situation and in shock that her mother had raised a hand to her.

'How far gone are you? When were your last courses?' she asked her daughter in exasperation.

'Three or four months, I think. It must have been the first time we made love back in early September, but he was so careful.'

Matilda snorted in contempt. 'Your young brother Henry was the result of being careful, as were half of the bastards scattered around Normandy. Does anyone know? Does he know? Your Horse Warrior.'

Constance shook her head. 'I have used chicken blood from the kitchen to fool my maid on my monthly cloths.' Matilda realised that her daughter had been living with this secret for several months, and her face softened for a moment in concern.

'I must think,' she said, pacing up and down the room. 'We must get you away from here; your father is preoccupied with Robert. He cannot know of this. This news would kill him, especially after the success of the alliance with Brittany that he desperately needs.

Constance watched her mother's face in concern. 'But where would I go?' she asked plaintively. It was as if her mother had not heard...

'God's bones,' she exclaimed suddenly. 'What are we to do about Alan Fergant? He will reject you immediately if a whisper of this gets out,' she said in a voice full of concern.

'I cannot possibly be betrothed or married to this man when I am carrying Morvan's child,' gasped Constance, standing up. Her mother raised a hand, pushing her back down onto the bed.

She continued in a tone that would brook no argument. 'You will go far into the countryside, and you will have this child. It will be taken away immediately, and then you will return. No-one will ever know.'

Constance looked at her mother in horror. She had thought

that her parents would just force Morvan to marry her. Now she realised that she had been naïve; the alliance with Brittany was far too important. She was about to lose Morvan and their child.

Her mother took her daughter's stricken face in her hands. 'By doing this, Constance, we may just be able to save Morvan's life,' she said emphatically.

Constance did not know how she got through the next few days with Alan Fergant; he took every opportunity to kiss and touch her, seemingly with her father's approval. They went hunting every morning, and then she was expected to entertain him every afternoon and evening. By the second day, when he managed to get her alone in the solar, he openly and explicitly talked about what he would like to do to her while trailing his fingers over her breasts. She was relieved when he said he was leaving for Brittany on the third day.

On her mother's advice, she had kept well away from Morvan although her eyes followed him, and she could feel his pain as he watched her walk hand in hand with Alan Fergant. However, she knew that she could do or say nothing or she would put him in danger. Her joy at carrying his child had dissipated to a continual ache of sadness. She knew that the child would be taken away by a wet nurse as soon as it was born.

That night, Toki and the outriders returned to Caen with the news; they had found Robert and his followers. The rebels had set up a temporary base at Thymerais, northeast of Remalard. It was yet another of Hugh's many chateaus, but this time they thought they were safe as it was outside the borders of Normandy.

Morvan woke suddenly from a restless slumber in the barracks to find his friend Toki standing beside him. It was still dark. 'The King has summoned you,' he said.

Chapter Twenty

Morvan stood before the King in the early dawn with Toki beside him. William stood on the top wall of one of the corner turrets in the chill morning breeze, and apart from nodding in recognition, he had yet to speak. Morvan was apprehensive, as he was not sure how much William knew about his relationship with Constance. In addition, he was not sure if William had forgiven him for working for the Queen. 'Are you loyal and trustworthy, Morvan De Malvais?' William finally asked. He did not wait for an answer but went on. 'Your brother Luc seems to think you are.'

Morvan bowed to the King. 'I am here to serve your majesty.'

William regarded him for several moments as if weighing him up. 'I know you have a friendship with my son Robert and his friends; they trust you. Robert knows that you have acted as a go-between for him and his mother behind my back,' he stated. Morvan nodded wondering where this was going. 'Well, now is the time to show your loyalty to me. I am sending you to Thymerais, but you will stay with Robert. You will become my eyes and ears, Morvan De Malvais. You will inform me of their intentions. I am sending Toki with you as a disgruntled Saxon as he also has a friendship with my son.' The young Saxon Thegn bowed in acquiescence. 'Malvais, you can use the excuse that Constance is betrothed. I have been told that the whole court has been talking of nothing but your dalliance with my daughter for months,' he growled.

Morvan could not meet his eyes as he looked up at the King but felt he had to say something. 'I am sorry if that news offends you, Sire, but my intentions were honourable; it is impossible to be with your daughter and not love her,' he said. William glared at him for several moments and then turned away. 'You leave today; do not let me down this time, Malvais.'

Morvan returned to his room at the barracks with mixed feelings. He was loyal to the King, but this meant that he would now be betraying Robert and his friends. However, he had no choice. He set off to the stables to groom Shadow, and it was here that Constance found him.

For a few moments, she stood just outside the doorway and watched him. He was absorbed in combing out the stallion's mane, and then he turned and saw her silhouetted in the doorway, the early dawn light highlighting the long auburn curls. Within seconds, she was in his arms sobbing uncontrollably. Morvan held her tight and, lowering his face to her neck, breathed in the smell of her skin. 'I have missed you so much, Constance,' he whispered as he lifted her tear-drenched face to his. He knew that she now belonged to someone else, but he was still unprepared for the naked pain he saw in her eyes.

'You have to help me, Morvan,' she stammered out between sobs. He held her at arm's length so that he could see her clearly in the doorway. 'What is it, my love? We knew this would happen, and my heart is breaking as well, but we cannot defy your father. You should not be here; we are not allowed to be alone together,' he sighed and stroked the side of her face.

She rested her face in his hand and looked at him longingly. 'I am carrying your child Morvan,' she whispered. Morvan's eyes widened in shock and alarm, and a gamut of emotions raced through him, joy, pain, fear for her and the child. He pulled her back into his arms and kissed her forehead. His mind whirled; at that moment, he had no idea what to say. He knew the consequences of this; William would kill him, and Constance would be interred in a nunnery, never to be seen again. The child would disappear, probably smothered at birth or exposed in the night air.

'What can we do? She asked, raising pleading eyes to his.

'Does anyone know of this? He asked, concern written on every line of his face.

'I have told my mother,' she said.

Morvan went stone cold; if the Queen knew then he was dead, she would surely be honour bound to tell the King.

'She is sending me away today to our home in Falaise to have the child; they will take it away. She is keeping this from my father and Alan Fergant. What can we do Morvan?'

The Horse Warrior wracked his brains. He was surprised that she was keeping it from the King. He could imagine William's fury if he found out, especially now the alliance with Alan Fergant and the betrothal was in place. He could not see a way through this, and turning away from her, he ran his hands through his hair in exasperation. Constance stood watching him in dismay.

'I will have to think on this, Constance. Unfortunately, I cannot see a way through, and I have to leave for Thymerais shortly on your father's orders.'

'Thymerais?' she questioned.

'Yes, I will join Robert; I have been given no choice. I may be away for months,' he said, grasping her hands.

Constance stared at her lover while tears streamed down her cheeks. 'I cannot stay here; I cannot lose you and our child. I will come with you, Robert will help us,' she said.

Morvan looked at her in astonishment. 'That cannot be Constance; your father will never forgive you.'

'We will run Morvan; someone will offer us shelter from my father's anger, my uncle in Flanders at first.'

Morvan's mind was in turmoil; he found it difficult to think clearly, his emotions were too close to the surface. 'You cannot be seen leaving with us. Pack a small bag of clothes and ride out to the village of Vimont. It is on the road to Thymerais; we will throw ourselves on Robert's mercy first. We will await you there but do not tarry.'

Constance smiled in relief. Reaching up, she kissed him and then whirled away to prepare.

Morvan leant his forehead against the cold wood of the stable door. He knew that if they took this step, there would be no going back. He led Shadow out into the morning light to brush his legs. Morvan turned back to get the brush and was startled to see Toki emerging from the stable door. They looked at each other for some moments in silence, and Morvan could see that the Saxon Thegn knew.

'You heard?' he asked. Toki nodded and shook his head in sadness.

'You are risking your life and hers, my friend.'

Morvan shrugged. 'Will you tell the King?' he asked.

Toki shook his head. 'It is your business, but I cannot see this ending well; he will kill both of you.'

Morvan bowed his head and turned away to finish grooming his horse; his stomach was cramped with anxiety and fear for

Constance. Toki stood for some time deep in thought outside the stables. He could understand precisely why the Queen was keeping this from William; there was so much at stake with the alliance with Alan Fergant of Brittany. However, if Morvan carried out his plan, all would be exposed, and the alliance would crumble. Finally, he came to a decision, and he went to the Queen.

Matilda was furious. Tight-lipped, she thanked and dismissed Toki after swearing him to secrecy and sent for Constance immediately, but although they searched everywhere, she was nowhere to be found. She had gone. Matilda sent a squire racing down to the stables, but it was too late; Morvan had now also ridden out with Toki.

Matilda knew she had to stop them, but she also had to keep this from William. She wracked her brain for some time before deciding to say nothing to him. She would tell him she had sent Constance to Falaise to prepare her for marriage, and she would convince him that it would be easier for Alan Fergant to visit her there.

Meanwhile, she had to get Constance back. Toki had mentioned that Luc De Malvais was on the borders near Le Mans; he could intercept them. She sat down to write him an urgent missive. If anyone could bring Constance back, it would be him; Morvan would listen to him. She summoned her Steward and told him to find a squire who could ride like the wind.

Chapter Twenty-One

Luc, Sir Gerard and their troop of Breton Horse Warriors had just made camp when the royal messenger rode in. Luc sighed at the sight of him.

They had just had an exhausting few days tracking a group of raiders that had burnt one of the local villages to the ground, killing the occupants and stealing their horses and animals. They had found their base in the forest, attacked at night and killed them; most of them were deserters or mercenaries from Anjou. Now he was looking forward to riding back to Morlaix to be with his family and to spend time with his infant son Garrett. However, an exhausted messenger on a winded horse, its flanks heaving, meant an urgent summons from the King. Gerard immediately went to see to the distressed horse while the squire handed Luc a roll of vellum. Luc could see two sides of writing as he unrolled it, and it was not from the King. Instead, this was from Queen Matilda. He read the missive in increasing anger and frustration and then gave a loud cry of exasperation.

'What was Morvan thinking?' he exclaimed as he handed it to a concerned Gerard. It was Luc who had suggested to the King that he use his brother's friendship with Robert and the rebels at Thymerais for his own good, and he hoped to put Morvan back in the King's favour. Now it sounded as if all that was in vain.

He turned and saw his men were all watching in anticipation; they all knew the significance of a royal messenger. 'Benedot, take the men back to Morlaix; I have to go north. I will take Gerard and five men with me. We leave shortly,' he said, crumpling the vellum that Gerard handed back and throwing it to burn on the fire. As he watched the flames consume the Queen's writing, he hoped she knew what she was doing; the King had eyes and ears everywhere. He had to go and save his brother from making the worst decision of his life, which would also taint the Malvais name for generations if known. The scandal of this would reverberate for them all if he could not prevent their flight. He looked at Gerard, who was as a father to them both. He just stared back and shook his head in disbelief.

Morvan met with Constance outside the small village of Vimont. Toki said nothing; he bowed his head in greeting to her and then just loudly sighed at the foolishness of it all. They were spending two nights on the road. It was about thirty-five leagues to Thymerais, and the horses and riders needed several rest breaks in between. Each night Morvan and Constance sat talking around the campfire until the early hours, making plans for their future together. Constance had decided to throw herself on her brother's mercy, asking for his support against her parents. Morvan was torn; he had sworn allegiance to the King who had sent him on a mission. He decided to take a middle path, assess what he found at Thymerais and send any information back to the King. He thought it would perhaps delay William's decision to have him killed.

They curled up each night under their blankets and quietly made love. Constance went to sleep almost immediately after the long ride, but Morvan lay awake staring at the embers of the fire, deliberating on what he had done and what his family would think. Even the thought of Luc's reaction filled him with anxiety. Every plan that he ran through his head was fraught with risk. He could not take Constance to his estates in Vannes as Alan Fergant as the Duke of Brittany could claim her and capture him; he had more rights over Constance as his betrothed than Morvan had. His mother and Luc would never accept her at Morlaix as they were loyal to the King, and it would put them at risk from William if and when he exacted revenge. He knew they had no choice but to run, but where to? He had connections in Ireland through Merewyn's mother, or they could go to Italy, where he would always find work as a mercenary. Still, it would be a hard life for Constance, always on the move and knowing that they would be hunted even there; William had a long reach in Europe. When they rose just after dawn, he was exhausted.

Luc and Gerard had ridden north at speed, snatching a few hours' sleep here and there; they knew they had to push the pace to intercept Morvan. Finally, at the end of the next day, they reached the road to Thymerais and camped beside it, just outside the village of Maillebois. None of the villagers had seen a party riding through, so they thought they had made it in time; Luc hoped so otherwise, he was riding into the lion's den at Thymerais after being responsible for the death of Gilbert de Sorrell.

Gerard had ridden in silence, but now he pulled alongside Luc, looking thoughtful. 'Do you think Constance will go with you willingly, Luc? She is running away from her betrothal to Alan Fergant, away from her father, and she is carrying Morvan's child. You are taking her back to a life she hates where the child will be disposed of or given away to some Knight's family who will stay quiet for a yearly stipend. Luc said nothing. He just stared into the campfire. He loved his brother dearly, and he hated what he was about to do, but he had no choice. He was saving his brother's life, and one day he may see that. He stood and threw the remains of the mulled wine into the undergrowth as Espirit suddenly whickered. The horses always knew when other horses were near. They immediately mounted and prepared to meet Morvan and his party.

Morvan was dog tired. He had slept little, and they had ridden all day through rugged wooded hills and streams. At first, he did not see the party who were spread across the road ahead; he was so absorbed in his thoughts about what they should say to Robert. Then Toki reined in beside him. 'Malvais, up ahead.'

Morvan paled; he would recognise that horse anywhere. The huge steel dappled stallion had its feet firmly planted across the track, his brother grim-faced in full battle array sitting in silence… waiting for him. Beside him was a frowning Sir Gerard, a man who had been his mentor and father figure since he was a child. He heard Constance gasp behind him, which filled him with determination to protect her; he knew why they were here.

Luc waited until they were only yards away before he spoke. 'Lady Constance, I am here to escort you to Falaise on the orders of the Queen. Your mother is distraught, as she believes that both of your lives are in danger. She also thinks that going to Robert Curthose will worsen the situation while she is trying to broker reconciliation between the King and his son.' Luc ignored Morvan completely as he watched the emotions play across her face. Gerard, however, stared directly at Morvan; the older man's face a mask of disapproval and disappointment. Morvan found himself forced to look away.

Luc continued in a soft, reasonable voice. 'At present, your father has no idea that you have left Caen to come to Thymerais. Therefore, now is the time for you to turn back with me to Falaise. Surprisingly Constance nodded her head in hopeless acquiescence, and Luc felt the tension leave his shoulders. The silence hung in the air for several moments, then, he spoke to his brother and Toki for the first time as if they were strangers.

'The Queen thanks you for your service in escorting the King's daughter so far, but you may now stand down and continue to Thymerais on the King's business; the lady Constance is now under our protection.'

Morvan found that his hands were sweating, and his knuckles were white as he gripped the pommel of the saddle. His emotions were in turmoil; he knew that what Luc had said was sensible, but Constance was the love of his life and carrying his child. He would lose both of them. He glanced across at her. She sat, head bowed and dejected on her mare; her cheeks were wet with tears.

'No!' he shouted, pushing Shadow forward in front of her horse. He saw Luc's eyes narrow and Gerard shaking his head at him in dismay. 'She is with child Luc, my child. I cannot let you take them away,' he cried, his voice breaking with emotion.

'I have no choice, Morvan. This is a situation of your making; you brought this down on her head as soon as you lay with her. If you continue, they will hunt you down and kill you. And Constance? She will be condemned to a life of imprisonment in some far away nunnery. Is that what you want for her?' he cried in exasperation.

Luc's words stung Morvan, as he knew he spoke the truth. This was his entire fault, but he could not let them take her. 'They will never find us, Luc. We will run. I can protect her,' he shouted.

Whirling Shadow around, he reached up and drew one of his swords. Both Constance and Gerard let out a gasp of shock.

Gerard shouted, 'No, do not be so stupid, Morvan,' and he moved his horse forward. However, Luc raised a hand and stopped him.

'I do not want to draw a sword against you, Morvan. You are my brother; I love you dearly. Nevertheless, I will do it if you stand in my way. Constance knows this is the only pathway to rescue you both from this unholy mess.' Luc had barely finished the sentence when Morvan rode straight at him and attacked.

Luc did the only thing possible, and reining back, he pulled Espirit up into a rear, making him strike out at Shadow while hastily drawing his sword. Despite Shadow's apparent reluctance, Morvan came back in for another attack, raining blow after blow down on Luc's sword. Physically they were equally matched, but this was Luc De Malvais, a master swordsman and Horse Warrior. Within seconds, he pushed Espirit to attack again. The huge stallion sank his teeth into Shadow's neck, viciously shaking him, which forced Morvan to turn and pull him away from the deadly Destrier.

Meanwhile, Luc stood up in the stirrups and launched a crushing blow on Morvan's head and shoulders with the flat of his sword, knocking him from the saddle. Luc leapt from the saddle and ran around the snapping horses to find Morvan struggling to his feet. He turned white-faced, sword in hand and launched himself at Luc, who parried and forced his brother backwards.

Blow after blow was exchanged as the horrified onlookers urged them to stop. Finally, Constance scrambled down from the saddle, and Toki separated the fighting stallions. Gerard was shocked to the core; he could never imagine any closer brothers than Morvan and Luc. To see them fighting each other like this broke his heart. As he watched, he quickly realised that the red mist had settled on Morvan, something he had always warned them about when training the brothers as teenagers. You must never let your emotions take control. He could also see that a grim-faced Luc was engaging with but purposefully trying not to hurt his brother. Time after time, he blocked his brother's blow, hoping that he would tire, but Morvan threw himself at Luc repeatedly.

Luc knew he had to finish this, so he took a chance. He suddenly dropped to his knees directly in front of his brother and rammed the hilt of his sword hard up into Morvan's stomach, winding him and sending him backwards, doubled up. Luc followed, raining blow after blow onto a gasping Morvan's sword hand until he dropped the blade and fell to his knees. Luc stood watching him for a few moments and then reached out a hand to pull his brother to his feet. However, Morvan ignored him and slowly stood back up, glaring at his brother.

'Is this what you want, Morvan? You want to fight or kill me so that you can steal her away into a life of impoverished misery as the wife of a mercenary. Always on the run, always looking over your shoulder for the many paid assassins that William employs? What of your child, what sort of life will they have?' he asked.

Morvan did not answer; he stood shaking, fists clenched as Luc walked over, picked up his brother's sword, and handed it back to him. 'I did not want to fight you, Morvan; you are my brother. I warned you over a year ago that this love of yours could never end well, but you paid no heed. Instead, you recklessly pursued a course that could ruin your life and hers and blacken our family name.'

Morvan slowly shook his head in denial. 'From this day, I have no brother. I have spent my life living in your shadow, and now I will make my own way without the famous Luc De Malvais name shadowing my every move. I will not work for the King anymore. Instead, I will join Robert as a rebel; I will help and support him against William and against you,' he snarled.

Luc could feel his own anger building which was rare. This move to join the rebels would sign his death warrant. Could Morvan not see that he was trying to save them?

'So be it, Morvan, if this is the path you wish to take. You are no longer welcome at our home in Morlaix. Our mother will be saddened but will understand why you are no longer fit to hold the family name,' he said in a tone that brooked no argument.

Luc took a distressed, sad-eyed Constance by the hand, led her back to her horse, and helped her into the saddle. He mounted Espirit, and without a backward glance at his brother, the group turned and moved back onto the road to Falaise. Morvan, watching them, cried with anguish and dropped to his knees. When, wracked by harsh sobs, he shouted after his brother, 'I will never forgive you for this, Luc; I swear I will never forgive you!'

Chapter Twenty-Two

Morvan stayed on his knees, head bent for some time after watching Constance disappear into the distant trees. Toki left him alone. His heart bled for both of them, but he knew that Luc De Malvais had made the right decision. Morvan needed time, but he would pull himself together. He may not be as ruthless as his brother, but he was strong and resilient in other ways. Toki knew that he was a fine warrior and a natural leader; he would have to find a way to deal with this.

Eventually, Morvan got to his feet. He wiped his arm across his eyes and looked at the blood on his sleeve. He had a deep slash across his cheek, which was bleeding. His head and ribs ached from the blows that his brother had inflicted, but this paled into insignificance compared to the pain he felt at losing Constance and his child. He stood and stared sightlessly into the forest beyond.

Toki walked over and placed a hand on his shoulder. 'It is time to go. Shadow has a nasty bite on his neck. I have washed it with water, but it will need a poultice if it is not to become infected. Morvan, tight-lipped, nodded in gratitude and followed the young Saxon back to the horses. Once mounted, he turned onto the road to Thymerais. Leaving behind the life and family he had known, he was filled with a cold determination to make his own way in the world without his brother's name or help.

Luc and his party rode swiftly west through the forests towards Falaise. They finally stopped for a night at the small monastery of Saint-Hilaire. Constance, who did not want to face anyone, went straight to her bed, a young monk leading the way, but Luc, Gerard and their men availed themselves of their hospitality. The abbot was a learned man who kept a good table but had little contact with the outside world, so he relied on travellers such as them for news. He did not think it strange that the King's daughter was travelling with such a small escort. However, one man had recognised both Luc De Malvais and Constance. He was a religious prelate travelling back to Brittany, as he had spent some weeks in France on his master's orders.

The three Horse Warriors accompanying Luc sat at the end of the long refectory table where the prelate was ensconced. He sat quietly and listened to their conversation. As he mopped up the meat juices on his trencher, he engaged them in conversation. He expressed admiration for their exploits in patrolling the borders. After several more jugs of wine, they were all good friends. When he left them several hours later, he knew all about the fight between Luc De Malvais and his brother; he also knew that they were delivering Constance to Falaise. This information would mean nothing in some other hands, but this man was Monseigneur Gironde, the chaplain to Duke Hoel of Brittany. He knew that what he had just learned would undoubtedly interest both young Alan Fergant and his other master, the papal envoy Piers De Chatillon.

The following day Constance was delivered to her mother's Castellan at Falaise. He was expecting her arrival; however, she had come directly from Caen as far as he knew. The Queen had sent him instructions that Constance was betrothed and was now to be kept in complete seclusion with her waiting women. Luc bowed in farewell to the King's daughter. He experienced a pang when she raised those sad, resigned eyes to his, but he knew in his heart that there was no alternative. He kissed her hand and wished her well before turning on his heel and heading back to his home, back to Morlaix in Brittany, back to Merewyn and his new son.

It had been far too long since he had been home; he told Gerard as they mounted and set off. Therefore, it was with heavy hearts that they rode through the large stone gatehouse, and up towards his castle. His younger brother would never set foot here again, and he had to break that news to his mother and his wife, who loved Morvan almost as much as he did.

In Thymerais, Morvan was greeted with much enthusiasm by Robert and his followers. The young nobles crowded around him with much backslapping; they were all grateful for the warning that Morvan had delivered at Remalard that allowed most of them to escape. Robert Curthose waited until they had settled back around the tables and the fire before he spoke to Morvan.

'Do you bring another message from my mother?' he asked. Morvan knew the young heir would be disappointed if he was expecting more gold.

'No, Sire, I have not come from the Queen.' This comment turned several heads in their direction. 'Unfortunately, your father found out about the gold. He was furious; relations between your parents are not good, and...' Morvan took a deep breath before he could say the next words. 'He immediately betrothed Constance to Alan Fergant.' Robert gave Morvan a sympathetic glance; he was not blind and knew the young Horse Warrior loved his sister.

Morvan continued, 'Toki and I have come to join you; I am no longer in the service of the King.' There was a stunned silence at this. 'I have broken with my brother and my family.' There was a ragged cheer at this news. 'This is because of Gilbert, because of the attack on Remalard by your brother and the Horse Warriors,' declared his friend Roger-Fitz-Richard. Morvan decided not to disabuse them of this thought, so he nodded, as he did not want to bandy Constance's name amongst them.

Morvan stared into the fire for a few moments. When, he looked up, he found Robert's puzzled gaze upon him. 'That must have been hard, I know how much you loved your brother; I used to envy your relationship with him.'

Morvan bowed his head, but Toki jumped into the conversation. 'They fought on the road here; his brother was trying to stop him from joining you. It was a fierce fight, but not even Morvan can stand against Luc De Malvais.' Everyone's attention was on Toki as he described the fight and the sword blows; they could all imagine the scene.

Belleme, leaning on the wall next to the fireplace, walked over and stood in front of Morvan. Leaning over, he ran a finger along the deep oozing cut on Morvan's cheekbone. The Horse Warrior did not move a muscle; he met his unblinking stare. 'He gave you this, did he?

Morvan glared at Belleme and nodded. 'You got off lightly; we have all seen your brother in battle. And you, Saxon, why have you suddenly decided to join us? Is it me, or does no one else find this suspicious?' he sneered.

Toki drew himself up to his full height. He was a big man, a broad-shouldered Saxon Thegn. 'I have never received the recognition or rewards that my family were promised for helping the King,' he stated.

Robert glanced at Belleme and waved him down into a seat. 'I believe them; Morvan would never willingly give up his family without reason.'

Belleme backed off with reluctance, but he determined to watch the Saxon, who could usually be found at William's side.

'Well, Morvan, I can certainly use you. Over fifty horses arrived from the North yesterday; they need training, as do their riders. Create a cavalry troop for us, Morvan, our own horse warriors as we have plans in place to get my father's attention,' he said while glancing at a scowling Belleme.

Morvan nodded and managed a smile. The noise grew around him as he downed goblet after goblet of wine to blot out the memory of the day's events. Inside, he was in a sea of pain at the thought of Constance. She would now be in Falaise, and he knew that he would never see her again; the memory of watching her forlornly riding away with Luc without a backward glance would stay with him forever.

The next three days were a hive of activity for Morvan and Toki as they assessed the quality of the mounts. Most were good, and Morvan could see a Belgian strain in the large build of many, so he presumed that Count Robert of Flanders had sent them. Then there were a few with spavined hocks that could only be of use as pack animals. Others would be suitable for riding horses for the vedettes and outriders.

Next, Morvan undertook the schooling of the horses, which was gruelling work, teaching them to respond only to commands from the rider's legs when the reins were dropped. Morvan needed this physical work; coupled with copious amounts of wine on a night, it meant that he dropped into an exhausted sleep each night.

Finally, on the fourth day, their work was interrupted by the blowing of horns. The large field they were using ran alongside the long tree-lined track that led to the walled chateau at Thymerais. Now a large colourful contingent of troops was cantering towards the chateau, standards and pennants flying. The riders were all sporting a blue and gold livery, and they were led by a dark man on a showy bay stallion. He was accompanied by two other Knights. Morvan thought he recognised the livery but could not place it. Then, as they drew level, he recognised one of the riders at the front, and he gave a sharp intake of breath: Piers De Chatillon, the papal envoy.

Toki came and stood beside him. 'There must be nearly a hundred men or more; Robert seems to be attracting significant support. Do we know who they are?' he asked Morvan, who shook his head.

'The livery looks familiar, but I cannot place it. However, the Pope's envoy is riding with him, so he must be important.' They stood and watched for a while as the three men dismounted and were warmly greeted on the steps by Robert, Hugh de Chateauneuf, and more significantly, his beautiful wife and young daughter Mabile.

It was dark and damp that early December evening as Morvan and Toki finally finished seeing to the horses and made their way to the Hall. The noise hit them as they opened the heavy wooden door into the light and warmth. The tables were packed with the newcomers, and the Hall was awash with the blue and gold livery. Morvan noticed that the standards and pennants were now in evidence held by squires at the back of the raised dais.

They made their way to the side tables on the dais, but Piers

De Chatillon greeted him as they took their seats. 'Morvan De Malvais, you are here again. Are you still coming from the Queen to support Robert?'

Morvan delivered an exaggerated bow to Chatillon, who smiled. However, Robert Curthose answered for the Horse Warrior. 'Morvan with Toki of Wigod has left the King's service to join us here.' Toki inclined his head to the top table and took his seat on the bench.

The leader of the troops was a large impressive man who sat beside Robert. He had an intelligent, penetrating gaze as he turned his attention to Morvan. 'Are you related to Luc De Malvais? He asked. Morvan gritted his teeth. How long would this continue, he asked himself. The silence around the table was palpable, and the dark stranger raised his eyebrows in surprise.

Morvan sighed and answered. 'Yes, he is my brother, although I have split with my family to serve Robert,' he said, bowing his head in Robert's direction.

'I have fought him in battle several times and always lost,' the man laughed, as did the rest of the table, which included two Breton Lords. Morvan gave a tight smile of acknowledgement as he took his seat beside his friends, Roger-Fitz-Richard and William de Breteuil. 'Who is he? He looks familiar,' he asked Roger.

'He is Gervais de la Ferte, the Seneschal of France, one of King Philip's right-hand men and his son, is about to be betrothed to Mabile, Hugh's young daughter,' he whispered. Morvan felt a cold wave of alarm pass through him. The Seneschal of France, was this pure coincidence that he was here?

Morvan was aware that the Lords of Chateauneuf en Thymerais were very wealthy, with extensive lands on both sides of the border with France. However, they had always vacillated in their loyalty, choosing either France or Normandy depending on their need. This match would be a significant alliance. Morvan looked along the high table, Hugh's only child, his daughter who would be his heir, was 15 years or so, and she looked like a frightened rabbit. Unfortunately, she took after her colourless father rather than her beautiful dark-haired mother; but the connection with France would be consolidated with this match. He also noticed that Belleme was again, sitting beside Piers De Chatillon; their dark heads were together, they seemed deep in conversation. Morvan was uneasy; there were so many undercurrents here, he felt that Robert Curthose was playing with fire.

Chapter Twenty-Three

Morvan continued the training of the men and horses the following day while most of the occupants of the chateau went out to hunt wild boar in the verdant forests surrounding Thymerais. He walked back to the Hall to partake of a nuncheon at noon while it was still quiet. On entering, he was surprised to find Piers De Chatillon sitting pensively by the fire, twirling a goblet of mulled wine. He nodded at Morvan, 'Well met, I could do with some company, Morvan De Malvais,' he said with a raised eyebrow. Morvan nodded while helping himself to some of the food laid out ready for the returning hunters, and Chatillon poured him a goblet of mulled wine.

'You must have found it difficult to dismiss your family's loyalty to the King so quickly,' he suggested. Morvan tore off a chunk of bread and dipped it into a steaming bowl of pottage before he answered.

'So it was, and still is in some ways, Chatillon. But as I am sure you know, sometimes a better cause is worth fighting for.'

The Frenchman looked sceptical. 'I had presumed that this sudden change of heart had more to do with the rejection of your suit for a certain lady.' He noticed the quick flash of anger in Morvan's eyes, and he knew he had hit home.

'You are well informed, Chatillon,' Morvan growled at him as he downed the wine.

The papal envoy nodded. 'I have to be, it keeps me alive, and I would not be as useful to my masters if I were not.' He gave a small smile of self-satisfaction.

Morvan finished his food, placed the empty goblet on the table, and stood to return to the paddock. 'Whatever my former allegiances, my loyalty is now to my new liege lord, Robert Curthose, so I will still protect him and his interests, Chatillon, no matter how many people try to put me out of action by sending warrior monks to punish me.'

'Yes, I heard about that; I can see by your face that you thought it was me. I hate to disabuse you of that fact. If I wanted you out of the way, I would just kill you. The wine you are drinking now would have a subtle poison in it that would take a few days to work but have the exact same symptoms of the bloody flux so that no one would suspect a thing.' Morvan glanced at the empty goblet.

They stared unsmiling at each other for some time before the Frenchman gave a short bark of laughter. 'I assure you, my Breton friend, I mean you no harm; I also have Robert's interests at heart; I am working to give him what he desires, the Dukedom of Normandy.'

Morvan raised a questioning eyebrow. The loud sounds of the hunt returning filtered in from outside. He turned and left him with a parting shot, 'But at what cost, Chatillon? At what cost?'

As he walked across the courtyard through the milling horses and hounds, his mind was churning over the possible agenda the Vatican might be pursuing. He did not doubt that they would use Robert to gain their ends. In addition, he believed Chatillon, if he had not sent them to attack him, who did?

He did not, at first, hear his friends hailing him, but he stopped while Roger and William regaled him for some time on the morning's exploits, the way Gervais de la Ferte had galloped his horse straight at a cornered tusker and dispatched him with one thrust of his spear. 'The man is fearless, Morvan; the beast was a huge old boar and could have disembowelled the horse.' Morvan smiled and watched them race up the steps for food. They seemed so young and carefree; he felt a small stab of envy.

He spent the better part of the afternoon teaching a group of riders to instruct their horses to rear and swirl on command. This resulted in several novices repeatedly hitting the icy ground. He stood with his hands on his hips for a few seconds, laughing with Toki whilst telling him what Gerard would have shouted at them. He suddenly realised that he would probably never see Gerard again, and his mood darkened.

He heard his name called and turned to see Hugh's wife standing at the side beckoning to him. He walked over and bowed his head in greeting. 'Can I be of service, my Lady?' he asked as she moved closer and looked him up and down with interest. For a second, she ran her tongue over her bottom lip as she looked at this powerful dark young warrior. She did not love her husband; he was a pale, colourless individual despite his wealth and huge estates. He had no presence; she was not surprised that her brother Belleme bullied him so easily. The silence hung between them for a few moments; finally, she sighed. This was not the time for a dalliance with an attractive young man, but maybe later; now however, she had a house full of important guests, and she needed Hugh.

'I have urgent need of my Lord Hugh, but I cannot find him. The grooms tell me he walked this way; if you could find him, I would be very, very grateful,' she said, raising her large dark eyes to his face and taking her bottom lip between her teeth. Morvan thought about what she was offering for only a few seconds. She was lovely, much younger than Hugh, but those dark eyes, they were Belleme's eyes as well, and he knew the whole family were poisonous in more ways than one. Their mother, her namesake, Mabel De Belleme, was a powerful and dangerous woman renowned for poisoning or killing her enemies in brutal ways before stealing their lands.

Morvan bowed and said he would look for Hugh immediately. Her eyes still held his; she put a hand on his arm in a possessive gesture, then her face clouded with disappointment, as he showed no inclination other than a raised eyebrow, so she thanked him and reluctantly turned away.

Morvan headed down to the path by the river; he had seen Hugh heading this way on a few occasions. He walked further through the frost-covered wooded banks; the river was wide and deep and fast flowing with the winter rains. He was just about to turn back when he heard voices. He stared through the trees, but at first, he could see nothing. So he moved closer, climbing the hill, following the sound until he could make out a low ivy-covered stone building. He realised at once that it was some sort of hermitage. There was a barred window on the side with an opening for people to leave food in return for prayers, but parts of it looked older than that. Then he saw the faint relief carved into the wide stone lintel; he could just make out the weathered shape of a man and a bull.

The wooden door stood ajar, yet the voices sounded more distant, and they echoed. Then it came to him; Luc had shown him something similar in Lombardy. It was a Mithraic temple. At the back, there would be steps down to a long chamber below where the Roman soldiers would make offerings or sacrifices to their god; this was why the voices had an echo. More recently, it would have been used by a monk who had chosen a life of isolation, prayer and abstinence. He stepped forward and flattened himself against the cold stone wall.

The men inside were arguing. He recognised Hugh's plaintive higher voice. 'We must move from here; my wife and child are in danger. William always seems aware of exactly where we are, and we all know how unforgiving he can be. We do not want a repeat of Remalard where we escaped by the skin of our teeth.'

'Gods bones, will you stop your whining, Hugh. Yes, we have spies here; that is why we are meeting in this godforsaken place. I am not sure about the Horse Warrior, but the Saxon I do not trust. I am sure that William has sent him; I think he needs to meet with a hunting accident; I will arrange it.' Morvan immediately recognised the bitter tones of Belleme's voice. A far deeper voice then joined in.

'Do not fear; the King has a plan in place for you. In a few days, we will move all of your forces to a fortress over the border, which King Philip has given you for your use. It is three times the size of this, well placed for raids into the Norman Vexin and nigh on impregnable. I will be sending a message to the King at first light to tell him where you will be as he will be sending over six hundred men, weapons and supplies.' Morvan knew in an instant that this was the French Seneschal, Gervais de la Feret.

Belleme was delighted. 'William will now take us seriously, and with luck, Robert will be consecrated in the cathedral at Rouen as the Duke of Normandy before the month is out,' he said.

'Where is this fortress, my Lord?' asked Hugh. Morvan moved closer to the barred window to hear the reply, and in doing so, he dislodged a stone, which unearthed others when his foot slipped on the ice.

'What was that? There is someone there,' shouted Belleme making for the steps. Morvan did the only thing he could; he pulled his hood up and ran down the incline towards the river.

He heard Belleme shout, 'There he is,' as he followed the path deeper into the forest. Fortunately, an autumn mist had settled around the river, and he was soon lost from their sight, but he could hear the sounds of pursuit; he knew it would be Belleme. He heard him shout, 'Get the dogs, Hugh, we will catch the bastard.'

Before long, Morvan came to the entrance of a long deep gully, and without hesitation, he jumped down into it and ran lightly over the large rocks at the bottom until dropping down further. He was suddenly confronted with a broad cliff face and a steep drop down to the river. He seemed to have run onto a large bluff, a peninsula of rock surrounded by the river. He could not go back. He stood panting and listened for any sounds behind him, but his own heavy breathing was the only thing he could hear. He let out a deep breath thinking he had thrown them off, when suddenly he heard the sound of a sword slashing at the evergreen undergrowth behind him.

It occurred to Morvan that the gathering of this group could mean they were reforming their previous alliance against William, the alliance which defeated him at the siege of Dol. Breton rebel Lords, Fulk of Anjou, Philip of France… and now the Vatican, except they had an even better advantage this time. They had Robert Curthose, William's insurgent son and the future Duke of Normandy in their midst. This alliance on these crucial border areas would weaken William's position in Normandy considerably. Morvan did not doubt because of what he had overheard, if they found him, they would kill him, and the only weapon he had upon him was the small dagger in his belt.

He looked down; he had no choice but to try to go down the cliff hand by hand. As he lowered himself over the edge, he heard the chilling sound of a barking pack in the distance. It seemed to take him an age to negotiate the crumbling rock as he scrambled for purchase. The sound of the dogs and shouting voices were much nearer as his feet reached solid ground. He flattened himself against the bottom of the cliff, hoping that they could not see him from above while he thought about his next move. The dogs were now directly above him, barking and yapping as they milled around on the top of the cliff.

'He went over here; the dogs can't follow,' he heard an unknown voice say.

Belleme answered. 'They can follow on the end of my boot.' Morvan heard a yelp as Belleme kicked a dog toward the edge.

He heard Hugh shout. 'No, Belleme, there is a way down over here; there is a path. I played here, as a child, and I know it well. If he is down there, they will pick his scent up immediately.' Morvan heard Belleme grunt his reluctant approval, followed by the sounds of them moving away from the edge.

He knew he had to move now, and there was only one way to go. He took off his heavy woollen cloak, bent down and, soaking it in the river, rolled it into a ball and threw it far onto the opposite bank whilst hoping that it might delay the dogs for a short while. He then lowered himself into the deep, fast-flowing water. He gave a sharp intake of breath as the icy cold water hit him, but he had no choice, and he began to swim as fast as he could downstream and back towards the chateau. Keeping as close to the icy banks as possible, he was still in sight of the cliff as the trees thinned here, and he prayed that they would not spot him or he was a dead man; he knew that Belleme would happily watch as the dogs tore him apart.

Chapter Twenty-Four

Robert de Belleme stood on the riverbank, a wet cloak ripped to shreds by the dogs in his hands. They had searched every inch of the woods to no avail, and he could feel the fury building inside him. The other two men stood nervously behind him, not venturing to suggest that they should call off the hunt as the light was fading.

Hugh coughed nervously as if he had built up the courage, but Belleme turned on him before he could get a word out. 'I will find him; he cannot have gone far.'

'We think he may have gone into the river; it's the only explanation for the pack not picking up the trail,' said Hugh.

Belleme turned and viewed the deep dark brown fast flowing river and its ice-encrusted banks. 'He would not survive long in there, so take the hounds a few hundred yards up each side,' he growled, stomping off back to the chateau, the wet cloak balled up still in his hands.

Morvan had dragged himself from the freezing river onto the bank where he lay in an exhausted, shivering heap. He could no longer feel his feet or his hands. The swim was much longer than he expected, and his teeth were chattering. He was aware that someone was approaching and tried to push himself up; he had escaped the dogs and did not want them to catch him now. He closed his eyes for a second and gritted his teeth to find the strength to get to his knees. Instead, he found himself being roughly pulled to his feet. He raised his eyes in alarm and reached for his dagger.

Toki's blue eyes looked at him in concern while gripping his shoulders to hold him up. 'You live a charmed life Morvan, not many men would escape a pack of the finest hunting dogs and survive a swim in an icy river in December. Now let us get you out of here before they discover us.' He took off his cloak and wrapped it around his shivering friend.

Fortunately, there seemed to be only servants in the Hall when they crossed it and headed to their room. Once there, Morvan stripped off his wet, freezing clothes, and Toki rubbed him down with a rough cloth to get the circulation moving again. He wrapped a blanket around his friend and summoned a servant to bring them tankards of hot mulled ale. He pulled a stool beside Morvan, who was beginning to get feeling and pain back into his numbed limbs.

'So tell me what happened?' he asked, his head cocked to one side.

Morvan related all that he had heard; especially worrying was the interference of Philip of France. Toki gave a low whistle. 'The King needs to know this information; we also need to know the name of this fortress. Do you have any idea?' he asked.

Morvan shook his head. 'It could be one of a dozen on the borders of Normandy.'

'We need to know as soon as possible.'

Morvan smiled. 'I think I know just how to find out.'

An hour later, a recovered Morvan with warm ale and food inside him decided to go down and check on Shadow. He believed the poultice on his neck had prevented infection, but he needed to see that it was healing. Espirit had torn the skin badly, and he knew that Shadow would always bear the scar, another reminder of his showdown with Luc. He automatically went for his cloak then remembered he had lost it. Toki had insisted that Morvan keep his, and so he flung it around his shoulders and headed out.

As he strode across the Hall, he noticed Belleme standing by the fire; he could feel his angry eyes on him as he went to open the door.

'Malvais!' he shouted. Morvan slowly turned and walked back towards him.

'Where is your friend the Saxon?' Belleme asked.

'I believe that, like me, he has gone to check on his men and their horses. Why? He asked.

Belleme stared back into the fire for a few moments. 'I like to know where people are in these dangerous times, especially people I do not trust,' he spat.

'You can trust Toki,' Morvan replied.

'That remains to be seen,' said Belleme with his usual sneer.

As he turned to leave, Morvan remembered Belleme's comment about arranging a hunting accident; he must warn Toki. However, he found he could not resist leaving Belleme without making one jibe. 'How was your hunt, Belleme? I believe it was exhilarating,' he said and smiled as he opened the door.

Belleme stared after him for some time. He stood, fists clenched, oblivious to the servants around him setting up the trestle tables for dinner. He replayed Morvan's comment repeatedly in his mind. Was he referring to the hunt for the intruder? He had noticed immediately that Malvais was wearing his cloak, so it had not been him in the forest, but he was now convinced that Morvan knew something and was taunting him.

Dinner that evening was a lively affair. Robert's followers were in good spirits after a successful hunt followed by an afternoon of horse racing and betting. As usual, Morvan and Toki were late arrivals; they bowed to the top table and took their seats. No sooner had they reached for their food and filled their goblets than Belleme's voice cut across the tables.

'Ah, our friends from the stables have arrived,' he laughed. It was evident that he was several goblets of wine ahead of them and his nearly black eyes glittered with malice. 'Tell me, Toki of Wigod; were you not cold out there in those icy winds without your cloak? Maybe like our Horse Warrior friends here, you have wrapped your horse in it.' There were several guffaws of good-natured laughter at this. The care and attention the Horse Warriors gave to their horses were often the butts of jokes until they saw them ride into battle. However, others at the high table knew precisely what Belleme was referring to this time.

Hugh de Chateauneuf glanced nervously at Belleme, shaking his head to tell him this was not the time. Gervais de la Feret calmly continued to tear the meat off the joint in front of him. He had taken no part or interest in their pursuit of the intruder.

Toki laughed good-naturedly at the comment. 'Ah, that is where the problem lies, Belleme; I think my horse has eaten my cloak.' This riposte produced more riotous laughter and banging of tankards on tables, especially from the men in the Hall who were close enough to hear the banter.

Without warning, Belleme stood, and Morvan watched him in alarm as he crossed to the side of the Hall. He returned and, walking to the side table where they sat, he slammed the wet, damaged cloak down in front of Toki. 'I believe this is your cloak, Saxon, I know that today you followed us through the woods. I believe that we have a spy in our midst that is working against us and is working for King William,' he shouted. The wet cloak had knocked the goblets flying, and the men sitting at the side table were now on their feet.

Roger-Fitz-Richard was angry. 'Have you proof of this Belleme?' he demanded, brushing wine from his clothes. 'Or are you just stirring up trouble again?'

Belleme was slightly taken aback; it was rare for the Lord de Clare to criticise him. 'I know it is him; get him to produce his cloak if this is not the one he was wearing when he jumped in the river.'

There was almost silence in the Hall full of men as the drama unfolded in front of the top table. Robert's face showed his concern, while Chatillon had an amused smile on his face at this unplanned entertainment. However, the smiles disappeared when a furious Belleme drew his sword. 'Get your cloak Saxon and prove me wrong,' he yelled into Toki's face.

To give him his due, the big Saxon stood calmly. He was not going to be provoked into a fight here in the Hall. 'My cloak was stolen a few days ago, Belleme, so what other proof do you have that it was me when we were working in the paddock training the men and horses?' he said, holding his hands out palms up as he looked at Robert Curthose.

'Oh, we can make you talk, believe me. Seize him,' he yelled to the men at arms, who did not immediately move as they looked to Hugh and Robert Curthose.

At this moment, a messenger had run down the Hall almost unnoticed until Hugh's wife Mabel waved him forward. She opened the vellum, gasped and then gave a loud wail that stopped everyone. Belleme turned and glared at his sister, who had a hand over her mouth, tears streaming unashamedly down her cheeks. 'For God's sake, what is it?' He growled, noticing the messenger in the Belleme livery for the first time.

'It is our mother; she has been murdered,' she gasped, offering him the vellum sheet.

There was a stunned silence in the Hall then Robert Curthose stood. 'Belleme, you will not fight in this Hall and especially now when you need to grieve. Therefore, Toki of Wigod, I suggest you leave us for the present. We will talk over these accusations in the morning.'

Belleme still stood, sword in hand, staring at his sobbing sister, shock and pain clear to see on his face. Ignoring the outstretched vellum in his sister's hand, he dropped his sword and walked over to the messenger. He grabbed him by the tabard, bunching and twisting it under his chin. 'How?' he shouted at the frightened man. 'How did she die?'

Robert walked up to his friend and unclenched his fingers. 'Let the man speak, Belleme.'

The messenger took a step back. 'It was at Bures, Sire. Hugh Bunel and his brothers, they gained entry to the castle. They came seeking revenge for the lands she took, and they...' the man faltered on the words.

'Continue,' Robert said, nodding encouragement.

'They found her room. She had just got out of her bath, and they beheaded her, Sire,' he stuttered.

Morvan heard the sharp intakes of breath that this brutal description provoked in the Hall. So many of Belleme's men were here who had served the family for years.

Robert dismissed the messenger and took Belleme by the arm. 'Come and sit with us; it will be better not to be on your own.' Hugh nodded in thanks to the prince as he led his weeping wife up to the solar.

Robert de Belleme sat and received the commiserations from his friends at the tables. 'Your father, Roger of Montgomery, will be devastated; it was a love match, I believe,' said Gervais de la Ferte.

Belleme nodded. 'Until she drove him away with her cruelty. She drove us all away, but we loved her. They lived most of the year apart, but my father was always drawn back to her like a moth to a flame. She is... was, full of energy, always exciting to be with or be near. We never knew what she would do next,' he said, staring into the distance. They left him with his thoughts, and conversation resumed on other topics until Belleme unexpectedly stood up.

'I have not forgotten that Saxon, Robert, we have a traitor amongst us. I will bring the hounds in here tomorrow; we have the scent they were following on the cloak. Toki had gone, as commanded, but Morvan heard those words with dismay. It was his cloak and his scent; he had to do something. He bowed to Robert and went to find his friend.

He found Toki laid upon his bed, his eyes closed. 'Do not think you can sleep. We have much to do,' he said, shaking him. The Saxon reluctantly swung his legs to the floor and looked at Morvan with a wary eye.

'Don't you think you have brought enough trouble and danger to my door?' he asked with a wry smile.

Morvan grinned. 'You must leave to go back to Caen in the early hours, but we have two things to do now. First, we must read the message that we know Gervais has written to Philip of France; I saw the Steward taking him vellum and ink earlier. Then we must retrieve the cloak from the Hall and destroy it; Belleme is bringing in the hounds tomorrow.'

Toki raised his eyebrows in amazement. 'It sounds as if you should be coming with me, Morvan; it is too dangerous here for you as well.'

Morvan shook his head, 'I cannot go back there, Toki. My path lies with Robert once I have found this information.'

Toki rolled his eyes in mock horror at the choices in front of him. 'You must go and copy the vellum scroll; you will need to go to his room now while they are still at the table. I will wait until everyone retires and remove the cloak if Belleme has not removed it.'

'I think Robert De Belleme has other things on his mind,' Morvan said and related the story of his mother's death.

The Saxon Thegn looked thoughtful. 'I met her several times; she was as beautiful as she was evil and cruel. As you know, Belleme's father, the Earl, ruled Normandy with Queen Matilda when William was in England, so his wife would often appear in court, often on a whim or because she was bored at Alencon. She would enjoy sowing seeds of discontent, create mayhem and disappear again, but he loved her. Our friend Belleme will now become even wealthier as he inherits all of his mother's lands.'

Morvan stood up. 'I must go while he is still down in the Hall. I may be some time, as I have to find the message, copy it and put it back. I will meet you in the stables.'

Morvan had no problem accessing the room of Gervais de la Ferte. His manservant, released from duties, was probably carousing with the other servants in the kitchens. Morvan had scanned the room and entered, closing the door behind him. A fire burned brightly in the large room. Morvan searched for some time, opening chests and looking under the bed and table, but there was no sign of the message. Finally, he sat down on the bed, glancing around in frustration. *Could he have sent it already?* He wondered.

Suddenly his eyes alighted on an unusual leather cylinder hanging on the chair by a long strap. He unfastened the top and took out the rolled vellum sheet inside. He tucked it inside his tunic and left to make his way down to the Steward's room to find ink and vellum to copy the message. He was relieved to find that this was also empty as he copied the ten lines of the message above the heavy seal of the Seneschal of France. Gervais de la Ferte described the forces gathering behind Robert; the list was impressive, with some Breton names shocking Morvan. He knew that King William would find this information helpful. The name and description of the fortress belonging to King Philip that Gervais asked him to give to Robert was there. He was right. It was formidable and famous for its defensive position. It was at a place called Gerberoi, and most people knew of it. More importantly, it was not in Normandy, it was over the border in the Beauvais region; it was in the Ile de France.

Morvan quickly sanded his copy. Then, tucking both into his tunic, he made his way back to his room to wait until the early hours to attempt to put the original back in the messenger's case. He just prayed that Gervais de la Ferte had drunk enough and was not a light sleeper.

Toki had waited for some time for the noise to die down in the Hall. Eventually, he made his way along the corridor and into the Hall. All of the tables on the dais were empty, although there were several warriors worse the wear for drink at the long trestle tables; many were snoring head on hands. He was pleased to see that the cloak was still resting where Belleme had thrown it.

He bundled it up and made for the main door when a voice softly accosted him. 'Removing the evidence are you, Toki of Wigod?' He stopped dead in his tracks.

Piers De Chatillon was leaning on a pillar, goblet still in hand, watching him. Toki said nothing. The papal envoy stepped forward, 'I suggest we put it on the fire and bank it up; that will have two advantages. First, it will be presumed that a servant has disposed of a bundle of rags when clearing the tables and it will most certainly be destroyed in the fire. Secondly, any pieces that could survive will be so damaged by smoke that no scent will remain. Belleme will no doubt rant and rave, but there again when doesn't he?'

Toki stood, rooted to the spot staring at the man with suspicion until Chatillon held his arms out for the cloak, and Toki reluctantly handed it over. The Frenchman raked over the embers and blew on them until they glowed. Then, he placed the cloak in the centre of the enormous fireplace and covered it with at least half a dozen more logs.

Toki watched him with interest. 'Why are you helping me?' he asked.

De Chatillon straightened up. 'We both know that is not your cloak. I am not helping you; I am helping Morvan De Malvais. I knew at once that it would be him; he has a penchant for following people and being in places where he should not be. He flung me headfirst into a wall once. I may even consider taking him on as an apprentice,' he chuckled.

Toki was still puzzled. 'But why are you helping him when you know he is still passing information to the King?' he asked.

'Unfortunately, my Saxon friend that is something I cannot share with you. Suffice it to say that the Horse Warrior is of far more use to me alive and at Robert's side than as breakfast for a pack of dogs. If you had not removed the cloak, then I would have,' he said and waved the young man away.

Chapter Twenty-Five

Morvan crept back along the narrow stone corridor in the early hours. He stood for some time outside the room of the French Seneschal but could not hear a sound. Finally, he lifted the wooden latch, slowly opened the door a crack and then stopped again. Still no sounds from within, he widened the gap and crept into the room, pushing the door behind him but not latching it. The fire had died down, but there was still enough light from the glowing embers to see the figure on the bed; Morvan could hear the steady breathing. He quickly glanced around; expecting to see the manservant on a pallet or truckle bed, but no one else was in the room. Morvan moved carefully around the furniture until he reached the table and chair beneath the window. He pulled the vellum scroll from beneath his tunic and slowly slid it back into the leather cylinder. While doing this, he kept glancing at the bed, but the Seneschal seemed to be deep asleep.

With a quiet sigh of relief, Morvan padded his way back across the room to the door, gently opened it and pulled it softly closed behind him. He had not noticed that the breathing in the man on the bed had changed or the dark, glittering eyes that had watched him cross the room to the door, his face clearly visible in the light of the fire.

Gervais de la Ferte rolled onto his back and smiled, Chatillon had been right about young Malvais, and by sending this information to William, he was playing right into their hands. King Philip would be pleased that their plan was working. He had attempted to break up the Anglo-Norman empire for several years, but he had never succeeded. Now, at last, it may be within his grasp as they hoped to draw King William into a trap at Gerberoi. Robert Curthose would become the new Duke of Normandy backed by the French King, and Normandy would be separate from England.

Morvan, oblivious to the manipulations of the conspirators, stood for a few seconds outside the door and let out the breath he had been holding. Suddenly a hand was placed on his arm. He jumped and went for his dagger when he realised it was Mabel, Hugh's beautiful wife. 'What are you doing coming out of the room of the Seneschal?' she hissed at him, her eyes huge in her pale face. Morvan had to think quickly, 'I was lost. I was looking for your room, my Lady; I thought you might need consoling after today's terrible news.' She looked at him, her eyes pinned on his face for what seemed like several long moments, and then she took him by the hand and led him down the corridor to an elaborately carved wooden door at the end. 'This is my room Morvan de Malvais, I insist on Hugh sleeping elsewhere so we will not be disturbed, and I expect you to console me over and over again for several hours, in return, I will not mention to anyone where I found you.' Morvan gazed down at that beautiful but cunning face and nodded as she opened the door and led him inside.

The room was lit only by a large fire, and she led him towards the large fur-covered bed; she peeled off her thin linen chemise and then sat naked on the bed, her knees up to her chin as she watched him. Her tongue encircled her lips in anticipation of what this muscled young warrior would do to her. 'Take your clothes off slowly, Horse Warrior; I want to enjoy this.' Morvan took a deep breath and slowly peeled off his tunic; he had no choice, he had come too far to be caught now, and he had to get out of here to get the information about Gerberoi to Toki.

It was fortunate that Mabel en Chateauneuf was so beautiful; she had alabaster white skin, almost translucent. She was slim but with perfect full breasts, which he admired as she uncurled on the bed to watch him. He unfastened his chausses and peeled them off until he stood only in his braies. She came off the bed and stood in front of him; she was almost elfin in appearance. Her dark curls and deep dark eyes met his as she ran her hands up the outside of his muscled arms and then she ran her fingers lightly over his broad chest and down his stomach. By now, he was fully aroused, and he gasped in shock as she slid her hand under his braies and grasped his manhood tightly.

'Not an inch of you disappoints me, Horse Warrior,' she said, gurgling with laughter as she untied his braies, and they dropped to the floor. 'I want you to take me fast and hard, do you understand? I want you to take me in a way that milksop of a husband of mine never could,' she demanded. Without letting her say another word, he picked her up and threw her onto the bed, his eyes glittering with intent. She stared up at him, her bottom lip between her teeth as he grabbed hold of her hair and roughly pulled her mouth to his, his tongue in her mouth, his fingers between her legs. He suddenly flipped her over, and still gripping her hair, he took her from behind, driving into her, consumed by hard anger for everything that had happened recently; he needed this release.

He lost himself entirely in the passion of the next few hours with her, taking her repeatedly, then lying back sated on the bed. He knew he had to go, he had to meet Toki. She lay curled around him, one leg hooked over his muscled thigh, a smile of utter satisfaction on her face. He had done precisely what she asked of him in so many different ways. What a lover he will be, she thought, thinking of the several weeks still ahead here at Thymerais, and she intended to have him repeatedly if he did not want his guilty secret sharing with her brother. For a few seconds, she wondered what he had been doing in that room; she did not believe for one second that he was looking for her. Then, she found that she did not care. Men and their plans. What was that to her? She only knew that she had a hold over him for a short time, and she meant to enjoy him.

Morvan made his way to the stables; he knew he was much later than expected and just prayed that Toki would still be there. Toki was pacing up and down, his distinctive black and dun horse saddled and ready to go. 'Thank God, I thought you had been caught, Morvan.'

Morvan shook his head, 'I was caught and waylaid coming out of the room, but I dealt with it.' He gave the copied vellum scroll to Toki and explained the significance of Gerberoi, and then taking his arm in a warrior clasp, he wished him 'God speed'.

Just as Morvan reached the doorway, Toki shouted after him. 'Chatillon knows; he knows that it was you and not me that they were chasing in the woods.' Morvan looked thoughtful; it did not surprise him – the man had eyes and ears everywhere, but would he keep the information to himself?

Later that morning, it was a more subdued group that met to break their fast. Belleme did not appear until much later.

When he came down, his glance swept the young men sat in the Hall and then he went straight outside. Morvan was already at work with his men in the frost-covered paddock. He had set up a line of targets, and the men had to command their horses to strike out at them. The riders were in a line listening intently to Morvan when Belleme came striding in between them.

'Where is he?' he demanded, his eyes sweeping the paddock.

'He is not here; I have not seen him this morning,' answered Morvan.

Belleme was spitting with fury. 'So it was him, and he has run. He was the traitor. You must have known,' he said accusingly to Morvan.

Morvan sighed and indicated to the riders that they should circle their horses to keep them warm. 'Listen, Belleme, I did not know him that well; he has only joined our group of friends recently. I did not invite him to come to Thymerais with me; he just tagged along. He seemed very resentful and angry with the King. I had no reason to suspect him.'

Belleme met Morvan's stare for a few moments, and then spitting on the ground at his feet, he left and headed back to the chateau. As he watched him go, Morvan noticed a messenger in the blue and gold livery come down the steps and mount his horse; across his chest was a dark leather cylinder.

Morvan was preoccupied at the midday meal; he thought it was ironic that he had left the King's service, but he had risked his life twice for him in the space of a day. His mind went back to the Mithraic temple, and he remembered his brother's words, that Mithras was the soldier's god, a god of war, but he was also the god of mutual obligation between a King and his warriors. He asked himself if that was what he still felt, some vestiges of obligation to William. Yet here he was about to fight on the same side as Philip of France against the King. He was struggling to reconcile the two despite his anger and pain over Constance.

Roger Fitz Richard brought him out of his reverie by digging him in the ribs. 'So, have you heard we leave tomorrow?'

Morvan pretended ignorance. 'No, tell me where do we go to this time? To another of Hugh's many chateaus?'

'We go to the grand fortress of Gerberoi; William will need at least a thousand men to get us out of there.' Roger laughed. Morvan smiled and raised his tankard of ale. His friends were exuberant, but Morvan found that he could not celebrate in the same way. He knew that he was betraying his King and the code of honour drilled into him by his family, but he could never forgive them for taking Constance and his child away from him.

The next day saw Robert and his followers riding out from Thymerais to leave Normandy. Hugh's wife and daughter came out with Hugh on the steps to wave them off; Hugh would join them later at Gerberoi. Mabel stared longingly at Morvan; she had only managed another night with him before they announced they were leaving. However, he had undoubtedly delivered just as much passion, and she felt bruised in all the right places this morning. Roger-Fitz-Richard saw the look she gave Morvan and smiled, so that was where Morvan had disappeared off to last night. He hoped Belleme did not notice, it did not take much to light his fuse at the moment, and Morvan swiving his sister would undoubtedly do that. He wished that he had the same effect on women; they seemed to flock to his Horse Warrior friend.

The party made quite a cavalcade as Robert had insisted

that all livery was to be worn and every flag and pennant would fly. This was no longer a group of young insurgents running from King William. Instead, a force of over six hundred strong, including the Seneschal of France, set off on the road to Gerberoi led by the blue and gold of Gervais de la Ferte and the rampant gold lions of Robert Curthose on a deep red background. Villagers came out and stood watching open-mouthed as the army passed through their hamlets.

They spent the night camped around a petite chateau at Vernon on the banks of the River Seine. Morvan commanded his troop to take their horses into the water to wash off the day's mud and dirt. He was gradually transforming this mixed group of forty men into something resembling a unit with pride in the appearance of themselves and their horses. There were very few of the large war Destriers for which the Bretons were famous, but the horses they had kept were big animals of solid but intelligent Flanders stock that responded well to training. He did not doubt that a small force of only ten elite Breton Horse Warriors could still wipe them out in a moment in a battle, but he knew that he had achieved a lot with them in the past weeks.

The next day they crossed into France, into the region known as Beauvais, and approached Gerberoi. The fortress given to them by the King of France was in an elevated position, large and imposing, surrounded by stone ramparts. It was surrounded on three sides by the River Tahier and could only be entered by fortified stone gateways. As Morvan sat on Shadow staring across the river, he agreed with Roger-Fitz-Richard; it was almost impregnable and could easily withstand a long siege if necessary.

As they crossed the river and began to ascend the winding

path to the top, Morvan was suddenly confronted with a sea of pavilions and tents in the meadows to the west. William Breteuil was riding just behind him, and he pulled Shadow back alongside him. 'I hope they are on our side,' he laughed.

William nodded, 'Yes, of course. It will be the siege of Dol all over again, except this time we will be on the winning side and not running away in a rout.'

As Morvan gazed down on the colourful scene below, he realised that he could see the standards of several Breton rebel lords. Fulk had also sent Angevin forces despite having just signed a pact with King William weeks earlier; he really was an untrustworthy, treacherous individual.

Morvan could see a contingent of troops from Robert the Count of Flanders, but the largest contingent there was at least six or seven hundred strong and they were flying the blue and gold French standard of King Philip. He was somewhat taken aback by the level of support for Robert Curthose. This was no longer a small rebellion by the King's son; this was open warfare on King William by combining his enemies hoping to put Robert in William's place in Normandy. Robert was a brave, almost fearless soldier, but Morvan knew that he was reckless; he lacked his father's cool head and strategy. He was no William when it came to battles; however, the pure numbers here may give him an advantage.

As Morvan stared down at the camp below, he saw two riders break from their column and gallop down to the meadows. They made for the largest pavilion in the French camp. Morvan pushed Shadow on into a walk while watching the men dismount. His rich clothes and distinctive hat gave the first man away, Piers De Chatillon, and at his side was Robert De Belleme.

As he rode through the solid stone gateways into the fortress, Morvan mulled over what he had seen. So Chatillon was the link between the French and Robert Curthose as he had suspected. He had been working behind the scenes to engineer this support for Robert around several courts in Europe. Pope Gregory had a problematic relationship with Philip of France; maybe this was his way of building bridges.

Morvan remembered what Luc had explained around the campfire on the beach in Brittany; the Church was determined to regain its position in Europe. The Pope had a vision that it should always be Church above state; he believed that Kings were appointed by and owed their first allegiance to God. Was Pope Gregory now using Robert Curthose as a pawn to achieve a united Europe under the Church? Morvan realised that a strong leader such as William the Conqueror stood firmly in the way of such a vision, so they needed to remove or weaken him. Looking at the numbers flocking here, Morvan thought that they just might achieve it.

As they pulled into the outer Bailey, a troubled Morvan dismounted. He hated his brother for what he had done. He hated William for forcing Constance into a marriage that she did not want, but at the same time, it was hard to shrug off his years of service and loyalty to his family and King. However, he now knew that he was about to cross the line. His fealty and service now had to be to Robert Curthose, and there would be no going back from this position; he would be fighting against his King.

Chapter Twenty-Six

It was a bitterly cold December night in Morlaix as Luc sat with his family around him in the solar in front of a blazing log fire. The westerly winds from the Atlantic were whipping and howling around his home in Brittany. His mother, Marie De Malvais, had put an extra shawl around her shoulders as she sat watching her grandchildren.

'I believe a messenger arrived today, and I hear the rebels have left Normandy,' she said, raising an eyebrow at her son and watching his face for his reaction.

Marie was half-French, tall and elegant. She had been brought up in the French court until Luc's father had swept her off her feet and stolen her heart. Until the recent events, she had lived the happiest of lives, riding out any storm that appeared on the horizon with a calmness that her eldest son had inherited. Her husband's death at the Battle of Hastings had been a blow, but he died as he had lived, riding into battle, and she had the consolation of her two sons.

Now there was a rift in the family that had torn her world apart. She would never have thought that the two brothers would fall out. There were only three years between them, and they had always been so close. She looked at Luc's face as he watched his children. Young Lusian had grown up so fast; he had his own horse now and had begun sword lessons in the pell yard with Gerard. He was the image of his father. Luc's daughter Chantal at three years old was adorable but headstrong; she took after her feisty but beautiful Saxon mother, who was nursing the new addition to the family, Garrett, a beautiful auburn-haired little boy with the sunniest of natures.

Luc looked up. 'Yes, Robert Curthose and his followers have apparently taken the fortress at Gerberoi. William is assembling a force to attack them, which he will lead himself.'

Marie looked pensive. They had talked for hours about Luc's decision to banish Morvan from the family home and lands. She had tried to get her eldest son to soften his stance, but he was implacable. Morvan had ignored their advice by continuing his affair with Constance. He had chosen a path that could destroy the family. Finally, he had raised a sword against his older brother. No matter how many tears she cried, there was no way back from that.

She fondly glanced down at her grandchildren and thought of the other child on the way, Morvan's child, who she would never know. It would be born in the spring and taken away in the night. Her heart bled for Constance; she could not imagine having a child taken away like that, the child of the man she loved.

Marie raised her eyes to Luc. 'Has William summoned you to join the attack on Robert at Gerberoi?' she asked with concern. Merewyn looked up in alarm; it was their worst fear that Luc would end up riding out to fight against his brother.

As Luc looked at their faces, he knew exactly what they were thinking, and if he was honest with himself, he felt the same. He could not forgive Morvan for what he had done, for raising a sword against him in anger, but he did not want to ride against and meet his brother in battle. He was relieved when he read the message from William that morning. 'No, William is sending us east again. Despite the pact that they have signed, Fulk is gathering his forces along the borders of Maine and Brittany. If, as we suspect, Fulk of Anjou is supporting Robert's rebellion, then it is a clever move. It is keeping the Breton Horse Warriors in Brittany, defending our borders.'

Both women looked relieved, Merewyn the most. She had married her Horse Warrior with open eyes, knowing that he would constantly ride out on patrols or into battle. However, she still had not forgotten the siege of Dol where he was so severely injured. She had thought for a time that he would never recover, never mind hold a sword. However, this was Luc De Malvais, and hours of sword practice and riding, every day had brought him close to how he was before the devastating sword thrust that had severed a tendon in his arm and almost ended his life.

She sat and watched him with Lusian; his dark, handsome head bent over his son. She was overwhelmed by the love she felt for her family, and the rift with Morvan made them even more precious. She felt for Marie. Merewyn had loved Morvan like a brother, and it not only left a massive hole in their lives, but she knew it preyed upon the minds of Luc and Gerard. However, like Marie, she could not see how to resolve this; the rift was too severe.

Falaise Castle was one of the coldest and bleakest of the Conqueror's strongholds. It had been his family home for many years, and little had changed in the last thirty years. Constance had been kept in seclusion since she had arrived. She was in all respects a prisoner. She was never left alone; her old nurse and her maidservant were always in attendance. They even slept in her room at night. She was allowed one accompanied walk along the walls once a day, but otherwise, she was never allowed out of her rooms. She was not allowed to eat in the Great Hall if travellers or guests arrived. She was not allowed any visitors.

All of the joy she had felt at carrying Morvan's child had evaporated as she realised that it would be taken away and put with a wet nurse immediately. She had little news of the outside world apart from the infrequent conversations with her mother's Castellan. As they moved into the Yuletide season, which she usually loved, nothing changed in her life. She had no idea where Morvan was or if he was even still alive. She had been as shocked as Gerard was as they watched the scene that unfolded on the road outside of Thymerais. She had always been in awe of Luc De Malvais, as was most of the court in Caen, but she knew that Morvan respected him and loved him dearly. To see them fighting each other was heart-rending.

Constance also felt a great deal of guilt; she had known her destiny was to marry well into one of the royal or ducal houses, she also knew what she and Morvan were doing was wrong, but they were reckless. They had been selfish in their all-consuming love for each other, and now they were reaping what they had sown. Morvan was probably in a rebel camp with her brother, his future as a Knight in William's household destroyed, estranged from his family and banished from his home and estates. She was now living a life of seclusion and solitude, a half-life, and she was dreading the birth of their child on her own there.

She could feel the child moving inside her, and it broke her heart to think of the life it may have as a bastard child in some other family. After the birth, they would bind her breasts tightly to stop the milk from coming, and she would be expected to return to court as if nothing had happened. How could her mother expect her to do that? Her mother had gone to these extreme lengths to keep this pregnancy hidden, especially from her father, as the alliance with Alan Fergant of Brittany was of such importance.

Constance shook her head in disbelief that she was still expected to go to Alan's bed as a virgin bride on her wedding night when she was still deeply in love with another man and had borne his child. She put aside the linen she was edging for the baby and gazed into the fire; the tears ran unchecked down her cheeks. In her heart, she knew she would never see Morvan again. Her mother would not take the risk of letting her leave Falaise until she travelled to Caen for her wedding to Alan Fergant, and that could be a year or two ahead.

Chapter Twenty-Seven

The rebels had been at Gerberoi for nearly three weeks before the news arrived that William was personally leading an army against them. During their time there, they had carried out numerous raids over the border into Normandy. They came back piled high with plunder from the villages and monasteries. Mainly food, livestock, horses, bags of grain, anything they needed to stock up for a long siege. Meanwhile, ever more of William's enemies were flocking to Robert's banners. He was now a force to be reckoned with, backed by the King of France, Robert Count of Flanders and Fulk of Anjou alongside several rebel Knights from Brittany.

Spirits inside the castle were buoyant; Robert was overwhelmed but pleased by his support, recognising him as the Duke of Normandy. Morvan was exasperated; Robert refused to see that he was just a pawn in the hands of Philip of France and the Pope. Robert had convinced himself that he was using them for his own ends, a view that Belleme spouted daily. Morvan kept pointing out the dangers of dealing with the likes of Chatillon and Gervais de la Ferte, but Robert refused to listen.

To counter this, Morvan threw himself into the training of his substantial troop of forty Horse Warriors. He was pleased

200

with their progress; they were beginning to shape up into a formidable unit. He knew that if Robert decided to risk an open battle against his father, they needed to be up to the task, so he put them through hours of sword practice on horseback and on the ground in the pell yard. His friends, Roger-Fitz-Richard and the Grandmesnil brothers, often came to help and participate; it was good for his men to confront Knights of their experience. At night, they were falling exhausted into bed, but every day they improved a little more.

Morvan often saw Belleme standing on the stone steps, watching them train as well, but he never took part; he had become even more belligerent and cynical since his mother's death, often picking arguments for no reason. No girl or woman in the castle was safe from his brutal attentions. The Steward of the castle had complained to Robert as yet another bruised servant girl came out of Belleme's room in tears after he had taken her up there from the kitchens that afternoon. After Robert had talked to him about his behaviour, Belleme had gone to find the Steward and had given him a beating. Still, he did listen and now left the women alone, becoming even more morose, sitting and glowering at his former comrades who avoided him.

On the third day, Gervais de la Ferte bade farewell and left the fortress of Gerberoi as the vedettes had informed him that William's army was now no more than three leagues away. Robert was taken aback that his French ally was leaving, but Morvan was not surprised. The Seneschal of France could not be found or trapped in Gerberoi. Morvan sat on Shadow and watched the departure of the Frenchman and his escort. Heading for the large fortified stone gate, the Seneschal suddenly pulled alongside Morvan.

'I wish you every success Morvan de Malvais; I hope that this forthcoming battle results in Robert receiving the title that is rightly his. A word of advice, my young friend, be wary of Chatillon, he is dangerous, a true puppet master, and there is steel and purpose behind that charm.'

Morvan inclined his head in a bow of thanks. However, the Seneschal made no move as he leant over and softly said, 'I enjoyed our conversations about horse breeding, and I hope you will survive this siege to come and see my string of horses race. One more thing, do not leave it too late to heal the rift with your family; they have your best interests at heart.'

Later that day, Morvan joined many other young Knights on the ramparts to watch William setting up his camp on a slight rise to the south. The atmosphere was subdued amongst the men as they watched the banners raised beside the striped pavilions. These were the banners that they knew, the banners of their own families and their friends. The following day two of them had crossed the lines back into William's camp; fighting against their fathers had been a step too far. This insurgency had now become a true civil war with loyalties split on both sides.

Morvan anxiously scanned the sides of the camp for his brother's distinctive banner of a black running horse on a blue background, but to his relief, he could not see it. He was surprised. Had William not summoned the Horse Warriors this time, or were they still on their way from Brittany? Would he have to face the furious onslaught of Luc, Gerard and the men he had ridden alongside for years? His stomach knotted at the thought. The impact of the choice he had made hit home as he stared down at the considerable force assembling below led by King William himself. Then the image of Constance came unbidden to his mind, her bowed head as she was led out of the clearing to her incarceration at Falaise, and his resolve hardened.

Once established, William invested the fortress, encircling and cutting it off from outside assistance or supplies. For the besieged, the monotony of siege life ensued. Gerberoi was very self-contained, with several wells and additional channels cut from the river that flowed through solid metal grills under the base of the walls. The force besieged inside also had enough food and fodder for several months.

Finally, on the fourth day of the siege, horns blew, and a herald appeared, followed by a small group of Norman nobles. From the ramparts, Morvan recognised Roger de Montgomery, the Earl of Shrewsbury, Belleme's powerful father, and Hugh de Grandesmil. Robert rode out to greet them, and they exchanged words with much head shaking. Within what seemed like only minutes, Robert had whirled his horse around and was riding back grim-faced. Morvan climbed down the steep steps to go and join the others in the Great Hall to hear what had been said.

'And how is my esteemed father?' asked Belleme as Robert came striding in and flung himself down into a chair. 'Obviously not prostrate with grief over the death of my mother then,' spat Belleme.

Robert peeled off his gauntlets and flung them on the table. 'They are not prepared to treat. My father will offer us nothing; we are to surrender to be dealt with at his mercy,' he said, shaking his head in disbelief. 'Even with the might of the French army and dozens of banners flying from our ramparts, he does not take me seriously.'

He leapt to his feet and thumped the table. 'We will show them how serious we are. Send the archers to the walls with orders to kill any man within range,' he shouted.

Morvan saw the two Grandesmil brothers exchange a glance; he had seen their faces blanch when they had seen their father beside Roger de Montgomery. Not Belleme though, he strode off towards the ramparts to direct the archers, shouting orders to the others.

For the next week, William's forces attacked the castle using escalade ladders, and were repelled from the walls. Gervais de la Ferte could not have chosen a better base for Robert Curthose; the fortress had been built to withstand a long siege. Most of the ramparts had solid wooden hoardings, which overhung the walls, protecting the men but allowing them to drop missiles or fire arrows on those below.

Gerberoi was built on a rocky outcrop with steep sides. On top of this, they had built a solid stone plinth to deter mining. By the end of the first week, it was abundantly clear to both sides that they were at a standoff. The fortress of Gerberoi, despite the large numbers inside, could withstand a siege for many months.

William and his army were camped outside, but it was late December when they had arrived. Now, in early January, the weather became bitterly cold with icy winds coming off the Atlantic. William's men in their tents became prone to chills and agues and huddled around the campfires in their blankets.

By the third week, Roger de Montgomery decided to act, and he approached William's pavilion where three large braziers were burning.

'Sire, we are at a standstill; we cannot use scaling ladders, the steep bluff cliffs are too high, and the ramparts are too well defended. On the other hand, our informers tell us that they have ample food supplies and water to hold out for many months. Surely it is time now for a rapprochement before our men freeze to death.'

William regarded his friend in silence for some time. Roger de Montgomery was a trusted friend, and he could see the wisdom of his words, but William was still furious at his son. Moreover, Robert had betrayed him by asking for support from the French, and this was such a heinous move that William was not prepared to forgive him. William turned away and picked up his goblet before sitting down heavily into his camp chair. He was now in his fifties and of a more portly stocky build. He was still a formidable warrior but not precisely the fit young man he had been; the worries and constant warfare of the last few years had taken their toll. He took a long draught of his wine before replying.

'We will parley Roger, but only on my terms,' he said, with a bullish expression.

Roger sighed; he knew what this would mean, although it was a step forward. 'I will arrange it for tomorrow, Sire.'

At noon the next day, a herald once more approached the gates of Gerberoi, and Robert Curthose rode out to hear what they were offering. This time, he was accompanied by Morvan, Roger-Fitz-Richard de Clare and Piers de Chatillon; as Belleme's temper seemed shorter with each day they were incarcerated, he became more unpredictable, and so to his fury, he was left behind.

Finally, William had come in person with seven of his senior Knights and a guard of ten men, all watching the gates and ramparts like hawks. Robert, seeing their concern, laughed. 'You do not have to be afraid, Father, I would not sink low enough to have you killed while under parley.'

William eyed his son narrowly; he looked well and full of

confidence, as well, he might be if the numbers of men and horses in the fortress were to be believed. 'You expect me to trust you ever again, Robert, after what you have done?' Morvan could see the anger inside the King, which never boded well.

'You left me no choice, Father. Others see me for who I am; they know that I am the rightful Duke of Normandy, and they treat me accordingly. My mother sees that!' he finished in a loud voice that was full of frustration.

Silence reigned for several moments as each man glared at the other before William replied. 'Your mother is saddened by the rift you have driven through the family. She wants you to cease this foolishness and return to court at Caen.'

Robert stared at the ground for a few seconds. 'I cannot do that unless you pledge to me now that the Duchy of Normandy is mine.'

The King shook his head, and Morvan could see the white of his knuckles as he gripped the pommel of the saddle. 'I will offer safe passage for your followers who have rebelled against me; I will not have them blinded or maimed as they deserve for their treachery. However, I will keep their lands in forfeit. As for you, I expect you to return to court and do penance for your actions against your father and your King.'

Morvan saw Hugh De Grandesmil and Roger de Montgomery look at each other in exasperation. Both father and son were as stubborn as each other, and neither would give way.

Finally, Robert shook his head. 'So be it. I will not accept your terms; they are not even worthy of that title. What happens next, Father, is on your head.' He began to turn away. 'Give my love to my mother and my sister, Constance,' he said.

William glared after him and then suddenly said, 'Constance is no longer at Caen; she is betrothed to Alan Fergant and is at Falaise. Your mother is preparing her for her marriage and position as wife of the Duke of Brittany; she is a dutiful daughter.'

Suddenly Piers De Chatillon, who had been silent throughout, intervened. 'I believe the church has received a request for her to be handfasted to Alan in the spring as Duke Hoel will not allow him to marry until he comes of age at twenty-five.'

William regarded the papal envoy with distaste. 'As usual, Chatillon, your web of spies keep you well informed. I have received the request from Alan Fergant as well and have agreed to it.'

Morvan reeled in shock and clamped his legs on Shadow's sides, which shot backwards and sideways into Roger-Fitz-Richard, who whispered, 'Get control of yourself and your horse Morvan.'

Meanwhile, Robert shook his head at his father. 'Another child is gone, Father; you are driving us all away or disposing of us.' Then he pushed his horse straight into a canter back towards the gates of Gerberoi. His entourage turned and followed except for Morvan, who stared at William for a few moments longer.

'Thank you for your timely information Malvais. See if you can use your powers of persuasion to make my son see sense and avoid the coming bloodshed, which we may all regret.'

Morvan was so angry at what he had just heard that he could not even answer the King. Instead, he turned and galloped after the others. Only as he dismounted outside of the stables did he realise that his cheeks were wet with his tears. He led Shadow inside and began to remove the tack while the word 'handfasted' went round and round in his head.

Morvan's stomach knotted as he brushed Shadow down. His

one hope had been that they would not be physically wed for another few years. In his heart, he always thought that he would find a way to go and get her. However, once she was handfasted that was impossible. It meant that Alan Fergant had all the rights of a husband; he could take her property and land, he could bed her as a wife, she could bear his children, and they would be recognised as legitimate by the church. This ceremony happened rarely, but it was often within families of the nobility who could not marry immediately for some reason. Constance would give birth to his child, who would be taken away. Alan Fergant would then claim her almost immediately, and he could do nothing about it…

Chapter Twenty-Eight

By the end of the third week, the camaraderie and spirit of the first few weeks were wearing thin. The failure of King William to come to terms with them, the threat of the fate that awaited them if they were captured or surrendered, now struck a chill chord with the young nobles, and the apprehension was tangible in the fortress. On top of this, they were in the very cramped environs of Gerberoi, living cheek by jowl with French Knights, Knights from Anjou, and Knights from Brittany. It was not long before trouble broke out.

The group around Robert had constantly bantered and bickered, but now the mood changed, and more severe arguments began to erupt. A sizeable group led by the Grandesmil boys began to discuss surrender as an option, and tempers were running very close to the surface.

Morvan, who was usually the voice of reason and a peacemaker, retreated into his own world of misery as he became ever more surly and uncommunicative even with his friends. Robert Curthose became more and more frustrated as he tried to keep the peace between the disparate groups. Over a hundred Knights had flocked to his banner bringing their men with them, and he felt some responsibility for them. Men and horses were crammed into every available space in the fortress. The stables were full, and dozens of horses were just left to wander in the outer Bailey or tied to rings in the outer wall with a net of hay. Robert watched the deterioration of his follower's initial enthusiasm with dismay, but he was not the strategist his father was. He found it became more and more difficult to sleep, and he often walked the ramparts for hours.

On one such night, he gazed down onto the campfires of his father's huge forces, which surrounded Gerberoi. He leant forward, rested his hands on the wooden supports of the hoardings, and stood there for some time trying to think through the moves available to him. He had to admit to himself that he had been flattered by the support he had been offered. However, now he had the men, horses, and weapons, he was unsure of his next move. Finally, he decided to call a council of his senior advisors tomorrow morning; they needed a plan. He heard a throat being cleared behind him, and he whirled, hand on his dagger, to find himself face to face with Piers de Chatillon.

'You are jumpy tonight, Sire,' he suggested, head on one side as he observed the young prince.

'You know my father's reputation better than anyone Chatillon; he has eyes, ears and assassins in every court in Europe, so what is stopping him here in Gerberoi?' he said with a wry smile.

Chatillon nodded. 'Yes, I have come across three so far, and I have dispatched them for you, Sire; their bodies went into the river.' He spoke in a chillingly unemotional voice.

Robert inclined his head in thanks, but his hand stayed resting on his dagger. He was alone late at night with one of Europe's most cunning and successful political assassins. Chatillon may have been supportive and had certainly supplied much of the gold for his success to date, but Robert had, in fact, listened to Morvan's warnings, and he did not trust him.

Chatillon smiled as he watched the emotions chasing across the face of Robert Curthose. Still, he had not invested so much time and money in this rebellion against William to have it crumble now. His concern had grown in the past few days as he watched the dissent and grumbling increase amongst the young nobles. They talked loudly and boldly of war, but when it came to it, few had the stomach for a prolonged war against their own fathers, families and friends.

'You are troubled,' he suggested to the young man.

Robert sighed, 'I cannot seem to see a way through Chatillon, there are so many options, and none of them are good.'

Chatillon nodded in sympathy. 'And of course, you expected your father to come to terms, as did we all,' he lied gracefully.

Robert met the dark eyes of the papal envoy in acknowledgement; he knew that he would not have admitted that to anyone else.

Chatillon turned and rested his arms on the wooden platform and gazed down at the camp below. 'A pigeon from my informers this morning tells me that William's force is not as large as we thought, and our unsavoury friend Count Fulk in Anjou has ensured that Luc De Malvais and his Horse Warriors are kept occupied on the borders of Maine and Brittany.' He looked meaningfully at Robert. 'A quick pre-emptive strike, something unexpected, may well just catch them unprepared and on the back foot,' he suggested.

Robert's eyes opened wide as he regarded Piers De Chatillon. 'You think we should ride out and attack?' he asked in an unsure voice.

'Think about what you have here. You have enough horses

in this castle at present to keep us fed for years, and you have a Breton Horse Warrior who knows exactly how to use them; he is almost as good as his brother in battle. Plan your strategy with him and ride out in two days just as dawn is breaking.'

Robert narrowed his eyes as he stared at Chatillon. 'You think we could succeed?' he asked.

'Look at it this way, Sire. You can stay here cooped up like rabbits in a hole waiting for a weasel or fox to dig us out, with tempers growing shorter. In addition, it will not be long in these cramped quarters before disease begins to spread as it does in these situations. Alternatively, you can take the initiative, give your father something to think about, something to respect you for so that he sees you as a force to be reckoned with this time. I suggest you go and get some sleep and....'

'God's bones, Chatillon, I believe you are right; we can do this,' he grinned, gripping the tall, dark envoy by the shoulders before turning away and striding off to his quarters.

Chatillon smiled. So far, everything had fallen into place, and his master would be pleased. He had brought the French to the table by persuading Robert to go to the French Court on the way back from Ghent; King Philip had been delighted to welcome the rebellious son of William the Conqueror and immediately offered him support. So the previous rift between Pope Gregory and King Philip was almost healed as they worked together to isolate King William.

Chatillon had supplied gold and weapons to Robert while manipulating Robert's followers to keep him angry with his father. Belleme had been particularly useful but had become more unstable and unpredictable in his grief over his mother's murder.

However, he had watched Morvan with interest from the

first time he met him in Ghent; he admired the young Horse Warrior. Still, he had seen that recently he was wavering and feeling somewhat guilty in his decision to join Robert and his rebellion, and the papal envoy could not have that.

Chatillon had made it his business to know everything about Morvan, especially about his forbidden love affair with Constance. He was delighted to receive a message from the Chaplain to Duke Hoel of Brittany, Monseigneur Gironde. The man was one of his many informers; he had immediately sent a pigeon to Thymerais to report the startling news he had heard about Constance and Morvan that night. Chatillon saw this as an opportunity to manipulate Morvan, so he had replied that Alan Fergant should be told that Constance was with child. He had heard that young Alan truly lusted after Constance, so he would still want her despite the child; he also knew that the alliance was just as crucial to Brittany as it was to Normandy. He told Gironde to plant the seed that the Pope might smile upon a hand-fasting ceremony to allow Alan access to his bride to be. He also suggested that Alan arrange for a servant to infiltrate Falaise. Finally, he had arranged for the Castellan's young squire to have an unfortunate accident by the river and told Alan to send a replacement squire who would pass information to him about the child's birth.

Chatillon had found at an early age that knowledge and information was power; it could often be used as a lever to move insurmountable obstacles, and he needed his young Horse Warrior to stay angry with King William and his brother. Morvan had also proved himself by relaying precisely the information to William that they had wanted him to have. Robert asking the King about his mother and sister had played right into Chatillon's hands and gave him the opening he needed to deliver a cutting blow to Morvan. He had seen the shocked white face as he rode back into the fortress. He realised that Morvan had obviously kept a glimmer of hope alive that he might perhaps ride off into the sunset and rescue Constance. Chatillon smiled at his romantic naiveté; William or Alan Fergant would have had him killed within days.

Now the young man's hopes had been firmly dashed, and the anger was bubbling just below the surface. He would stir up that anger even further tomorrow, and he would ensure that Morvan and his Horse Warriors were the vanguard of the attack on William's camp the following day.

Robert called an early meeting of his key followers, including the most senior Knights from France, Anjou and Brittany. When Morvan strode in to join them, about thirty men were seated around the Great Hall tables. Robert arrived minutes later with Chatillon at his side. The envoy came and sat beside Morvan while their tankards were filled with hot mulled ale, and trenchers were placed out with warm bread, cheese and platters of cold meats. Then, the group set to on the food with a vengeance while Robert placed a large vellum sheet on the table and weighted it down at the corners.

Chatillon rested a hand on Morvan's shoulder. 'I noticed that you seemed shaken by news of the hand-fasting of Constance,' he said in a conspiratorial whisper. Morvan swallowed and tight-lipped, he nodded. 'I really feel for you, but to William, the alliance with Brittany is everything,' he said, tearing off a chunk of bread and stabbing a piece of cheese with his dagger. 'It is unfortunate when a princess is forced to love not where she will, but it is their lot, and it often happens to many sons of the nobility as well,' he continued.

Morvan turned pain-filled eyes on Chatillon, which for a

slight moment gave the papal envoy pause for thought, and suddenly he felt a wave of empathy for the young man; he had also suffered misfortune in love when a young man in the French court, so he recognised that pain. However, strategy and manipulation was his trade, and so he continued. 'I believe that Alan Fergant has now found out about the child; he is still prepared to take Constance but has insisted that the child be exposed in the night rather than given away. It is one of his stipulations to Matilda for continuing the alliance. He has also promised the Queen that he will not betray Constance to her father.'

Morvan pulled in a ragged gasp of air and stood up. Chatillon grabbed his wrist in a steel-like grip. 'If you are going for air, do not be outside for long. Robert needs you here; he intends to attack his father tomorrow. Pull yourself together; only you can lead and organise this attack.' Morvan stood for a moment, wild-eyed, and then he brought his hand down over his eyes and his face. Chatillon pointed at the bench with an expression that gave him no choice, and Morvan reluctantly sat back down.

As Robert began to speak and announce his intention of attacking, Morvan felt himself filling with rage against Matilda, William and Alan Fergant. His child would be born in three or four months, a dark-eyed boy or a beautiful blue-eyed girl like her mother, and they would murder it at birth. He gripped the edge of the table, his knuckles white, whilst staring down at the wood. He hardly heard a word of what was said until Chatillon nudged him hard, and he looked up to find all eyes were on him. He quickly recovered.

'My Horse Warriors will lead a three-pronged attack in alliance with the French and Anjou cavalry,' he said, standing and striding forward to stand beside Robert Curthose. He outlined precisely how the plan would work, attacking the camp on three sides at once.

Chatillon smiled in approval, and watching him; he thought how much like his brother he looked and sounded. He may want to reject the Malvais name, but he commanded the same respect as his brother; the Knights were listening intently, nodding in agreement and approval at his strategy. They needed this Horse Warrior strategy combined with the element of surprise to work against a man who was one of the greatest and most experienced warriors in Europe, William the Conqueror.

Chapter Twenty-Nine

It was bitterly cold and dark as hundreds of men tacked their horses up as quietly as possible in the inner and outer Baileys of Gerberoi. The stable boys had been up for hours, ensuring that the horses had a warm oat mash to give them the energy they would need for hours of battle. Morvan had his troop of forty Horse Warriors in the western part of the large inner Bailey. He went over with them exactly what their role would be in the attack for one last time. The last three weeks he had spent with them had paid off threefold, and he now considered them a cut above the enemy cavalry. In the last week, the double scabbards had finally arrived from the saddle makers and smiths in the castle. Every day since, Morvan had concentrated on teaching them how to use two swords effectively in battle whilst controlling their horses with their knees.

Now they were mounted and lining up four to a row behind him. Apart from Shadow, the horses were not the substantial war destriers, but they were still big, powerful animals who had undergone months of training and had been brushed until they shone. Their tails had been docked for battle, and their manes knotted. Although they were not the famous Breton Horse Warriors, they had undergone the same training, and they rode proudly in their leather doublets, their crossed swords on their backs. Morvan had confidence in them, they were his men, and he had volunteered them for the most dangerous assignment, the vanguard charge into the centre of the enemy camp. He felt proud of them as they rode down towards the colossal fortified stone gateway. Men stopped what they were doing to watch them and raise clenched fists in salute.

Morvan raised a hand in farewell to Robert and his friends as the heavy gates swung open and the portcullis was raised; both had been heavily greased to reduce the noise they would make. He glanced over his shoulder to see the other troops of cavalry lining up further back. Following his strategy, they would come in two timed waves after him and attack the left and right wings of the enemy. Robert Curthose, Belleme and the other nobles who followed Robert were on the right wing.

The sound of hooves as they trotted down the track would give them some warning below, but there would still be that element of surprise. As the last of his men emerged from under the walls, he gave a loud rallying cry and shouted, 'On Y Va!' They broke first into a gathered canter down the hill and then into a full gallop when they reached the meadow below.

As they swept towards the camp, they spread into rows of eight across. Morvan could hear dozens of warning horns blowing from the camp in front of them, and he could see men frantically scrabbling for horses. As they approached, several dozen had already managed to mount and were forming up. Morvan knew that they were taking a risk; it was rare that William was ever caught napping. He had dozens of sentries and mounted vedettes in concentric circles around his camp. Morvan had heard the first horn when they had appeared at the top of the track. He just hoped that the two cavalry formations inside the fortress had heard it and moved their attack forward;

otherwise, he and his men could end up in real trouble on their own in the centre.

William held his arms up as the two squires lowered the chain mail hauberk over his soft leather tunic; he could hear the increasing clamour and shouting coming from outside. Still, he was confident that his senior Knights and captains would be rallying the men into action. As he pulled on the thick leather gauntlets and strode out into the breaking dawn, he felt a twinge of admiration for his son Robert and his followers to have the audacity to launch an attack like this. It was a good move by the insurgents, but he was sure that his far more experienced and battle-hardened force would win the day. His only concern was how his senior commanders would feel as they came up against their own sons. They had made light of it just yesterday. 'If we come against them, we will give them a good hiding and send them home to their mothers and wives with sore heads,' had been the comment of the peppery Earl De Clare who was furious with his son Roger-Fitz-Richard.

Roger de Montgomery, the Earl of Shrewsbury, was waiting for William outside the pavilion, as was his faithful Saxon retainer Toki of Wigod, who was holding his big bay stallion for him to mount. The thunder of hooves and clash of swords greeted them from the meadow below as William mounted. His standard-bearer and almost twenty Knights followed him as he cantered out onto the small bluff in front of his pavilion to view the scene below before he rode down to engage his son Robert in battle.

Morvan's first charge had been successful as they still had the element of surprise; they had smashed through the centre of the camp, destroying the thin line of mounted Knights and men who had arrayed themselves across the meadow. As Morvan delivered blow after blow, he whirled around and glanced up at the fortress. The first troop of cavalry led by the French and Angevin Knights were only just cantering down the track. This put Morvan and his men in a dangerous position; they were now being attacked on three sides by much larger numbers. Morvan shook his left foot out of the stirrup and leant as far to his right as he could, literally hanging down the right-hand side of Shadow. Then sweeping his blade across the front of the pikemen as he galloped across the front of the troop who were just forming up and stabbing the end of the long pikes into the ground. Several of his men followed him in the same manoeuvre, one they had practised repeatedly, and they effectively snapped or shattered the long wooden poles as the pikemen jumped back in alarm.

He loudly shouted the order to withdraw, and most of his men disengaged and retreated towards the end of the meadow near the fortress to reform. A glance around showed him he had lost three men; he scanned the meadow but could not see them. He sighed; that was to be expected, as they were untried in battle, mistakes would be made. William's army was now swiftly forming up and spread across the meadow in a broad curve, six or seven men deep. He turned and stared at the fortress as his men caught their breath; over a hundred mounted men emerged on the path with Robert leading his cavalry. Morvan was frustrated that they would lose any advantage if they did not make haste, but fortunately, Robert pushed them all into a furious gallop. He watched as the French and Angevins, who were now down in the meadow, successfully slammed into the enemy's left flank.

There was a sudden blare of horns from the enemy, and Morvan saw King William emerge on a small bluff overlooking the meadow. He spotted the long blonde hair and beard of Toki, who rode beside him along with a large group of Knights. The banners of most of the famous Anglo-Norman families were there, and, as he watched, over half of them wheeled away to take up different commands in the field. William's army was an experienced force, and he noticed that several shield walls were appearing. Robert's foot soldiers and pikemen were now emerging, including several hundred archers and crossbowmen courtesy of King Philip of France and Count Robert of Flanders. They were an impressive sight as they marched briskly down the hill. Still, they poured out of the gates of Gerberoi, a considerable force to be reckoned with. Morvan readied his men to attack again.

William sat on his bay stallion and watched this display of arms with some alarm; this enemy insurgent force was far more significant than he had expected. He looked at the banners of Anjou and France; his son had garnered more support than he had realised. He should have taken Morvan's report more seriously. He sat at first with composure and watched the large groups of cavalry attack his army's left and right flanks. His men at first seemed to stagger back from the blow, but soon his own cavalry engaged, and it had turned into a melee of swords and horses. He felt confident as he looked at the centre. His experienced men were now in position, row after row of shield wall with smaller troops of Norman cavalry on their wings to protect their sides. He narrowed his eyes as he watched Morvan and his Horse Warriors; he could see they were readying for another attack, but they would not find it so easy against a solid shield wall.

At that moment, he decided he needed to be there amongst it, and against the shouted advice of Roger de Montgomery, he turned and cantered down towards the centre.

Belleme was burning with a dark fury; he was delighted that they had finally attacked, and he slashed his way through the Norman troops that he had once fought alongside with a zealous viciousness. As he rested for a second and wiped the blood from his sword, a squire rode up. 'Sire, Robert asks that you take control of the crossbowmen as their commander is dead.'

Belleme lifted his helmet and wiped the sweat from his brow before nodding at the squire who bowed his head and galloped away. As he watched him go, Belleme felt a small spark of nostalgia for his days as a young battlefield messenger, risking life and limb to take messages to the commanders and captains. Of course, back then, that was for his father and King William, the very men he was fighting against today. He pulled his helmet firmly back into place and cantered through the melee, slashing down on both sides as he went to join the line of crossbowmen standing in a ragged group at the side near the trees.

He pulled his horse up in front of their Serjeant. 'God's Bones. Why are you just standing around watching the battle?' he shouted at them. Glancing around, he could see an ideal position for them. 'Run your men over to the bluff, put half on the raised bank below, and as for the rest, get them lying down with their crossbows on the bluff, so they are not such an obvious target for the archers.'

The man jumped into action while Belleme engaged with and dispatched a Norman foot soldier who, running forward, had decided to try to disembowel his horse from behind. He whirled the horse away and, leaning forward, slashed his sword across the man's exposed throat.

Sitting up in the saddle, he pushed his horse forward to the side of the bluff where he scanned the battlefield. 'Do not waste your quarrel bolts; I want accurate fire to bring down the horses of every Norman Knight that you can see; it is easier for us to kill them if they are unhorsed. Take care, I will take off the fingers of any man who brings down one of our men,' he growled as he glared at them. The crossbowmen exchanged glances; they did not doubt that this madman would.

He spotted one burly Norman Knight who seemed to be getting the better of William De Breteuil, one of the few young men that Belleme respected. His face red with emotion and anger, he rode down from the bluff straight at the burly Knight. In a sweeping blow, he galloped in from behind and took off his head, which clattered along the ground in its helmet. The body, pumping blood, slipped sideways from the saddle. William De Breteuil, a serious young academic and mathematician, probably as a younger brother destined for the church, sighed with relief. He lifted a weary arm in thanks to Belleme for intervening.

'Go and protect my crossbowmen on the bluff and try to stay out of the centre of the field, you fool,' he shouted at him.

Suddenly, there was a space and lull in the fighting where his horse was standing, the ground already littered with bodies, the metallic stench of blood in the air. Belleme surveyed the battlefield. Robert seemed to be holding his own, driving William's men back on both flanks. In the centre, however, hundreds were engaged in fierce fighting, and the noise was tumultuous, the cries of men, the screaming of horses and the clash of metal on metal. He could see King William's standard flying in the middle, and as horses moved, he could suddenly see the King and his senior Knights cutting their way through Robert's men and cavalry.

He recognised his father, Roger De Montgomery, still a formidable warrior, and decided to turn away. There may be no love lost between them, but he had just lost one parent, and he did not yet want to lose another. In addition, he was not yet ready to step into his father's shoes as the Earl of Shrewsbury, with all of his responsibilities. He realised that, with her death, he would have inherited all of his mother's estates at Alencon. That was, of course, if King William let him keep their lands after this debacle.

Morvan had regrouped yet again, and they recharged the shield wall, but it was solid; they were repeatedly turned away by the wall of bristling spears and pikes. He found himself considering what Luc or Gerard would do in this situation. He had watched his brother in dozens of skirmishes and battles. Luc was absolutely fearless, and he would smash his way through a shield wall with his men in a relentless wave of fury that terrified the enemy. Morvan's men did not have the enormous powerful Destriers to do that. He turned and thoughtfully surveyed the group sat behind him. He summoned his Captain forward.

'Get ten of our best men on the biggest horses behind me; we are going to jump the shield wall. As soon as we do, we will turn and attack them from behind. I need you and the rest of the men to follow me and attack the front again as soon as we are behind them.'

The man swallowed and looked at Morvan as if he was mad. 'But Sire, there is another shield wall behind them.'

'Yes, but we have seen that there is a sizeable gap, and we have the element of surprise. They will jump back when they see the big horses coming at them over the top of the men in front. Just do as I say; I know this will work,' he said, shortening his reins and preparing Shadow for what was to come.

William had made it through to the right flank with some of his Knights, where he was fighting against Robert's cavalry and the young cadet nobles. He smiled to himself as he saw the awe and worry on their faces as he and their fathers cut down the French Knights in front of them with comparative ease. He watched as some of them, including the Grandesmil boys, turn away rather than face their fathers. Suddenly, he felt his faithful big bay stallion lurch. It staggered sideways, and William, an experienced rider, presumed that it had been speared or stabbed. He quickly kicked his feet out of the stirrups so he would not be trapped when they collapsed. Sure enough, the big horse fell to its knees, and the King threw himself off as it fell onto its side.

William, sword in hand, jumped back, spotting a sizeable crossbow quarrel embedded low down in his horse's neck. The lifeblood of the horse pumped out around it as it flailed on the floor, eyes rolling in fright. William, teeth gritted, strode forward and, with his dagger, opened the large artery in its neck to put it out of its misery, placing his hand over its eyes. He sighed; the big bay Destrier had carried him faithfully into many a battle for the last five years. Now, however, he had other concerns; he was unhorsed and on the ground surrounded by dozens of Knights fighting at close quarters around him on horseback. He was vulnerable, and he was an easy target; the French or Angevin Knights would revel in the glory of killing the 'Norman King'.

A hand clamped down on his shoulder, and he whirled around, his sword raised to strike his attacker. However, Toki stood there, holding out the reins of his horse to the King. William laughed, took him by the shoulders and embraced him.

'Well met. In many ways, you have been more of a son to me than my own sons have; I will not forget this Toki of Wigod,' he said, mounting the stallion. Once in the saddle, William looked ahead; he could see Roger de Montgomery and De Clare slicing their way through the French blue and gold livery. 'Pull one of those French bastards out of their saddle and follow me,' he shouted over his shoulder as his horse leapt away.

Toki grinned as he watched him ride away; William was one of those people who took joy in battle when he was in the middle of it. Even in his fifties, he was a warrior to be feared. He insisted on not wearing insignia in battle; there were no rosettes or ribbon tied around his arm, as some Kings were wont to do to mark themselves to their followers. He wore the same red and gold tunic as his Knights. With his chain mail coif over his head and a helmet with a wide metal nosepiece, he looked no different from any other Norman Knight.

Toki now turned his attention to getting a horse when he suddenly felt a massive thud in his chest, and he found himself falling. A large square crossbow quarrel had embedded itself in his body, piercing straight through his breastbone and knocking him backwards onto the ground. As he lay there winded, he lifted his head with effort and looked down in amazement, purely by chance it had hit the bottom v of the neck of his chain mail tunic. He found it difficult to breathe or raise himself as the pain radiated out over and deep within him. He stared up at the grey winter sky above him, aware that his life was about to end on a battlefield far from his home on the banks of the Thames in England. A shadow fell over him, and he closed his eyes for a moment. When he opened them, Toki found himself looking up into the grinning face of Belleme; he had a crossbow resting on the crook of his arm.

'So I was right, Toki the Saxon, you were the traitor in our midst all along, feeding information back to the King. Now as I promised you, I am making sure that you pay the price for betraying us. However, I have not used one of these for some time, and my aim was somewhat rusty, so I have come to finish the job. Toki watched, struggling to draw a breath as Belleme cranked the crossbow and inserted another long vicious metal quarrel bolt. He then placed it on Toki's throat before smiling and releasing the catch.

Morvan had successfully jumped the shield wall, a dangerous move as any of the pike or spearmen could jab upwards into the underbelly of the horse. However, the unexpected suddenness of the manoeuvre acted in their favour, and within moments, they had landed, turned and attacked the shield wall from the rear. As the horses charged into them, the men had no chance, the Horse Warriors slashing, stabbing and trampling them. The second shield wall broke as men panicked or ran to help their friends in front and were cut down in turn as the rest of Morvan's troop galloped through the increasing gap. This sight was too much for even some hardened Norman troops in the second shield wall, and they turned and fled.

Morvan sat for a few moments at the edge of the forest catching his breath. Several sword fights were still going on around him as he gazed out at the carnage that filled the meadow below Gerberoi. The battle was still viciously fought on both flanks between mounted Knights. He could see the King wielding his sword; recognisable on his big bay stallion, then suddenly he was gone. Someone had brought him down. Morvan stared at the spot where he had last seen him for what seemed like an age, and then he pushed Shadow forwards towards it. As he fought his way through, he saw that the King was back, this time on a distinctive dun and black coloured mount that Morvan recognised as Toki's horse. Swinging his sword around his head, the King charged back into the fray.

Although he felt a wave of immense anger against William, he did not want him to die in this battle. That would not be good for Robert, Normandy or England, so he was relieved he had escaped without harm. Morvan had now almost reached the spot where he saw the King fall, and looking around, he saw several blood-spattered bodies on the ground. William's big bay horse lay prone on its side.

Morvan began to turn away to regroup his men when his attention was drawn to the edge of the fray and a fallen Saxon warrior. The dawn winter sun shone on his long blonde hair where he lay on the ground. He knew at once that it was his friend Toki. He had been seriously wounded, and now he saw that a crossbow was being brought to his throat as someone stepped forward to finish him off. Morvan heard himself shout, 'No', as he leapt from the saddle. Scrambling across the churned-up ground that was now slippery with blood, he threw himself at the man who held the crossbow. However, he was too late; he reached him just as the bolt slammed into his friend's throat.

Glaring up, Morvan found himself staring into the glittering black eyes of Belleme. Below him, he heard the last gurgling sounds of his dying friend as, with a cry of pure rage, he swung his sword at the Seigneur, and sweeping the crossbow from his hands, he sliced deeply into his upper arm, knocking him backwards.

Belleme lay in shock on the ground. He only just managed to get himself to his knees when Morvan smashed the hilt of his sword into his face, breaking his nose and cheekbone and laying him out cold. Morvan wanted to sink his sword into

228

the black heart of this man, but for some reason, he found he could not do it, so he punched him repeatedly, standing over him with a stare that was full of hatred as he looked at him lying amongst the bloodied corpses of the dead. Belleme had blood pouring from his nose and trickling from his mouth, his arm was bleeding heavily. Part of Morvan knew that he should get him off the battlefield because the injured were usually put to the sword and then stripped of their clothes, boots and anything of value. Despite that, Morvan found no sympathy for Seigneur Belleme after what he had just witnessed, so instead, he left him to the fates, his men might find him. He turned on his heel and returned to Shadow.

Once mounted, Morvan stood up in his stirrups and scanned the battlefield looking for his Horse Warriors, although he knew his Captain and Serjeant would have rallied them together. The height of Shadow at over seventeen hands gave him an advantage, and looking around, he could see that the element of surprise had given Robert's attack an advantage. William's forces were being forced back towards the river, and he could see that some of the King's men were already crossing the ford at a run. The fighting was still fierce in the centre, and he cut and slashed his way through to where Robert and his followers were bunched together. Morvan looked for the King or Roger de Montgomery's standards, but he could not immediately see them. Had they left the field? If so, it was time to call a halt. He pulled up behind Roger-Fitz-Richard, who was just dispatching a large, aggressive pike-man. Roger turned in alarm at first as Shadow pulled alongside but then realised that it was Morvan and gave him a wry grin.

'Well met, Morvan, we seem to be driving them back.'

Moran nodded. 'We need to make a stand and sue for terms

to end the slaughter. Where is Robert?'

Roger agreed, and they both stood in their stirrups to locate the prince. Roger suddenly pointed, and Morvan could see the unusual black helm that Robert Curthose wore into battle. Like his brother, Luc, Morvan tended to avoid metal helms and helmets, especially one like Robert's, as they restricted movement and vision with a very broad noseband of metal. Instead, the Horse Warriors would wear a chainmail coif, which covered the neck and head but left the face free. Morvan could see that Robert was attacking a large burly Knight on horseback. He was about to say farewell to his friend when he realised that he recognised the horse of the burly Knight, and yelling at Roger, he suddenly pulled Shadow up into a rear. He shot forward, pushing his way brutally through the other mounted riders. At first, Roger reeled in surprise, but then the words shouted by Morvan resonated, and he followed in his wake as he realised that Robert was fighting the King; it was his father on Toki's dun stallion, and they could not let them kill each other.

Robert had ridden into battle glowing with pride and en-thusiasm, the size of the force he was bringing against his father's army, the element of surprise and the sight of the Horse Warriors smashing into the centre had almost overwhelmed him. He had lived in his father's shadow the whole of his life, and now he was establishing his own identity, his own success in the field. He did not doubt in his mind that his forces would carry the day. Like his followers, they had spent the day staying as far away from the King and his senior nobles as they could; they left them to the French and Angevin Knights. However, William and his Knights were some of the most experienced fighters in Europe and winning a battle was not just about youth and the strength in your sword arm, it was when to deliver a

230

blow and what type of blow. Fighting in the centre of a mell came naturally to these men; they had done it so often it was second nature, whereas the men they were fighting against had done most of their training in the pell yard. It was different when you had the smell of blood and gore in your nostrils, the never-ending cries and crash of steel on steel and your horse sliding on the entrails and bodies of slain men.

As Robert Curthose surveyed the field, he decided to head for where the fighting was at its thickest with a few of his followers to try to force the battle to a speedy end. He saw the sizeable burly Knight on the dun horse; he was laying about him and dispatching men with ease. Robert saw his opportunity and sweeping around, he rode up beside him on the Knight's left side so that he would have to reach across to his left to engage. However, the Knight was far swifter and supple than Robert expected, and as he whirled his horse round to face him, the Knight rode straight at him, and he found himself on the receiving end of punishing blows.

For several moments, their blades were engaged, and they strained against each other, but the Knight was far stronger. Robert remembered seeing a trick that Morvan had used in training, and he suddenly disengaged, leant backwards out of range, and then dropped forward down the side of his horse's neck to bring a hard flat blow up under the man's wrist.

To Robert's relief, it worked, and the Knight dropped his sword. As he grabbed to catch it, the man was unbalanced, so Robert rode his horse straight at him. The man was unhorsed and hit the ground. He was obviously winded, so Robert dismounted to finish it on the ground. He realised that this was one of his father's Knights, he was wearing his colours, but this Knight had killed many of Robert's men. At that moment,

Morvan pushed Shadow forward and pulled him up into a rear, striking out with his hooves in front of Robert to get his attention; Morvan feared that a red battle mist had descended as often was the case and needed to stop him.

'What are you about?' he yelled angrily, reeling back from the flailing hooves and glaring at Morvan. Morvan indicated the man on the ground who was now swearing profusely, struggling to his feet and shouting for Montgomery.

'It is your father,' he shouted at the prince.

Robert turned in horror to stare at the man in front of him, the man he had nearly killed, and he recognised his father's voice. He immediately sheathed his sword and pulled his father to his feet, kneeling and bowing his head to him.

William glared at his son and moved away; he tried to mount his horse, but his hand was too severely injured. He suspected that his wrist was broken. Robert stepped forward, and cupping his hands, he helped his father back up onto the back of the big dun stallion. At that moment, Roger de Montgomery and Eustace De Boulogne rode up swords drawn to protect the King.

'Sire, are you hurt?' Montgomery shouted above the clamour. William shook his head and pulled his horse around, his reins in his uninjured left hand. Without a word to his son, he left the field, his Knights and followers cantering behind him.

Shortly afterwards, the Norman horns sounded the retreat, and Robert Curthose was left triumphant. He had unexpectedly beaten his father in battle, one of the most warlike and successful military leaders in Europe.

As Morvan sat on Shadow watching the remains of the dispirited Norman army cross the river, he considered Robert's success. He knew that there were many winners and losers in this defeat. There was no doubt that a humiliated and defeated William would now be forced to come to terms. Indeed, he was sure that Robert would now become Duke of Normandy; there was surely no doubt. The successful manipulation of Robert by both Pope Gregory and King Philip of France had paid off; they would undoubtedly hope to gain from this situation. Morvan thought that the repercussions of this unexpected defeat of King William would be felt for some time all over Western Europe.

In fact, as Morvan was to find out, it was not many months before the news of the defeat of William at Gerberoi by his son and the resulting damage to the King's prestige had filtered far over to England and into Scotland. King Malcolm III was delighted that William was so occupied in Normandy, and he immediately began planning a significant campaign of punishing raids over the border into Northumberland.

Chapter Thirty

Morvan stood on the ramparts of Gerberoi, gazing down at the land stretched out below, wrapped up in his own thoughts. It was almost March, but there was no hint of spring in the cold late afternoon air that assailed the fortress from the north. The meadows below still bore all the signs of the battle; the bodies had been removed, returned to their families where possible or buried with quick lime in a mass grave. Hundreds had died; the battle may only have been short, but it was brutal, and the French and Angevin troops had certainly given no quarter.

The detritus of warfare still lay scattered on the churned earth, broken helms and leather straps and stirrups, the odd leather gauntlet lay on the ground. It had been a decisive victory for Robert, and William had retreated injured to Rouen, but Robert and his father were still not reconciled. William could not forgive Robert's betrayal; the fact that he had allied himself with his father's enemies was a step too far. What is more, William had not returned to Matilda's side in Caen. Instead, he had stayed in Rouen. He was furious that he would now have to come to what might be damaging terms with his enemies because of his humiliating defeat at the hands of his eldest son.

His senior Knights and advisors were an influential and powerful group of the Anglo-Norman aristocracy. It included

Roger de Montgomery, Hugh de Grandesmil, Eustace de Boulogne and the Earl de Clare, who used all of their skills to try to negotiate a truce for their sons and younger brothers. King Philip, who had, for his own ends, made their cause his own, supported Robert, and William found that he had no choice but to come to the table.

As Morvan stared out over the vast forests surrounding Gerberoi, he heard the blowing of horns in the distance. They heralded the approach of Roger de Montgomery, the Earl of Shrewsbury. How he would feel when he faced this man; after all, he had purposefully left Belleme, his son and heir, out there on the battlefield to die. He watched as they galloped out of the trees, pennants flying, a considerable escort of armed men and other lesser Knights now turning up the track to the fortress. He took a deep breath and walked along the ramparts to the narrow circular stone staircase. He trailed his hand on the rough cold stone as he descended. It had been a quiet few months since the battle, and now they were to sit down with William's negotiator to find out if it had all been worthwhile.

Robert had felt triumphant at first at the end of the battle. His father had lifted the siege and retreated to Rouen. However, to Morvan, there was no doubt that the incident on the battlefield had affected him. Robert had lived his life in the shadow of his father, but he respected him, and despite their constant arguments, he was proud of what his father had achieved. He was shocked by how close he had come to killing him on the battlefield. As he lay in the dark of the night, Robert knew that it would have been something that he would have found very difficult to live with. In addition, how would he ever have been able to face his mother? His parents still loved each other deeply. This had softened his stance towards his father, and although he still demanded recognition, the burning rage and anger that he had initially felt had diminished. Now, as he welcomed Roger de Montgomery, Robert found that he wanted reconciliation with his parents.

When Morvan reached the Great Hall, Robert was just greeting his guests. As expected, Chatillon was one of those seated around the table. Although he had left on other matters for several weeks, Morvan was not at all surprised to find him back here in time for the negotiations. Gervais de la Ferte, Seneschal of France, had also arrived as King Philip's representative, ostensibly to support Robert but in reality out to get what they could. Therefore, yet again, Robert Curthose was in the hands of these arch manipulators of their own or joint agendas.

Morvan was pleasantly surprised to see that Robert took control; he had a forceful and charismatic voice, and soon he had the attention of all the men at the table as he welcomed them all to Gerberoi. Roger de Montgomery inclined his head with the others in thanks, but then he turned to Morvan.

'I believe that Robert has you to thank for the strategy that was so successful in putting us to rout,' he said, pinning him with his hawk-like gaze. Morvan was somewhat taken aback.

'I believe we all played our parts in that Sire,' he said, indicating the others around the table and the young nobles standing listening in the background.

'It is a shame that it came to open warfare with so many lost, but hopefully, we can now resolve this!' The senior nobleman said

Robert nodded. 'I was sorry for the loss of your son, Belleme, he has been a good friend to me over the last few years, and he certainly facilitated the alliances that made my victories possible,' he said, indicating Chatillon and the Seneschal of France.

Roger de Montgomery sat back in surprise. 'Oh, Belleme is not dead; one of my Knights found him badly beaten and wounded on the battlefield. He took his mother's death very badly, so I have sent him away to her estates in Allencon to recover. He has also decided he is ready to make his peace with the King.'

Morvan felt a flash of what felt like anger at first that Belleme had survived, but he had to admit that he also felt a small amount of relief that he had not killed him.

For the next few hours, the men around the table discussed and disputed what was to be gained and lost after the battle of Gerberoi. William was still not prepared to name his son as Duke of Normandy, but he was prepared to publicly confirm him as his heir and give him far more power in the ruling of the Duchy.

William was also forced to concede and recognise King Philip's right to the eastern Vexin, which meant that France would now run right up to the River Epte on the border with Normandy. It would be a massive blow to any further Norman expansion in this area. Morvan noticed the smile of satisfaction on the face of Gervais, the French Seneschal; his master would be pleased.

Chatillon was also quietly pleased; the King had been humiliated and brought to heel. In addition, the Pope's fractious relationship with France was now a more powerful alliance, which meant that the church could extend its influence in Western Europe unchecked for a while. Chatillon hoped that Robert would be in their pocket for years to come. Belleme may be gone, but he hoped to use Morvan to good effect to keep

Robert engaged.

Morvan found that he was clenching his fists under the table. Negotiations over, people were now moving and chatting together.

'Are you not pleased with what Robert has achieved?' Chatillon asked him, looking at Morvan's white and angry face.

Morvan turned narrowed eyes on him. 'I am pleased that my friends will be pardoned and that their lands will be returned, but what has Robert actually achieved for himself? He is still not Duke of Normandy.'

Chatillon could see the anger building in the Horse Warrior. 'Robert has certainly strengthened his position and attracted powerful allies. Come outside, let us get some air,' he said, standing up. He could feel Morvan's simmering discontent as they walked into the Bailey.

They stood in silence in the cold still of the night as he waited for Morvan's anger to dissipate. Then he spoke quietly, 'I believe that Robert has rewarded you well for your service.'

Morvan nodded. 'Yes, a large estate in northwestern Maine, right on the border with Normandy and France, close to Hugh's estates. It has a small chateau on a lake, which I may make my home. It is somewhere out of the reach of William and the Duke of Brittany but always under the threat of attack from Fulk.' He laughed bitterly. 'Which, of course, means that every time I visit, I may find that my farms and villages have been burnt to the ground.'

Chatillon gave a wry smile. 'These are troubled times, but you still have the huge estates in Vannes, I believe.'

'Yes, but I believe it may be many years before I visit them. Fortunately, I have a good Steward and Captain in Beorn who will manage them for me.'

Chatillon felt some sympathy for the young Horse Warrior; he knew what it was like to wander homeless. 'You may not think it at the moment, but you will find love again, Morvan. You will find someone, marry and have a family. It is what we do; we go on. Our instinct is to survive.'

Morvan found that he had to turn away at the thought of Constance. In a rasping emotional voice, he turned back to Chatillon. 'In a few months, they will kill our child, Chatillon, a perfectly healthy boy or girl whose only mistake was to be born to the wrong parents. How do we survive and recover from something like that?' he said as his emotions became too much, and he turned, bowed his head and walked away.

Chatillon stood for some time deep in thought. He needed Morvan; he had plans for the young warrior. He made a decision that he hoped he would not regret. He would send a pigeon in the morning.

The following day Roger de Montgomery returned to Rouen with the terms agreed around the table to see if they could persuade William to accept them. Montgomery hoped so, as the King's son Robert was coming to meet his father halfway.

Morvan was just riding in on Shadow after an early morning gallop as they were preparing to leave.

'Wish me luck, Morvan de Malvais,' Montgomery said to him. 'The pardon I am requesting from the King includes you as well as our cadet sons.' Morvan inclined his head in a bow of acknowledgement. Montgomery continued. 'I heard about the rift with your brother. I hope you can resolve it; families are stronger together.' He raised a hand in farewell and trotted out of the gates with his large colourful entourage.

Morvan dismounted in the cobbled yard and spotted Chatillon on the ramparts with his basket of birds. He wondered what devilry the papal envoy was up to now; probably ensuring the Pope or his uncle had the terms of the treaty before anyone else. No one would have been more surprised than Morvan to find that the bird was flying south on business that concerned him.

A week later, when flurries of sleet were still hitting the west coast of Brittany, Matthew, the Steward of Morlaix, appeared upstairs in the solar to inform Luc that a visitor had arrived. 'At this time of night, in this weather, Mathew? Who is it?'

'I believe that it is a priest of some standing, Sire. He did not give me his name, but he is dressed in very rich garments.'

Luc raised an eyebrow at his wife, Merewyn, who just shrugged. 'Go and see who it is; he will not have travelled all the way to Morlaix to see you without reason, Luc,' she said, smiling up at him.

They had been together for eight years, but as he watched her sitting in the firelight, her blonde hair shining and her huge green eyes smiling up at him, he had never loved her more. He reached out, stroked the side of her face, and then headed for the door and the staircase down into the Hall.

His visitor was huddled by the fire, a warm mulled ale in his hands. He stood as Luc approached, but Luc waved him back down. In the light of the fire, Luc recognised the pinched cold face immediately. He was not a man he liked.

'Monseigneur Gironde, what brings you here to Morlaix from the warm halls of Duke Hoel in such weather? I hope you are not the bearer of bad tidings. The Duke and his family are in good health?'

Gironde shook his head. 'No Lord de Malvais, the Duke of Brittany, and his family are well. I serve more than one master, one temporal and one more spiritual,' he said in a soft voice that still had a slight Italian lilt to it.

Luc pulled up a chair beside him. 'Alright, Gironde, I am prepared to listen, but you should know that I will not act against the King in the interests of the Pope.'

Gironde gave a slight smile. 'For once, Lord De Malvais, my master Piers De Chatillon is not acting in the interests of either his uncle the Cardinal or Pope Gregory. This is what he would like you to do. Believe me; it is in the best interests of your family.' Luc was intrigued and sat back to listen.

What he heard made him sit forward again and gave him a great deal to think about. He arranged for Gironde to have a bed for the night, but he then sat for another hour in front of the grand fireplace in the Hall as he weighed up his options.

Merewyn eventually came looking for him; she was surprised to see him sitting staring into the flames on his own. 'Luc, it is late. There were not bad tidings, I hope,' she said, staring at his troubled face.

He took her hand. 'No, my love. I cannot explain yet, but I must leave tomorrow; I must go to Caen.'

She looked perplexed. 'Has William summoned you?'

Luc looked at her and wondered how much he could say without embroiling her in this. 'No, William is still licking his wounds in Rouen. I am going to see the Queen on an almost impossible errand, but I cannot say more because no one must ever know.' He pulled her onto his lap and held her close, she was the centre of his life and family here in Morlaix, and he could never imagine life without her. 'Let us go to bed, but not to sleep yet,' he said with a twinkle in his eye as he ran his hand lightly over her breasts. 'I am leaving with Gironde tomorrow, so let us enjoy tonight. I may be away for over a week.' She laughed, and climbing off his knee, she ran up the stairs like the girl he first saw running across a meadow away from him in Ravensworth many years before. As a Saxon girl, he had been the enemy she was running from; now, he was her husband and lover.

Chapter Thirty-One

On the last day of April, William returned to Caen from Rouen. It was the longest he had ever stayed away from his wife while in Normandy, and Matilda knew that it was a sign of his displeasure with her. However, Robert was her eldest son and her favourite. She recognised all of his faults, but she thought he did have a case for being awarded the Dukedom before his father died. Using her influence with Roger de Montgomery, she had engineered a compromise between Robert and his father behind the scenes. William would agree to a public affirmation of Robert as his heir and give him more power to rule the Duchy in his absence. She had sent several messages to Robert begging him to accept these terms and heal the rift, and she was pleased that he had done so. She had also extracted a promise from Robert to return to Caen and meet with his father in late summer. That gave her time to build her own bridges with William, whom she loved dearly.

Her second son, William Rufus, was now firmly established in the English court, and everyone there knew that he was his father's heir to take the throne of England after his father's death. Her youngest son, Henry, was still young enough not to cause her many problems. However, she knew that he was highly intelligent, cunning and manipulative; she imagined that he would attach himself to the tail of his brother William Rufus's success in England, as he had always been closer to him than to Robert.

However, the child that filled her waking thoughts was her daughter, Constance. Her heart went out to her all alone at Falaise. She was about to experience one of the most heart-rending moments of her life, the loss of a child.

Matilda had been surprised by the sudden arrival and request for a private audience from Luc De Malvais a few weeks earlier. She had not seen him for over five months, but she knew, of course, about the falling out with his brother when Morvan had refused to hand Constance over and had fought his brother before going over to the rebels. This rift between the two brothers had been the talk of the court, and of course, it had been impossible to keep Constance's name out of it. However, so far, there was not a whisper of her carrying Morvan's child. Fortunately, The Court had accepted her betrothal to Alan Fergant and her removal to Falaise for the hand fasting to the future Duke of Brittany. She trusted her Castellan and the two women she had put in charge of Constance at their home in Falaise; one of them was the childhood nurse of Constance, so she expected to be able to keep the child's birth a secret. She went cold at the thought that William might find out that she had done all of this behind his back; her transgression in giving money to Robert would pale in comparison.

She had been wary and on guard when she sat down opposite Luc De Malvais in her solar that afternoon. They owed this proud and intimidating warrior several times over for his service and, more recently, she certainly did for the rescue of Constance, which had cost him a high price with the loss of his brother.

She indicated that he had her permission to begin. He explained why he was there and told her about the sudden and unexpected involvement of the Duke of Brittany's chaplain Monseigneur Gironde… She could feel herself gripping the arms of the chair at the news; the more people who knew about Constance, the more dangerous it would become. However, his following sentence took her breath away…

'Your Grace, Alan Fergant now knows about the child.' Matilda's heart seemed to leap into her mouth at that news.

'God's bones! If William finds out, we are all done for, especially if the alliance with Brittany crumbles after his recent defeat at Gerberoi.'

Luc, grim-faced, agreed. 'Gironde tells me that Alan Fergant still wants to marry Constance; he is very taken with her. He also wants the alliance to go ahead. He has agreed to stay quiet on the condition that the child is disposed of; it is to be taken into the forest by one of his men and Gironde and left to be exposed to the night so that none of them has the sin of a child's murder on their souls.'

Matilda felt her eyes fill with tears, and she could see the anguish in Luc's face as he turned away to hide his emotions. 'I have already arranged for the child to go immediately to a Knight's family in the Vexin, an honest man who I knew from the court of Flanders. His wife is barren, and the child is to be brought up and treated as theirs, so he would be trained as a Knight if it was a boy.

Luc nodded, but his subsequent request took her totally by surprise as he put forward the plan he had come up with to save the child. He needed her permission to put it into place and a letter to her Castellan at Falaise to give him access. At first, Matilda was unsure; she did not want to do anything to enrage

Alan Fergant now he knew about the child. That might risk exposure; the alliance with Brittany was more crucial than ever for William.

'Stay here for a few days, Malvais. William is not back for a few weeks. You can use the excuse that you have come to check on Morvan's troop of Horse Warriors that were left behind. I need time to think on this,' she said, frowning.

'If it helps, you should know that this suggestion came not from Gironde but from his master, Piers De Chatillon, the papal envoy,' he suggested.

Matilda gave a sharp intake of breath. 'He knows?' she asked. 'This makes it worse; he can hold this information over us forever. We will become his pawns; he is a dangerous and cunning man, totally ruthless,' she said, beginning to pace across the room.

'Usually, I would agree with you, but this time I do believe that he has the interests of Morvan and Constance at heart. He has known all along about the child; it makes no difference to his plans if the child lives or dies,' said Luc standing up and holding out his hands in supplication.

She stared at him long and hard and then nodded. 'What you have said is true. I may agree to your plan when I have thought through all of the implications and risks, but you must ensure that no one ever knows of this apart from you and me.'

He bowed his head in acquiescence. 'I will return tomorrow at noon to find out your decision, and if we decide to go ahead, I will need a message to the Castellan,' he said, and standing, he left her to her thoughts.

Matilda stood gazing into the flames of the fire, weighing up the pros and cons of what he had suggested. Could she live with the death of her daughter's child on her conscience when she had a chance to save it? She eventually decided that she could not and that she would agree to the plan that Malvais was putting forward; the child would be saved and go to the family in the Vexin as planned. She hoped that she would never regret this decision; it was such a risk. However, she also felt a spark of hope that if the child were born whole and healthy; it would go to a life with another family far away from Brittany.

She felt a wave of sadness. It would be her first grandchild, and she would never see the child

Chapter Thirty-Two

Morvan was in Paris. He had not been in the splendour of the French court since he was a very young man on a visit with his mother to see her family. The Palace de la Cité was an impressive fortress built on the Ile de la Cité, an island in the centre of the River Seine. It had been the home of the French Kings for hundreds of years, and each King had rebuilt or extended parts of it until it was a considerable sprawling fortified complex. It soon became apparent to Morvan that King Philip, the present incumbent, had grandiose plans for the expansion of France, and he expected Robert Curthose to help him achieve that. Philip saw the natural borders of France as the Alps to the east, the River Rhine to the north and the Pyrenees to the south. He intended to gradually drive out the invaders who had taken land from the Frankish and Gaulish Kingdoms.

At Chatillon's suggestion, King Philip had invited Robert to his court for a month before returning to Caen and the reconciliation with his father. After all, they did not want this to go too smoothly, so they needed to keep the anger and ambition burning in Robert Curthose. Although this was the court of his brother's and William's enemy, Morvan was pleased to be away from Gerberoi. The constant training and long monotonous evenings in the fortress had given him far too long to brood. He found himself counting the weeks to the birth of his child, and one night after too much Rhenish wine, he found he had to stop himself from waking his Horse Warriors and galloping to Falaise to try to take Constance. Fortunately, his friend Roger had found him in the stable block, his bridle in his hand, and he had talked him out of it. Piers de Chatillon had heard of this and suggested to Robert that he take some of his entourage with him, especially Morvan and Roger-Fitz-Richard.

The French court was a hive of intrigue and entertainment, musicians, strolling players, jugglers almost every night; King Philip liked to be kept amused. They went hunting every day with the King, and the young nobles of the court and Morvan's great Destrier Shadow was greatly admired. At night, the young and even the married women of the court tried to get his attention, and although he embarked on several flirtations, his love for Constance stopped him from going any further, the forthcoming birth of his child occupied his thoughts.

In the second week, the Seneschal of France, Gervais de la Ferte, arrived at court with his large family in tow. He had five sons and four daughters, and they were undoubtedly a lively addition to the court. The older sons were seemingly game for any adventure or prank, bet, or demonstration of horsemanship or arms. They also brought an impressive string of horses with them; Arab horses crossed with the French thoroughbreds built for horseracing, a sport, which had recently taken off in the courts of Europe. Morvan's interest was piqued. It was the first time he had come across horses bred purely for sport and speed rather than for battle, although he was aware that in the east, the Arab nations, and the Mamelukes, used the horses for both.

Morvan soon became firm friends with Etienne, the eldest

son of the Seneschal, obviously destined for greatness himself as the heir to an exceptionally powerful and wealthy family and, of course, now betrothed to Mabile de Chateauneuf. Each day found him down at the paddocks watching these high stepping, glossy, beautiful animals being lunged. They had much shorter backs and smaller heads; their eyes shone with intelligence. Morvan noticed that one of the younger brothers, Ette, was an extraordinary rider, a 'neck-or-nothing' daredevil who would take any fence and who stood up in the stirrups to gallop. The other brothers teased him unmercifully, but he just laughed and thumbed his nose at them.

One day, Morvan mounted up to take part in a race around the fields when a hay wagon rolled unexpectedly out in front of them and the horse young Ette was riding shied violently. The young man was flung from the saddle, landing like a bag of sticks. Morvan quickly reined in and ran over to the lifeless figure lying on the ground. Etienne arrived seconds later, knelt beside him, slapped his face, and said, 'Ette, Ette,' while Morvan gently unfolded each limb to check that nothing was broken.

'Get some water or wine, Morvan,' Etienne said, scanning around. Morvan asked a bemused and frightened peasant who produced a battered leather bucket and pointed to the stream. Morvan returned and was about to wet the boy's neckerchief when Etienne just emptied it over the boy's face. Ette came up gasping and spluttering and then launched a string of obscenities at his older brother. Seeing Morvan standing over him, he coloured up. Morvan looked at the boy with interest. He did not have his brother's blonde hair and ruddy complexion; he had huge dark eyes and pale white skin. He must take after the second wife of the Seneschal, who was an acclaimed Italian beauty.

The young man was helped to his feet, and to Morvan's astonishment, within moments, was running to remount while shouting over his shoulder. 'Do not on any account tell Papa I had a fall, Etienne,' he said, narrowing his eyes at his brother before swirling his horse around and galloping off.

Morvan stared after him in amazement while Etienne just laughed and shrugged. 'Ette will get us all in so much trouble one day,' he said as he mounted and galloped after him.

That night the vast Great Hall of the palace was packed; most of the French nobility seemed to be in attendance. It was the feast day of St Germaine, so they had all attended mass in the cathedral of Saint-Etienne earlier in the day. There had been feats of combat and skill between the squires and then between the Knights in the sizeable sandy ménage.

Morvan was invited to take part by Chatillon in one of the supposed mock battles. In no time at all, Morvan and Shadow had put paid to half a dozen French Knights while Philip and Gervais de la Ferte had watched in admiration. They had both seen the Breton Horse Warriors in battle, usually on the receiving end of their ferocity, and Philip wanted his cavalry trained on similar lines. Morvan was half-French, and many of the older nobles fondly remembered his beautiful mother Marie, so Morvan suddenly found he was enjoying life as a fêted guest in the French court.

Later that evening, during the dancing and singing, Gervais de la Ferte approached Morvan. He introduced his lovely wife Alina, who gracefully bowed to him and then swept a hand over three of his daughters and two of his sons trailing behind. Morvan bowed his head to them all, and, raising his eyes, he met the eyes of Ette. Then, he realised that it was not Ette; this was obviously his sister. She had the same large, dark, long-lashed eyes like their mother. She gave him a wry smile, and then the truth dawned on him; Ette was a girl.

Gervais watching this smiled. 'I believe you have met my disgraceful daughter Minette, who sometimes thinks she was born a boy. I believe she parted company with her horse today, and you helped her.' Morvan could not help smiling back at him and his wife, who was laughing and shaking her head at the way her husband always knew everything.

'Ah, but it was not her fault, Sire,' he said gallantly, and he received a smile from Gervais in reply as he looked fondly down at his errant daughter. Now that she was dressed as a young woman in a soft green gown, she looked older than the sixteen years or so that he had thought.

Her father brought his attention back. 'Chatillon and I are meeting with the King in the morning; I would like you to be there, Morvan de la Malvais.'

Morvan bowed and agreed while wondering why these men thought he was so crucial to their discussions. He was a provincial Knight, out of favour with his famous family and banished by Alan Fergant from his estates in Brittany. However, his brother Luc, a consummate diplomat, had taught him years ago that you learnt more by watching and listening, so he would go and say little, but he would find out what was afoot.

The family of the Seneschal moved away and headed through the archway and out onto the terraces. As they went through the arch, Minette turned and stared at him for a moment with those huge dark-lashed eyes before turning away.

'An extraordinary young girl, engaging and so intelligent, she could have been a Count or a Duke if she had been a boy. However, she will make a name for herself, I have no doubt,' said Chatillon, who had appeared beside him in that annoying silent way that he had. Morvan just grunted non-committedly, but his eyes were still on the archway, and Chatillon smiled.

After that, he saw her almost every day, always sitting on the fence in her boy's clothes or riding hell for leather through the forests. She rarely spoke to him, just gave him the odd glance. However, at the end of the week, he found her sitting on the edge of the water trough watching him groom Shadow. 'I think he is one of the biggest and most impressive war horses that I have ever seen,' she said.

'You should see Espirit Noir, his father.'

'Do you have him as well?' she asked, with her head on one side.

'No, he is my brother's horse; he is still used in battle, but he will go out to stud in the paddock soon.'

'Ah yes, your brother, I have heard of him. He is a very famous warrior, but you have fallen out with him, yes?' Morvan inclined his head but said nothing. 'So, Horse Warrior are you going to bet on me tomorrow?' she asked.

Morvan raised his eyes to her face in a shocked glance. 'Your father is going to let you race against the other Knights and riders?' he asked incredulously. He knew that these races could be dangerous.

'He wants his horses to win. If I ride, I will win, so he will... How do you say it?' she asked.

'Turn a blind eye?' suggested Morvan.

She laughed and nodded. 'Now I must go before mamma misses me. Bet on me, Horse Warrior, I will win,' she threw over her shoulder as she ran out of the courtyard.

Two days later, the court assembled in the broad meadows on the banks of the Seine. Pavilions and seats had been set up, and crowds gathered to watch the race and to see the King and his court. The many soldiers kept the crowds back.

It was a long race over several leagues, up hills and through forests, so it was about speed, strategy, and stamina for riders and horses. Morvan, who had used the Arab strain in his horses for years, knew they had both. There must have been about forty riders in the race jostling for position and striking out at their opponents. Morvan could see three of the distinctive shorter-backed horses of the Seneschal. He noticed that the third horse was being ridden by a small rider who kept out on the crowd's edge. The horns blew, and they were off in a riot of coloured caparisons, noise and thundering hooves as they disappeared up the hill and around the edge of the forest.

The course had been plotted carefully; it meant that at the end, the leaders would have a good gallop over the far hill and down along the riverbank in full view of the King and his court. Morvan found himself in demand with some of the Knights as they drank their wine and waited, but before long, there was a halloo from the watchers, and the first horses galloped into sight. It was a strung-out group, but in the lead was Minette, distinctively standing up in her stirrups, leaning over the horse's neck, her head almost between its ears. Morvan had never seen anything like it, and he hallooed along with the rest cheering her on.

Then a strange thing happened as she approached the finish line; she looked back over her shoulder and saw her brother Etienne behind her. She slowed her horse and let him streak past her to win. Morvan looked at her in astonishment as she trotted the glossy chestnut towards him, but she just smiled. She had won the race, but she knew that some of the French Knights would not be happy, so she had pulled back. Like her father, she was a clever diplomat, but Morvan thought that she had made her point, and he found himself shaking his head but smiling back.

Morvan was called into several meetings with Robert and King Philip. He watched, listened, and answered honestly when asked a question, and he could see that they valued his opinion. They all knew it was his plan and strategy that had been used at Gerberoi; Robert was generous in that way and had given all the glory to Morvan. After several weeks in the company of King Philip, Morvan found that he could not like him. At least with William, you always knew where you stood, but with King Philip, you always felt that there was another agenda. He knew that King Philip had met with Chatillon on his own several times, and he wondered what devilry they were planning and how it involved Robert Curthose. He determined to find out.

One summer evening, he sat on one of the walls of the fortress gazing down at the swallows sweeping over the waters of the Seine. Robert and Chatillon were at his side, so he took the opportunity to ask their opinion of King Philip. Morvan knew that Chatillon was French, but he served the Vatican first and foremost, and Morvan had picked up that he had been instrumental in healing the rift between the Pope and Philip.

Chatillon laughed at the question. 'They are all the same; they will use you, abuse you if you do not deliver and then dispose of you when you are no more use to them. Always remember that my friends,' he said with a wry smile. Then, he saw his surly manservant beckoning to him. 'I must go; duty calls,' he said, indicating the pigeon in the man's hand.

Chatillon unrolled the tiny vellum scroll from the small leather tube strapped to the bird's leg. He read the message and stood thoughtfully for a few moments; it was from Gironde. He glanced over at Morvan, Etienne the eldest son of Gervais, had

255

joined them, and the Horse Warrior was laughing at something he said. Chatillon was pleased that Morvan had developed friendships with the family of the Seneschal, as it could certainly prove useful. Chatillon decided to wait before sharing the news he had received. In two days, they would return to Gerberoi; he would tell Morvan then that Constance had given birth. That would also leave time for the child to be taken far away.

Morvan enjoyed his last days in Paris; they had hunted and raced the horses. Etienne had invited him to ride one of the Arab racehorses, and he found it so different to the powerful Shadow. Galloping hell-for-leather across the meadow on the short-backed thoroughbred, he felt that all the horse's power was bunched underneath him.

'Gods bones, they are fast, Etienne!' he said in a breathless voice as he came back into the stables.

Etienne nodded. 'It had been a dream of my father's for many years after he saw some Arab traders racing them in Spain.'

As usual, Minette was there and now beckoned him over. 'You leave tomorrow, Horse Warrior?' she asked, raising her large dark eyes.

'Yes, we have to return as we are all leaving for Caen shortly to make our peace with King William, hopefully.' He had discovered that she was astute on political and diplomatic matters, not surprising given her family.

'You are not married, I believe?' she asked, staring into the distance. The silence hung in the air for some time as he struggled for the words. 'Do not fear. I know about your love for the Lady Constance, and now she has gone to someone else,' she said in a matter of fact voice. Morvan looked at her in astonishment, and she gave a small snort of laughter. 'I find I can make myself relatively small and insignificant in so many rooms that people disregard me when they are gossiping.'

Morvan was rendered temporarily speechless. She continued, 'So now you are heartbroken, but you will find that it will wear off; everyone says that it does,' she said, raising her eyes back to him. She turned and jumped off the fence to head back into the fortress to dress for dinner. As she walked away, she suddenly looked over her shoulder and smiled at him, a smile, which lit up her face and made her look very feminine.

'I will wait for you, Horse Warrior. I like you very much, and I think we would suit. Also, my father likes you.'

Morvan was left staring after her, entirely bemused by the conversation that had just taken place.

Morvan did not see Minette that night; he missed dinner completely. He went to his room with his friend Roger-Fitz-Richard, but on the way, he noticed Chatillon's taciturn servant cloaked and booted, hurrying along the corridor. He bade farewell to a surprised Roger, and he sprinted off after him. Remembering his previous experience with following Chatillon and his servant, he took far more care to stay entirely out of sight. The burly man crossed the bottom courtyard to a postern gate in the wall, and Morvan gave it a few moments before he followed him.

It was not dark; the beautiful summer twilight was just darkening over the river. The man got into one of the many boats tied up on the banks of the Seine, and a boatman helped him in and settled him in the stern. Several boats were out on the river as this was a busy crossing. Morvan waved one boatman over and asked him if he could follow that boat without being seen, offering an extra payment. The old man grinned and nodded. He pushed the boat off and kept as close to the banks and trees as possible.

The boat ahead continued down the Ile de Cité and then, reaching the end of the island, turned to follow the left bank of the Seine for some way before the boatman was tying up at a landing stage. Morvan could see large stone buildings in the distance.

'What is that building? He asked the boatman.

The older man looked at him as if he were mad. 'You are a visitor to Paris, Sir? Or you would know. That is the Abbey Saint-Germain-des Pres, one of the oldest, largest and wealthiest Abbeys in France and the home of Cardinal Odo the Prior of Cluny, when he is in Paris.' They say he will be the next Pope,' he added.

Morvan asked the boatman to wait and dropped a coin into his hand with the promise of another. His mind in a whirl, he ran up the path through the trees to try to catch the servant. Chatillon's master was here, and Morvan needed to know what they were planning. He had sworn allegiance to Robert, who had been good to him, and now he would defend both his person and interests.

As he reached the solid Abbey walls and made his way along, he heard the closing clunk of a wooden door ahead. On reaching it, he found that it was a heavy wooden metal-studded door. He pushed against it hopefully, but it was locked. However, he knew he had to get in and find out what the servant had brought or what he was delivering to Chatillon. He quickly ran further along the walls until he came to a tree. It was not precisely overhanging the wall, and he knew it would be a risky jump to the top of the wall, but he had to give it a go. He climbed as high as he could along the branches towards the wall; the one he was on creaked ominously, it was an old tree. However, he managed to inch along the branch and gain purchase with his feet in one of the forks to push himself up. Then, he pushed off and flung himself at the wall. His hand grabbed the rough stone on the top and his feet scrabbled for a foothold. The many years of sword practice had paid off; Morvan had an impressive muscular physique that helped him pull himself up the wall. He sat on the top and surveyed what was beneath him; the boatman was right, the grounds, churches, chapels, gardens and cloisters all lay spread out in front of him. It was a massive site over several acres. How on earth would he find Chatillon's servant?

Morvan dropped to the ground. He reasoned that the monks would be in the refectory at this time of night, but Odo would likely go back to the Abbot's house, where he would be staying, to attend the arrival of the manservant. Fortunately, he had spent a lot of time staying in Abbeys over the years while travelling with Luc. He just needed to find it.

Morvan walked through the well-tended vegetable gardens towards the more significant buildings, bringing him into the cloisters. He had just turned into these when he found himself face to face with a hooded monk.

Morvan made a quicker recovery than the man did. He bowed his head. 'I beg your pardon, father, but I am here as a guest of Cardinal Odo. I went to get some air in the gardens but lost my way. How do I get back to the Abbot's house?'

There was a moment's hesitation from the monk, but then he put back his hood. He was an older man who narrowed his eyes at Morvan as he took in his warrior attire. Morvan smiled and shrugged at his own foolishness, which seemed at first to allay the monk's suspicions.

'The Abbot's house is at the end of the Abbey; it faces down towards the gardens,' he said, turning away. Then he turned back. 'Who did you say you were? I think perhaps I should accompany you; we do not allow strangers to wander the Abbey grounds.'

At that moment, Morvan knew that he had no choice, and he quickly pushed the man backwards and banged his head against the wall, rendering him unconscious. The man slumped to the ground, and Morvan pulled the prone figure into the shadows where he divested him of his habit, putting it on over his clothes before setting off on his mission to find the servant.

The hooded 'monk' skirted the edge of the gardens and crept along the side of the imposing building that had to be the Abbot's residence; he could see the light shining out of a window above, which had fortunately been opened due to the summer heat. It was a beautiful stone building that had recently been constructed with impressive arched doorways and leaded windows with wide stone lintels. Morvan carefully climbed onto the top of one of these so that his head was just below the open window above. He took a deep breath and clung to the stonework. He could hear two voices, neither of which was the servant.

'Well, my nephew Piers seems to have succeeded in his task; this missive from him sets out the terms of the treaty and describes the improved relations with King Philip,' said a deep voice. Morvan realised that this was Odo. The second voice, however, had a strong Italian accent.

'Yes, he has done well, and I shall report as much to Pope Gregory. However, there is more work to be done, Odo. We need William out of Normandy and back to England as soon as possible. The Pope has plans for that area under the Dukedom of Robert. My sources tell me that Robert is softening toward his father due to an incident on the battlefield.' Morvan heard Odo snort.

'You are well informed, Dauferio, even I have not heard this. You, man! Come here and tell us what happened between Robert and his father, William, during the battle.'

Morvan clung to the stonework as Chatillon's servant related the tale. Then there was silence. Morvan's feet and fingers ached from balancing and gripping the rough stone, but he knew he had to hear more.

'We need to fire up Robert's anger once more; we need to push him into a second rebellion as soon as possible,' said the Italian.

Morvan wracked his brains for where he had heard that name. He had spent time in Italy; he must have come across this man there. He was obviously at the same level or higher than Odo, so he must now be a significant cardinal or Archbishop.

Odo grunted in agreement. 'I will set the wheels in motion; this man will take a message back to my nephew. We need as much discontent and rebellion in the region as possible, in Normandy itself, in Brittany to try to disrupt the alliance they have formed. With the help of Fulk of Anjou, we will raise trouble in Maine. William will not know in which direction to look first,' he laughed.

At that moment, Morvan's numb fingers gave way, and he crashed to the ground below. He was winded, but he had heard Odo shout, 'What was that? Someone is there. Were they listening?'

The next minute heads appeared at the window, and he scrambled quickly to his feet and set off at a run.

'Get after him!' Odo shouted at the manservant. Morvan ran as if the hounds of hell were after him. He headed back in the direction of the gate, but he found it was locked inside as well when he got there. He kept running, the sounds of a hue and cry now building behind him. Fortunately, he ran under the wall's shadow, but he could see figures pouring from the buildings in the distance. He reached the end of the vegetable gardens and noticed a large heap of mouldy straw. Without hesitation, he ran ahead, threw off the monk's habit under a tree near the wall and running back, he dived under the straw, pulling as much of it back over him as possible in the hope that he was covered. Fortunately, the sun had set, it was much darker in the shadows, and that was where they were searching for him along the walls. He heard shouts as they found the monk's habit.

Gradually, the sounds of the search dwindled away, but still, he stayed put. Despite the heat, smell and dust of the straw, he knew there could still be guards and patrols everywhere. He must have fallen asleep, but the Abbey bells calling the monks to Lauds or dawn prayer woke him. He reasoned that the prayers would keep most of them occupied and gently removed enough straw to look around. Being close to the Seine and low lying, there was a slight summer ground mist around the Abbey grounds, but he could not see any sentries or monks in evidence. He carefully extracted himself and, knowing he had to be well away from the sentries on the gates, made for the large tree and clambered up it onto the Abbey wall.

He expected his boat to have gone hours before as he raced down to the banks, but he found the boatman curled up under a dirty, rough blanket with a skin of wine. He pulled him awake and told him to row him back up the river as fast as possible while he looked back at the Abbey and listened for any signs of pursuit.

'They came looking for you, those monks and their big servant. Threatened me he did if I didn't tell them your name, but they didn't get anything out of me,' he said with a gap-toothed grin.

Morvan nodded in gratitude and then sat wrapped in thought as they rowed back upstream to the Ile de Cité. Suddenly, a thought occurred to him. 'You didn't know my name, so you couldn't have told them.'

'Ah well, I was clever, I said that to them, but I got away with saying you were a warrior in a laced leather doublet, and they let me be.'

Morvan groaned and put his head in his hands. He paid the man and walked back up into the palace in the encroaching dawn light, creeping into the stables. He curled up under a blanket in Shadow's stall; he wanted to look like he had been here early, grooming his horse.

He was kicked awake by Roger-Fitz-Richard. 'Where were you last night? You were missed; I had to make up some cock and bull story to cover for you.'

Morvan grinned. 'I am eternally in your debt,' he said.

'I just hope she was worth it,' his friend said, shaking his head and heading for his horse.

A few hours later, they assembled, ready to depart. They took their leave of King Philip and the assembled court, including the Seneschal and his son Etienne. Everyone was sad to see them go, and an open invitation was issued to come back anytime. As they rode out and over the bridge, south onto the mainland, Morvan heard the gallop of hooves, and there was Minette, back in boy's clothes on one of her father's fiery racehorses.

'Do not forget about me, Horse Warrior. I made this for you for the winter; this will remind you of me when you have mended your broken heart,' she said. She pulled her horse alongside his and presented him with an expensive, deep-blue velvet, hooded coif before smiling and galloping away. There were cheers from the men as Morvan, surprised at first, took it in good stead. Turning to look behind, he noticed Chatillon's dark eyes were on him, but the papal envoy was not smiling along with the others. It was a very uncomfortable stare, and Morvan looked away. As he expected, there was no doubt that he knew where Morvan had been...

Chatillon knew, but what would the papal envoy do about it? If Cardinal Odo ordered his disposal, Morvan was a dead man walking while Chatillon was by his side; it was his trade to make men disappear.

Chapter Thirty-Three

Matilda had arrived at Falaise on a beautiful summer evening, having received a message from her women that Constance would give birth in the next few days. She was determined to make sure that nothing went amiss; this alliance was too important. As far as William was concerned, she was visiting Constance at Falaise and would stay for the hand-fasting ceremony to Alan Fergant a week or so later. She also had to deal with significant estate business, as they had not visited William's childhood home at Falaise for some time. She had almost forgotten how its stark shape dominated the skyline as she rode towards it.

As it was a first child, the labour was prolonged. Constance clenched her teeth and suffered in silence from the first dull ache in her back to the fourteen hours of difficult labour and ongoing pain. She finally gave birth to a boy in the early hours of dawn. Matilda watched him swaddled while the women saw to Constance to ensure that all of the afterbirth came away. Childbirth is often dangerous, and they all knew that childbed fever was a killer.

Constance heard the cries of her child and held her hands out in supplication to her mother. 'Please, if only for a short time,' she begged. Matilda's gaze softened, and she nodded as the newly hired wet nurse picked up the baby and placed him in his mother's arms. Constance gazed down at the dark shock of hair; he will look like his father, she thought as she gazed into his face, his unfocused blue eyes looking up at her. She loosened the tight swaddling and took hold of a tiny hand. 'I will always love you, and I will always love your father,' she whispered as the tears came and ran down her cheeks. Matilda found it heart wrenching as she watched, but she had to be strong for both of them. She reached over, lifted the baby boy, and handed him to the wet nurse, who was now cloaked and ready. Without another word, they disappeared out into the night, leaving the stricken Constance to give a wail of anguish.

Matilda followed the wet nurse out and along the dark stone corridor. 'This way,' she said and led the way to a narrow stone staircase that went down to a bleak guardroom at the bottom. She opened the door, and two men were waiting. She nodded to both. 'It is a boy. Here he is,' she said, waving the wet nurse forward. The nurse was a stranger purposefully brought from many miles distant so that she did not recognise anyone.

The younger of the two men bowed his head to the Queen. 'We must go immediately; a wagon is waiting on the track outside the castle.'

The Queen nodded and then said,' Wait! Do you have the second child?' He nodded sadly and indicated a carefully wrapped bundle on the bench. The Queen walked over and pulled the corner of the blanket back. A small pale face was uncovered; he looked as if he were asleep, not stillborn. She looked at the young man. 'Thank you, but now you must go; you have done your part, and no-one must ever know,' she said. He bowed, and the three of them disappeared out into the night, taking the child of Constance and Morvan with them.

Chatillon had purposefully distanced himself from Morvan. He knew without a doubt that it was Morvan at the Abbey; he had undoubtedly followed his servant, but why? What game was this young Horse Warrior playing, and for whom? He had plans for Morvan; he was about to become very useful to him, and he did not want anything to put that at risk. Therefore, he waited several days back at Gerberoi before he approached him.

Morvan was dicing with the young men one evening when Chatillon arrived and stood beside him watching the game. Glancing up, the Horse Warrior became increasingly uncomfortable, as if he could feel Chatillon's eyes burning into him. He had always had an arm's length but good relationship with the papal envoy. He would have likened it as to how a rabbit watches a snake, warily, but always giving itself time to outrun it.

'I want you to accompany me to a nearby Abbey tomorrow, Morvan de la Malvais; I hear you have a particular interest in them at the moment. At this one, you may learn something to your interest,' Chatillon said smoothly and softly into his left ear. Morvan had only just stopped himself from flinching as he felt the man's proximity.

He did not reply at first but mulled over his options. Chatillon was a famed assassin; if he had wanted to, this man could kill him anywhere. Morvan had to admit his interest was piqued; what would he learn? He threw several more dice before he replied.

'I am training the men for two hours in the morning, but I can make myself free from noon,' he said. Chatillon smiled and turned away.

They spent over an hour at the Abbey. Morvan heard nothing of the slightest interest, and so they set off back to Gerberoi with a brooding Morvan wondering what this was about and if indeed, he had men waiting en-route to dispose of him. He was even more alarmed when Chatillon took a narrow foresters' track to the left.

As Morvan reluctantly followed, he shouted to Chatillon, 'Where are we going?'

Chatillon turned in the saddle and looked at him, then smiled. 'Be patient, my friend; all will be revealed.' Shortly afterwards, the track came out at a small but beautiful lake. 'I come here when I want to think and get away from the noise and pell-mell atmosphere of the castle,' he said as he dismounted and invited Morvan to do the same. They knotted the reins to let the horses graze, and Chatillon invited Morvan to sit down on a large log. For a while, they gazed out across the water; there was an abundance of wildfowl.

Chatillon had struggled for some time with what he would tell Morvan about his child. Should he let him believe that his son had been killed as they had promised? Would that not be for the best? Alternatively, would it be better to tell him that he had, in fact, put the wheels in motion to save the child? That he had arranged for it to be delivered to a Knight's family to raise. It was the news of Morvan's visit to the Abbey of Saint-Germain-des Pres that decided him to choose the latter as it would give him a hold over Morvan and the Horse Warrior would be indebted to him for saving the life of his son.

'Robert returns to Caen in a week to make his peace with his father. What are your plans, Morvan? Will you go with him, bend the knee to the King but stay in Robert's entourage? I have also heard you talk about selling your sword to the highest bidder in the wasp's nest that is southern Italy.'

Morvan stood and picked up a handful of stones from the

pebble beach. He skimmed them across the water before replying. 'I have pledged my allegiance to Robert. I doubt the King will be pleased as I was his man; he now sees me as a rebel, but I will also return to Caen. King William will no doubt decide all of our fates. If he has found out the reason why Constance is at Falaise, I may be riding to my death,' he said, running a hand through his long hair.

'He does not know yet and hopefully will never find out. The child was born a week ago,' Chatillon said in a soft voice.

Morvan stopped what he was doing and looked at him. 'It must have been born a few weeks early; what was it? He whispered.

Chatillon's eyes did not waver as he stared directly at Morvan. 'It was a boy,' he said. Morvan could not breathe; a weight seemed to be pressing on his chest. He dropped to his knees and finally managed to drag in several ragged breaths, the last one of which ended on a broken sob. He stayed there, his hands covering his face for some time. Chatillon did not say a word.

'So he came into this world. Did Constance hold him? Did he have any comfort before they killed him? He asked in an anguished voice.

Looking into Morvan's eyes and seeing the pain there, Chatillon suddenly found that he was more affected than he thought he would be. Unexpectedly, something in this young warrior had struck a chord with him from that moment in the alleyway in Ghent when Morvan had calmly handed him his own dagger back. He found he had to look away before he answered.

'He is not dead Morvan, he lives. I arranged with the Queen and your brother for him to be taken away. They swapped him for a newly stillborn child, and they stole him away in the night. He will be brought up in the family of a good Knight that the

Queen found, far away from Brittany.'

Morvan looked at him in disbelief. Chatillon watched as a gamut of emotions raced across his face, joy, hope and despair followed by sadness that he would never see his son. He pushed himself to his feet and, stepping forward; he pulled Chatillon up into a bear hug. He then held him at arm's length, and searching his face, he asked, 'Is he healthy and whole? And Constance? Is she safe and well?'

'I believe so,' replied Chatillon.

Morvan nodded. 'Thank you,' he whispered. 'I thank you, Chatillon, from the bottom of my heart; I am in your debt.' Chatillon smiled; that was just where he wanted him. Then a thought occurred to Morvan. 'But why did you do it?' he asked in a puzzled voice.

'I have asked myself that repeatedly young Horse Warrior,' he laughed. 'Despite the way you constantly meddle in my plans and cause me endless problems, I like you for some reason. At times, I see a younger me when I look at you. You are intelligent and charming, but you have proved you can be ruthless and unforgiving when you need to be. I know what really happened to Belleme on the battlefield, but I think you have a great deal of potential. You can become someone like me, someone of importance in the courts of Europe if you wish.' He finished and stood, hands-on-hips, head on one side, regarding the young Breton.

Morvan gazed at him in astonishment and then burst out laughing. 'I do not think I am a diplomat or a spy Chatillon, although I could probably be an assassin with practice.'

Chatillon gave a thin smile. 'Just think on it that is all I ask. You could become my apprentice, and I could make you very wealthy. Together we could be unstoppable,' he laughed. It was meant as a joke, but as Morvan watched him mount, he knew that Chatillon was deadly serious.

Chatillon gathered up his reins and brought his horse closer. By the way, your Warrior Monks were sent and paid for by the Seigneur Robert De Belleme. He used my name to invoke their attack, describing your attack on me and implying that you were a threat to both my mission and me. Morvan met Chatillon's gaze and gave a curt nod of thanks, as he cantered after the Papal envoy suddenly he felt no remorse at all for what he had done to Belleme.

Chapter Thirty-Four

Constance stared at but did not really see Monseigneur Gironde as he explained to her and her mother the hand-fasting cere-mony condoned by the church. It had been three weeks since the birth of her child, and Constance still felt the sharp pain of her loss. She found herself automatically going through the daily tasks with her mother and the Castellan: morning and evening prayers, household tasks, needlework, walks to the herb garden, menus for the dinners, preparations for the arrival of Alan Fergant and his party. She moved, spoke but was not engaged, and her mother, who had rarely left her side, cast a worried eye over her. Although she had physically recovered quickly from the birth, being young, fit and healthy, walking each day to get her strength up, Matilda thought she still looked pale and wan, and her eyes were in a faraway place.

For Constance, this morning was different though; her mother had come early to help her maid dress her in her finery, arranging her hair and pinching her cheeks to bring some colour to them. She sat Constance down, and taking her hands, she talked at length about her expectation that Constance would be a dutiful daughter. Alan Fergant would be arriving with his entourage and Monseigneur Gironde today, and Constance must be pleasant to them. Matilda had then left Constance sitting in the chapel with her maidservant while she went to have a whispered conversation with Gironde.

'She must never know that the child is alive, for if Alan Fergant found out, it would be the undoing of us all,' she said.

Gironde bowed his head in acquiescence. 'I ensured that the new squire Alan Fergant put in place in Falaise was in the party that took the child to the hillside in the woods. He was also there the following day when they checked the child was dead and buried it. He was white-faced when he returned, but I know he sent a pigeon back to Brittany.'

The Queen thanked him and led him back into the chapel.

Moments later, Alan Fergant strode in with several of his Knights behind him. He bowed and greeted the Queen, and then he turned to Constance and, taking her hand, kissed it. 'You look more beautiful than ever, Constance; your stay in Falaise away from the hustle and bustle of Caen has obviously suited you. I must arrange for you to stay here longer.' Constance looked at him in a startled way as if she had just realised what was happening. He seemed such a huge, vibrant presence in the small chapel, this man she was to marry in the next year or two. She was now resigned to her fate; maybe the pain of losing Morvan and his child will have lessened by then. She fixed a smile on her face as he led her to the front of the chapel.

Alan noticed with pleasure that some of his Knights smacked their lips in appreciation of his future wife. Her shining, deep-auburn hair was braided in a band across her head, but the rest flowed down her back in waves. Her tall figure had filled out with the pregnancy, and to Alan, she looked beautiful, curvaceous and very desirable.

Pregnancy had obviously suited her; he thought with a quick flash of anger that he quickly subdued. He wanted her, no matter what had gone before; he intended to have her, and she would now bear his children. They stood in front of the Monseigneur as he intoned the words in Latin. He then motioned for them to come forward, and placed her small hand in Alan's large one. He gripped it tightly, making Constance look up at him in surprise again. Gironde removed the embroidered tasselled stole from around his neck and wrapped it repeatedly around the hands and wrists of the couple, binding them tightly. He followed this with more prayers and then sprinkled their bound hands with holy water, bowing and making the sign of the cross over them. Finally, he held his hands up to God and announced that Alan Fergant of Brittany and Constance of Normandy were now handfasted with the blessing of the Holy See.

At that, Alan pulled Constance close to him and kissed her, a deep kiss as she tried to pull away. A cheer broke out from the Knights behind as Alan finally released her and turned and grinned at his followers.

Constance had been surprised at the ceremony and response of his Knights in the chapel. Surely, this was just an affirmation and blessing by the church on their betrothal; Fergant and his followers were clearly more pleased than she expected with the alliance. She had thought before that her father's need for this alliance was greater. He would be pleased to know this, and she was sure her mother would tell him. For Constance, the long celebratory meal in the Great Hall that night was interminable.

Matilda had invited several Norman Knights as well. She wanted as many witnesses as possible to this event; it would not be a hole-in-the-corner affair. So over fifty had sat down to the laden tables on the dais above the crowded Hall. There were many toasts and lewd comments and jokes about the couple, and Alan grinned and took it all in good heart.

When it became very late, Matilda rose to retire and gestured to Constance to join her. However, Alan grasped her hand and pulled Constance down onto his lap, where he kissed her soundly and squeezed her breast. 'I will see you soon,' he said. Dismayed by his kiss and caress, she nodded dumbly and hurried after her mother.

Once in her room, Matilda saw the panicked white face. 'Constance, you are the daughter of a King and Queen; pull yourself together and act as we expect. Think of your father. We have managed to keep your sin hidden. I love you dearly, but it is now time for you to atone for that sin and do your duty,' she said firmly. 'The church has handfasted you; this rarely happens and needs a papal dispensation which Alan obtained. You are now his wife in every way but name, and shortly he will arrive through that door expecting you to behave like a wife. Do not disappoint us,' she said as she turned and left her quietly, closing the door.

Constance sat on the edge of the bed in a state of shock; how had she not realised what was happening? She stared wildly around the room as if in search of escape. For a second, she thought of barring the door but noticed that the drawbar seemed to have been removed. Then she heard laughter and loud voices, and the door was flung open. Alan Fergant stood there, his Knights crowded around the doorway behind him.

He was a young, tall and attractive man with an imposing physique, and she felt a wave of panic as he firmly closed the door on his laughing friends and came towards her, unbuckling his sword belt and hanging it on a chair. 'At last, we are alone; I have waited a long time for this moment, a long time for you,' he said, pulling his tunic over his head.

Constance watched him wide-eyed, her hands gripping the edge of the bed. 'No, this cannot be; you would not want me if you knew the truth,' she gasped desperately. Alan laughed as he undid the laces of his chausses, carefully removing each one and laying them on top of the nearby chest but never taking his eyes off her until he was standing in just a pair of fine, thin, linen braies. She could see that he was fully aroused.

'Ah, but I do know Constance. Like your father, I make it my business to know everything. I know all about you and that damned Horse Warrior. I know he swived you repeatedly. I know about the child you bore. However, for the Queen's sake, I have agreed not to tell your father or to kill Morvan de Malvais, and you are my reward for my silence. You are mine,' he said, staring down at her with an angry intensity that produced a flutter of fear in her stomach, but she also now knew that she had no choice.

She was white with shock; her mouth had dropped open as she looked up at him towering over her, and she realised what he knew. He pulled her firmly to her feet and began unlacing her gown. 'Now, you are my wife, and you will do what I say. I will be here at Falaise to enjoy your company for several days or even weeks, every month until our marriage takes place. Gironde assures me that any children will be recognised as legitimate by the church,' he said as he became impatient with the lacing on the back of the gown and ripped it open so that it dropped to her waist.

He suddenly lifted her back onto the bed and, pulling her gown up to her waist; he undid and dropped his braies. Spreading her legs, he stood and gazed down at her, his face a mask of lust. Constance closed her eyes, not believing at first that this was happening to her. She felt his hands running up the inside of her thighs; then he knelt between her legs, his large muscled thighs pushing her legs wider apart. As his mouth and teeth descended onto her breasts, his hands firmly kneading and gripping them, she shuddered at first, but she forced herself to suppress it; she now had to accept that this man was her husband. She knew that this had always been her destiny as the daughter of King William, she would just find a way to live with it, and she forced herself to weakly smile up at him and rest her hands on his muscled arms.

As she lay there, she knew that she was obeying her parents, and more importantly, she was saving Morvan from being killed. Alan Fergant would be here every month in the future at Falaise until she went permanently to his bed when he was acclaimed Duke in a year or so. They would then have a full marriage ceremony in the cathedral in Rennes, and she would become Constance Duchess of Brittany as her father wished. The alliance would be safe.

'Let us see if a Duke of Brittany can do better than a lowly Horse Warrior, shall we?' he muttered as he thrust himself into her. Before too long, he had finished, and he lay heavily on top of her. The tears ran silently down her face as she turned her head to one side and thought of Morvan. She would never forget him; he was and would always be the only man she would ever love. He was her first and last love. She vowed then never to bear Alan Fergant's children; there were ways to prevent it, and she would find them.

Chapter Thirty-Five

Robert and his followers returned to Caen at the end of August. They knelt for pardon as expected in front of the King, and overall, he granted them the return of their lands. However, as they got to their feet, he turned back and added that if any of them ever rebelled against him again, he would take their lands permanently, hunt them down and maim them. It was a subdued group of Knights who gathered in the Great Hall that night. Despite his stern demeanour, William was pleased to see his eldest son and the young cadet sons back at court.

Morvan had dropped back into his place with the Horse Warriors, and his men who had stayed behind were overjoyed to see him despite the strict training routines he threw them back into immediately. With the addition of the troop he had trained at Thymerais and then Gerberoi, he now had a contingent of nearly a hundred; he determined to spend the next six months finding the best warhorses he could for them. However, he noticed that William no longer came down to watch them train. The King may have been pleased with the information Morvan sent from Thymerais, but he had yet to forgive Morvan's change of allegiance to Robert.

Morvan struggled with the thought of sharing his recent information from the Abbey in Paris with the King. What he had heard was a threat to both Robert, who yet again would be manipulated, and more directly to William himself. However, his anger at William for forcing Constance into marriage with Alan Fergant still burned bright, so he waited, although he had yet again warned Robert Curthose that there were plans still afoot from the Vatican and Philip of France.

'There will always be intrigue between the Church and Kings. Do not worry, Morvan, I will be vigilant,' he replied, shrugging. Robert was enjoying the carefree life of being back at court, and of course, his mother was delighted.

In early September, Robert was standing at the paddock fence watching the Horse Warriors carry out complicated echelon manoeuvres on each other; he was a common sight there and often joined in to keep in shape. However, Morvan, who now knew him well, saw that he had news to impart today.

'I will be taking twenty of your men for a few days,' he said.

Morvan raised his eyebrows. 'May I ask for what purpose?

Robert did not answer for a few moments. 'I go to see my sister Constance in Falaise; it is less than a day's ride. I know that you loved her, so I am not asking you to accompany me. My mother tells me that Alan Fergant is there for almost a full two weeks each month since they were handfasted. Mother tells me they are happy, and they will no doubt have children soon, and I need to build a friendship with him. When I succeed as Duke of Normandy, he will be one of my main allies.'

Morvan turned stone cold. He automatically nodded and assured Robert that he would sort out the men for him. He turned away, his stomach in knots, he found that part of him was pleased that she had moved on and found some happiness, but part of him was torn by a dreadful sense of loss for what they had.

A week later, a ship arrived in Caen from London with a message from William Rufus. Malcolm, the King of Scotland, had taken advantage of William's defeat in France. From mid-August, he crossed the border and ravaged the north of England from the Tweed to the Tees. These were severe and brutal raids that had given him significant hoards of plunder which he had taken back across the border.

William was frustrated, with the situation still so unsettled in Normandy he did not feel as if he could leave to return to England. Malcolm had broken the treaty of Abernathy signed in 1072 when Malcolm had paid homage to William and had acknowledged him as his feudal overlord; he even gave him his son Duncan as a hostage. There was no doubt that Malcolm had to be punished for these raids, and plans were made for Robert to put together a force for the following year to sail to northern England.

Morvan decided to go with Robert; Constance was now beyond his reach, gone forever to another man. He had never been to England, and, as he was banished from Brittany and his home in Morlaix, there was nothing to keep him here. However, having thought long and hard on his information from the Abbey in Paris, he decided first to go and see the King.

William was surprised to get a request from Morvan; he was aware that the young Horse Warrior had kept out of his way, and he had to admit he was still angry and piqued that he had gone with Robert to Gerberoi. He also knew that it was Morvan's strategy that had dismayed and defeated his forces. While he admired the moves he made, William also remembered that Morvan had stopped Robert from striking him down in the heat of battle, so he agreed to see him.

The first thing William noticed was that the young man in

front of him had changed. He was harder, leaner, he looked older, and there were the marks of suffering on his face. Luc De Malvais was fearsome and ruthless; Morvan had always been a softer version of him, still as lethal in battle and with a sword but without that cold killing instinct that made Luc so feared. Now, looking at the young warrior in front of him, he could see far more of his older brother in him. William wondered if the rift in his family had been the cause of this. 'You wished to speak with me? He asked.

William's eyebrows were raised and leaving his chair, he walked over to the window. Morvan stepped forward and related what had happened when he went to the Abbey Saint-Germain-des Pres. He related the conversation he had over-heard between Odo the Cardinal and Prior of Cluny and a man called Dauferio. 'Tell me, Morvan, why did you risk your life to follow Chatillon's servant and go to the Abbey?

Morvan stared at the floor for a few moments before he replied. 'I have pledged to protect Robert, and I do not think that they have his interests at heart for all of their bluster and praise.'

William nodded. 'My son is fortunate to have you by his side; the same way I was when I had Toki of Wigod by my side. Also, I need to thank you for your timely intervention on the battlefield; if it had not been for you and Toki that day, I might not have been here now,' he said, piercing Morvan with his hawk-like gaze. 'Leave the matter in my hands; I will deal with the Pope and Philip of France. I hear you are thinking of taking the Horse Warriors to Scotland.'

Morvan nodded.

'Good, you have my blessing to do so, we need to teach King Malcolm a lesson,' he said as he dismissed him.

As he reached the doorway, Morvan turned. 'Sire, who is Dauferio?'

William took a while to reply as he gathered his thoughts. 'He is a man with fingers in many pies. He has held many positions of power; he was the Abbot of Montecassino, the Pope's legate to Constantinople. At present, he is the Cardinal of Santa Cecillia in Castile-Leon in Spain. Some say that Odo of Cluny, Chatillon's uncle, will be the next Pope when Gregory dies, but I would lay a fortune that it will be Dauferio; he has more influence and power. A dangerous man Morvan, you did well to get out of there with your life, and if you heed my advice, I would watch my back and tread carefully for some time.'

Morvan inclined his head, and, going out, closed the door behind him and stood for a few seconds. Yes, what he had done was dangerous, but he had to admit that he enjoyed the adrenalin and he found he needed that in his life now.

He thought of Chatillon's offer. Did he want to work for this master spy and assassin? He decided to mull it over; he had time to think over the following months of training ahead in preparation for the Horse Warriors to go to Scotland and the wild northern borders of England.

Epilogue

In Morlaix, Gerard and Luc were training the young horses on lunge reins when Merewyn came out to join them in the early autumn sunshine, bringing a servant carrying two jugs of cold cider from the cellars. Luc smiled at his beautiful wife as she came over to him. He reached out, put an arm around her and pulled back a fold of linen to reveal the child nestling quietly in her arms.

The little boy with the dark shock of hair and wide blue eyes was the image of Morvan. They had called him Conn, a good Breton name for a boy. Luc knew that the servants thought the child was one of his by-blows, and for a while, Merewyn had received sympathetic and understanding looks that had amused her. However, they both knew that they would have to keep the truth of his birth a secret while William lived, and even then, Constance and Alan Fergant must never know. Even Queen Matilda and Monseigneur Gironde did not know that he had brought the boy back to Morlaix, back to his rightful home. They both thought that the child had been sent to the Vexin. Luc had sent a message to the Knight's family to say that the child had unfortunately died shortly after birth.

Merewyn smiled as young Conn opened his eyes, regarded

them solemnly for a moment or two and then smiled and waved his hands, trying to grasp her finger. As an honorary grandfather, Gerard had immediately walked over to see him, smiled down, and had taken his little hand.

He turned to Luc, 'You will have to tell him some time; you cannot keep this from him. It is his right to know that his son is alive and safe with his family.'

Luc shrugged at first, but then, under Gerard's stern gaze, he inclined his head, but his lips were set in a thin stubborn line that Gerard recognised so well.

'Yes, but not for some time. We will wait. It is far too dangerous at present for all of us involved in this; we have too much to lose. Also, I believe that Morvan will still be far too emotional over the loss of Constance. I will tell him one day, Gerard, I promise. One day...'

Glossary

Angevin – Soldiers, cavalry or citizens from the province of Anjou.

Bailey - A ward or courtyard in a castle, some outer Baileys could be huge, encompassing grazing land.

Braies - A type of trouser often used as an undergarment, often to mid-calf and made of light or heavier linen.

Cadet son – A cadet son is a younger son, not the heir, usually in the nobility.

Castellan – The Governor of a castle, sometimes called a Pincenar.

Chausses – Attached by laces to the waist of the braies, these were tighter fitting coverings for the legs.

Coif – A chain mail hood and collar.

Dais – A raised platform in a hall for a throne or tables.

Destrier – A Knight's large warhorse, often trained to fight, bite and strike out.

Donjon – The fortified tower of an early castle later called the Keep.

Doublet – A close-fitting jacket or jerkin often made from leather, with or without sleeves. Laced at the front and worn either under or over, a chain mail hauberk.

Escalade - The art of scaling walls with ladders during a siege.

285

'Give No Quarter' – To give no mercy or show no clemency for the vanquished.

Hand-fasting – A legally binding ceremony for a couple, it could replace marriage.

Hauberk – A tunic of chain mail, often reaching to mid-thigh.

Holy See – The jurisdiction of the Bishop of Rome – the Pope.

Investment - Surrounding and preventing entry or escape during a siege.

Liege lord – A feudal lord such as a Count or Baron entitled to allegiance and service from his Knights.

Monseigneur – A title and honorific in the Catholic Church.

Motte – An earth mound, forming a secure platform on which a Donjon would be built; initially, this would be made of wood until the earth settled and compacted.

Patron – An individual who gives financial, political, or social patronage to others. Often through wealth or influence in return for loyalty and homage.

Pell – Stout wooden post for sword practice.

Pell-Mell – Confused or disorganised action, often in street riots or battles.

Pottage – A staple of the medieval diet, a thick soup made by boiling grains and vegetables and, if available, meat or fish.

Prie-Dieu - A type of prayer desk to kneel on for private use.

Quarrel – A large, often square-headed bolt for a crossbow.

Retainer – A dependent or follower often rewarded or paid for their services.

Rout - Disorderly withdrawal from a battle.

Seneschal – The senior position or principal administrator of the royal household.

Serjeant – The soldier Serjeant was a man who often came from a higher class; most experienced medieval mercenaries fell into this class; they were deemed to be 'half of the value of a Knight' in military terms.

Vedette - An outrider or scout used by cavalry.

Vellum - Finest scraped and treated calfskin, used for writing messages.

Author's Note

William of Normandy spent almost all of his life involved in warfare of one kind or another. The battles became more defensive as he became older, and formidable alliances were built against him in Europe. He faced some of his biggest challenges in the late 1070s and 1080s, rebellions in England, Scotland and attacks on his borders in Brittany and Normandy. He suffered two significant military defeats during this time—one at Dol in 1076 when the arrival of King Philip of France routed his army. The second one was even more humiliating and damaged his prestige at home and abroad when he was defeated at the siege of Gerberoi and wounded by his son Robert who had rebelled against him. Again, the hand of King Philip can be seen here as he sent a significant force to support and encourage Robert.

William is a fascinating man. There is no doubt that he loved his wife Matilda dearly; he was devastated by her death in 1083. However, his relationship with his eldest son, Robert Curthose, was a troubled one. The incident with the chamber pot at L'aigle is well-documented, and Robert then went on to rebel using various bases on the borders. He did go to his uncle's Robert's court at Ghent in Flanders and then to the court of King Philip of France for support. This was quite shocking as these were his father's sworn enemies, this move was seen as a significant betrayal.

The Anglo-Norman noble cadet sons got off lightly, considering they rebelled and supported Robert against William and their own fathers. Still, one of them was killed in the retreat from Remalard.

On an interesting note, Hugh d'Airelle, who with his son claimed their land was stolen when the cathedral of St Etienne was built in Caen, reappeared again. He interrupted King William's funeral in 1085 and refused to let the ceremony and burial go ahead until he received compensation for his lost land. Unfortunately, there is no record of whether he received any.

Robert de Belleme, the son of Roger of Montgomery, the powerful Earl of Shrewsbury, was reportedly just as cruel, vindictive and sadistic as I have made his character here. His mother, Mabel de Belleme, was far more notorious, and several books have been written about her skill as a poisoner and her gruesome death.

Toki of Wigod was a faithful young Saxon retainer of William. He did rescue the King by giving him his horse in the battle for Gerberoi, and he was killed by a crossbow bolt shortly afterwards...

Constance was Matilda's favourite daughter and was kept at court for far longer than expected for a King's daughter. She was betrothed and then married to Alan Fergant. Some sources from the period suggest that it was not a happy marriage, and there were no children. She died in 1090, and the gifted 12th century historian William of Malmesbury alleges that Alan Fergant had her poisoned by her servants because she was barren. She was only thirty-three years old.

Malcolm of Scotland did take advantage of William's preoccupation with events in Normandy, and Robert Curthose, having reconciled with his father, was sent with a force in the autumn of 1080 to defeat him. During this foray, Robert Curthose built a defensive castle on the River Tyne at a place, which is now called Newcastle.

But… that is the next story… in Book Four of the Breton Horse Warriors series.

Read More

The Breton Horse Warrior Series
Book One – **Ravensworth**
Book Two – **Rebellion**
Book Three – **Betrayal**
Book Four – **Banished**

The fourth book in the Breton Horse Warrior Series, 'Banished', tells the story of Morvan De Malvais, a leader of the Breton Horse Warriors in Normandy. He has lost Constance, the young daughter of King William and the love of his life. Their child has been taken away in secret by the Queen and his brother Luc De Malvais to be raised by others. He has been banished from his home and estates in Brittany by Alan Fergant, the heir to the Duke of Brittany, who has married Constance against her will, and Morvan sees very little now to keep him in Normandy.

King William's eldest son, Robert Curthose, is taking an expedition to attack and punish King Malcolm of Scotland for his recent savage raids across the border into Northumberland. Morvan decides to take his Horse Warriors and go with him; he wants to carve a new life for himself away from the torment and loss he has experienced in the last year. However, two people have other plans for him.

Minette, the young daughter of a powerful nobleman, Gervais de la Ferte at King Philip's court in Paris, has fallen in love with Morvan and intends to win his heart. She is willing to use her influence to bring him back to Paris.

Piers De Chatillon, papal envoy, spy and assassin, wants Morvan to join his web of spies and work for him; he has valuable knowledge that could put Morvan's child in danger. Chatillon is an arch manipulator and usually gets what he wants by fair means or foul, leaving a trail of bodies in his wake in the process. **Read the First Chapter on the next page...**

Banished

Normandy at the mouth of the River Orne – early autumn 1080

Morvan was supervising the loading of the big warhorses into the wide-bellied ships for the third time, and tempers were becoming frayed. He had been here for the best part of a week, back and forwards from Caen to the mouth of the River Orne where new wooden quays had been constructed over the last year. The campaign they were about to embark on had been in the planning for six months, and now it was finally happening. Suddenly there was a crashing and squealing from below as one of the stallions objected loudly and violently to the proximity of other horses. Two of the new light wooden partitions had been kicked to smithereens already. They had been taking the horses on and off the boat for two days, feeding them on board on purpose, calming them and getting them used to their new surroundings.

'God's bones, what are you doing down there? I told you to keep his eyes covered,' Morvan shouted, running his hands through his shoulder-length dark hair in frustration.

These horses were not the usual mounts; they were primarily

huge war Destriers trained for battle; Morvan had scoured the countryside to find many of them in the past year. So much time and effort had gone into training each horse that they could not afford to lose one due to the carelessness of a stable boy or squire.

Eventually, all twenty were loaded on each of the boats. They had rigged large canvas covers over the decks, which were lashed to the gunwales. This would provide both protection from sudden squalls and keep the horses calm on the long voyage. They were heading north shortly, clinging to the coast and sailing up to Ghent in Flanders, where they would disembark for several days. Then, waiting for and following favourable winds, they would sail across the North Sea to the vast estuary of the River Humber in Northern England. They were going to war, this time against the Scots.

King Malcolm had been raiding across the border into Northumberland for years, but now he had broken the Treaty of Abernathy where he had sworn to pay homage to King William of England. William, who was still occupied with events in Normandy, decided to send his son, Robert Curthose, to the borders with a large force to deal with the problem. They were to cross the border and subdue the Scots. Robert, only recently reconciled with his father William had agreed to the task with enthusiasm and immediately requested that Morvan accompany him, with his eighty strong cohort of Horse Warriors.

Morvan de Malvais stood on the raised foredeck of one of the horse transports in the early autumn sunshine. He was a tall, good-looking man with deep brown eyes dotted with gold flecks. He had the well-muscled but lithe physique of a Horse Warrior. His signature laced leather jerkin and crossed swords on his back declared his trade. Although he was a Breton, he loved this time of year in Normandy, the giant oak trees with their leaves just beginning to change, the abundant apple crop ready to be turned into cider or brandy. He gazed out over the lush meadows and then turned back to the task in hand.

Morvan was respected, not only as a leader and fearsome swordsman but also as a clever strategic commander in battle. He had proved himself repeatedly to his liege lord Robert Curthose. He had to admit that, for the first time in over a year, he felt exhilarated by the coming expedition and excited at the thought of taking his men into battle. He wanted to leave behind the tragic events of the last eighteen months. He had lost the love of his life, Constance, the daughter of King William and Queen Matilda. She had been handfasted to Alan Fergant, the heir to the Dukedom of Brittany.

When he thought of Constance, the pain of how they had loved and lost each other was unbearable at times, but he knew he had to forget her; she was another man's wife. Their forbidden liaison had produced a child. This boy had escaped a death sentence and had been taken far away to be brought up in another Knight's family.

Morvan was estranged from his own family, something that was unthinkable as they had been so close. His older brother, Luc De Malvais, could not forgive him for his foolishness in lying with Constance and getting her with child. He could not forgive Luc for taking Constance back to the Queen and into a marriage she did not want. Morvan had ended up fighting his brother on the road at Thymerais, and had lost. In retaliation he joined the rebels led by William's eldest son Robert Curthose against the King. This was the final straw for Luc, whose family motto was duty and loyalty, and he banished Morvan from the family home at Morlaix in Brittany.

Through the papal envoy, Chatillon, Alan Fergant found out about the child and ordered it to be killed as soon as it was born. He also put a price on Morvan's head and banished him from returning to Brittany. Therefore, although the thought of leaving these western lands was bittersweet, this expedition was a new beginning for him.

A cloud of dust in the distance told him that Robert was on his way for his usual daily visit and inspection. There were over twenty boats now tied up at the quays that were full of weapons and supplies. As the group galloped nearer, Morvan could see by the pennants flying that King William was accompanying his son. The large group of horsemen pulled up further down the quays. The King and his son dismounted, and Morvan saw they were now in deep conversation with the two quartermasters in charge of victualling the hundreds of men and horses on the voyage. He walked down the quays to join them, and Robert greeted him with a grin gripping his arm in a warriors clasp. The King turned his hawk-like gaze on Morvan.

'How are the horses?' He asked; the King always had a keen interest in horses, especially Destriers.

'We have eighty-five mounts boarded and settled without them killing each other,' he answered with a wry smile.

King William snorted in amusement; he knew just what it was like to have so many ungelded stallions in close proximity on a crowded ship.

'We are just about to feed them on board, and then we will lead them off back into the meadows for a run. We will reload them at dawn ready to sail tomorrow on the early morning tide,' Morvan finished.

William looked at the Horse Warrior in front of him; he knew he was about thirty years old, a year or so older than his son Robert. Although Morvan had moved his allegiance to his son, William respected Morvan; he had a lot to be grateful for from this Breton. This young man had saved his life twice. Once by whisking him away to safety from a French army at Dol and then at the siege of Gerberoi. Robert had almost killed him, not realising that it was his father he was fighting, but Morvan had recognised him and stepped in to stop it.

'Well, God speed to you both tomorrow, I expect you to show that Scots renegade, King Malcolm, that he cannot treat us with impunity. Now, Robert, show me this change you have made to put more sail on these wallowing pig-like boats,' he said as he stomped off further down the quays where a dozen ships were moored at the furthest part of the river mouth.

Morvan smiled; Robert Curthose often had a burst of enthusiasm for new or different ideas, some of which were disastrous. Now he had spent days with an Italian master mariner who swore he knew how to double the speed of these boats; William was always interested in new ideas.

The many Knights and courtiers who had accompanied the King had dismounted and were milling around the quayside and ships. However, Morvan noticed one man who was still mounted on a large horse that was cropping the grass. Morvan was facing into the western sun, and so he shaded his eyes. With a jolt, he recognised the horse; most Knights in Western Europe would recognise that horse and its tall rider with his dark shock of hair and signature crossed swords on his back. The horse was Espirit Noir, a huge, steel dappled war Destrier lethal in battle. Sitting calmly on his back, staring across at him was his brother Luc De Malvais. They had not seen each other for two years since they had fought on the road at Thymerais, and Luc had defeated him.

Morvan stood rooted to the ground as they stared at each other, and then Luc gathered up the reins and walked the big horse towards him. Espirit recognised Morvan immediately and playfully head butted him so that Morvan, shaken out of his shock, stroked the long noble nose. Then Luc spoke, 'I was in Caen, and I heard you had joined the force leaving for Scotland.' Morvan nodded but did not reply. 'As we never know what the Gods or fates have in store for us, I thought it best to bid you farewell as you may not return.'

Morvan weighed up his brother's words, it was not so much an olive branch as an olive leaf, and he considered whether to respond or whether he wanted to accept it. Then he remembered the words of the papal envoy, Chatillon that Luc had helped save his newly born son from death when Alan Fergant insisted on having him killed. 'I have little choice but to go, Luc, I need to get away from Normandy, and I am unable to return to Brittany. Luc acknowledged this with a slight tilt of his head. 'You seem to have made your peace with the King after the rebellion, and you have carved a name for yourself after your successful strategy at Gerberoi, Gerard talks of little else.' He said with a sad smile.

There followed a silence for some time as each man was deep in their own thoughts. Things had been said between them on that day in Thymerais, which were difficult to take back. As Morvan struggled with what to say, he finally burst out, 'You know I can never forgive you for taking Constance and my unborn child away.'

Luc nodded. 'I hope that one day you will see that it was the only option to save both of your lives.' Morvan snorted with derision and then took a deep breath. 'I was told that you helped to save my son; Alan Fergant was about to expose him on the hillside.'

At that moment, Luc decided to tell Morvan the truth about that night; he could see that Morvan had changed. What he had been through, the battles, the sadness and grief at losing the woman he loved and their child all had left their mark on him. He seemed older, more responsible, less emotional and hotheaded.

'There is one thing you need to know, I was not going to tell you, but now I think you have the right to know.' Morvan watched Luc apprehensively as he dismounted. He came and stood in front of him and told him the events of that night, how they swapped his son with a stillborn child to trick Alan Fergant while they whisked Morvan's child to safety. Luc then gripped hold of Morvan's upper arms.

'Your son is not far north in the Vexin in some strange Knight's family. He is at Morlaix with his family, his cousins, his grandmother, where he should be. He is now fourteen months old, is walking, almost running, his name is Conn, and he is the image of you.'

Morvan's mouth dropped open. He looked at Luc in amazement; he shook his head as shock and then joy was reflected in his face. Then he pulled Luc into his arms and hugged him, tears streaming down his face. Luc held his breath, hoping against hope that this may go some way to healing the rift between them. He pushed Morvan away to hold him at arm's length. 'Listen to me, this is important; no one must ever know that he is alive, certainly not while King William and Queen Matilda are alive. If Alan Fergant ever finds out, as Duke of Brittany, he may turn on us at Morlaix and still have the child killed. Not even the people who were there that night, Queen Matilda or your devious friend Chatillon know that the child did not go far away as intended to the Knight's family in the Vexin. You can never risk telling anyone, Morvan, do you understand me?' Luc could see the deepening frown on Morvan's brow, and then to his relief, he nodded and raised his eyes to Luc. 'Can I come and see him?' he said in a whisper.

'You are welcome home in Morlaix again; in these troubled times, we are stronger together no matter our differences,' he said.

Morvan let out a breath in relief; the split with his family and home had been heart breaking.

'However, Alan Fergant is not so forgiving; he has let it be known that he has banished you from Brittany and put a price on your head. He has done this privately; he could not do so publicly, or he would give away his wife's perfidy and dishonour his name and hers, and of course, the truth has to be kept from William.' Luc saw Morvan wince at what he was telling him and clench his fists.

'Listen to me, Morvan. I will ensure that your estates at Vannes are well managed and that you receive the revenue. Beorn and a hundred of the Horse Warriors are still based there; he is a good and competent man. Those estates will become Conn's inheritance if you never return. I suggest you come to Morlaix on your return from Scotland but sail directly into the harbour below the castle and make sure you are not seen. Some people in the port are in the pay of Alan Fergant. He is a highly intelligent man who is fast gaining a reputation as a warrior; do not underestimate him. He is not called 'Iron Glove' for nothing. I am told that he is obsessed with Constance, and he will kill you for what you have done to her.'

Morvan nodded in understanding while his heart was filled

with joy at the thought of his son, who would be able to take the Malvais name. Suddenly, a thought occurred to him. 'Where do our people at Morlaix think the boy came from?' He asked in a perplexed voice. Luc gave a wry smile. 'They think he is one of my by-blows; it has done my reputation no end of harm with the women on the estates who all love Merewyn.'

Morvan gave a sad smile, 'so he calls you papa then?' Luc nodded. 'For the present only, he will be told when he is old enough to understand. The good thing is that he bears our name. He is Conn Fitz Malvais.'

Morvan took his brother's arm in a warrior's grip, 'thank you, Luc.'

'Just come back home to him and us, Morvan. I fought the Scots for several months on one of William's campaigns that led to the Treaty of Abernathy, which has been recently trampled in the border mud by Malcolm. They are cunning, fierce, and often undisciplined, but they are still a force to be reckoned with. Do not turn your back on them or believe what they say when they are at their most charming. Moreover, be wary of King Malcolm if you have dealings with him. He is a worthy and clever opponent. Now I must leave,' he said. Mounting his horse, he raised a fist in salute to his brother and was gone, leaving Morvan, his mind in a whirl staring after him...

The Breton Horse Warrior Series

'Banished'
Subterfuge
Seduction
Sacrifice

The Breton Horse Warriors – **Book Four**
will be published by Moonstorm Books on Amazon in
November 2021

To find out more and to join our mailing list and newsletters, contact us at:

Website: www.moonstormbooks.com
Email: enquiries@moonstormbooks.com
Facebook: S.J.Martin Author
Instagram: S. J. Martin author
Twitter: @SJMarti40719548

About the Author

S. J. Martin... is the pen name of a historian, writer and animal lover in the north of England. Having an abiding love of history from a very early age influenced her academic and career choices. She worked in the field of archaeology for several years before becoming a history teacher in the schools of the northeast, then in London and finally Sheffield.

She particularly enjoys the engaging and fascinating historical research into the background of her favourite historical periods and characters, combining this with extensive field visits. Having decided to leave the world of education after a successful teaching and leadership career, she decided to combine her love of history and writing as an author of historical fiction. With her partner and a close friend, she established Moonstorm Books, publishing The Breton Horse Warrior Series...

When she is not writing, she walks their two dogs with her partner, Greg, on the beautiful beaches of the northeast coast or in the countryside. She also has an abiding love of live music and festivals, playing and singing in a band with her friends whenever possible.

Printed in Great Britain
by Amazon